For Kevin,
and Thanks!

8 Nov 18

My Cousin, Charlene

A Novel

Charlie Rowell

For my sister, who kept me sane.

Copyright 2005

WITNESSETH

ONE

This story doesn't have a surprise ending, or any other ending right now, because my cousin Charlene is alive and well and still going along and getting along.

I didn't know I had a cousin Charlene until about five years ago. I was home alone, watching television, being bored. The doorbell rang and there was Charlene, full grown and sassy, saying, "Hey, cuz."

I'm just as moral and upright as the next guy, meaning that any woman who looks like Charlene and isn't my sister is fair game. So I said, "Do come in and be comfortable," or maybe just, "Uh, hi."

Charlene stands about five-nine in stockings, right about six feet in heels, eye to eye with me. We're talking drop-dead gorgeous. Legs that won't quit, perfect ankles, the cutest rear end and smallest waist you can imagine, a rack that can stop traffic and a face that can get it going again.

A voice that ranges from a rich contralto to a mezzo-soprano, clear and lovely.

And hair! Soft and silky, shoulder length glossy brown hair, and deep brown eyes with the longest lashes I have ever seen. Add to that a killer sense of style and it's no wonder that every head turns whenever Charlene enters a room.

All of that in my living room, in black leather: gaucho hat, bolero jacket over a white silk blouse; skirt not quite a mini, slit along the left thigh so that each step showed stocking top. The garter belt wasn't visible, but the pull of the stocking top showed it was there. Black patent leather sandals of thin straps and stiletto heels.

Blood red nail polish, fingers and toes. Deeper red for lip gloss.

"And so, I decided to move to Toledo. It's such a lovely town."

Of course, Charlene is entirely nuts.

"What does one do for excitement around here?"

Hell if I know. Look around this apartment. Do I look like I have a life?

"I thought you might let me take you to dinner, maybe go

somewhere for drinks and dancing?"

Charming.

And fearless, which I learned later, at a dive bar named 'LENNIES.' It tries to be a biker bar; some of the trade is rough without being especially tough, which any guy can tell you is a bad combination.

Some unnamed, addle-headed hillbilly came up to us as soon as we cleared the door, leered and said, "You're with me, sugar," reached for thigh and higher, then bent forward, gasping from a knee to the groin which likely drove his package back to where it was when he was born.

"Not now, not ever," which was followed by a dainty lift of skirt hem and the ball of Charlene's right foot applied forcefully to Billy's forehead.

Followed by Billy falling backwards, unconscious.

"Hey, we don't allow no fightin' in here." Lenny - I guess - was indignant.

Charlene leaned across the bar, hooked one elegant forefinger under his chin and pulled him forward with the delicacy of a tow truck moving a stranded bus. "Margarita, rocks, salt. And for you, darling?" The casual, inquiring turn of the head.

I shrugged, "Same." No need to complicate matters.

"Excellent." To Lenny, "Use the good tequila, won't you? The cheap stuff spoils the taste and makes me mean." From beneath the skirt, I guess kept in a stocking top, an Andy Jackson offered in payment. "Keep the change and," a dismissive glance at the inert Billy, "tidy up a bit. We may be staying and I hate clutter."

That was my reintroduction to Charlene who, in the years since I have learned, has a pair of balls unmatched by anyone I know, myself included.

Really.

Charlene is a free-lance hit man.

Born Dwight Charles Lewis. Charlene endured an insanely vicious mother and a Milquetoast father, and taunts such as you wouldn't believe. I always felt a little sorry for him, and tried to keep him out of harm's way, not that I was any good at it. But I tried and he knew it, and now I am really glad I did, because as long as he doesn't tell me what he is going to do, I'm ok. I'm his lawyer.

Charlene - or Charlie; he hates being called Dwight and I don't blame him - knows a lot of truly rich people, and he knows just how to tease them along. So now I have three lawyers working for me and a half-dozen secretaries and a paralegal, and a private investigator on retainer. The irony is, I'm not that good a lawyer. But Charlene likes me and that's good enough for the clients, and those three lawyers know a hell of a lot about law and trials and procedure, and they win. They win a *lot,* and the clients like that. They don't pay us to lose.

And with Charlene as a reference, we don't have any unpaid invoices and our suppliers - recommended by Charlene - never overcharge us.

Life is good; uncomplicated.

Mostly.

But every now and then, Charlene needs a favor. Sometimes, it's a whopper, and when it's not, I wish it were *only* a whopper. Like now, with the Randolph case.

Benny Randolph is the cutest kid you can imagine. Big blue eyes, trusting eyes. Rosy cheeks and blond hair, and a truly poisonous grandmother who wants him to live with her. Children Services thinks his grandmother is a fine woman, and his father isn't around any more - no one knows why.

Anyway, how Charlene knows what he knows escapes me. I gave up arguing with him six months after he showed up, and if he told me to bet everything I owned on the lottery - "Here are the numbers" - I'd do it.

I mentioned that to him once and he said, "Are you nuts? No one can guess the lottery numbers."

Anyway, Charlene said to save the kid so here I am, back in Juvenile Court and hating it. The clients rarely wash, the cases last forever and the children aren't always the victims we claim they are. I especially hate being here on the Randolph case because, like the gypsy curse about having an innocent client, he really is a victim and I really have to win this one.

"Mr. Compton, we haven't seen you for a while. Identify

yourself for the record, please."

"Daniel Rodney Compton, your honor, entering my appearance as counsel for the child, Benjamin Randolph." Magistrates aren't really stuffy. It's just that the record is made with a tape recorder instead of a live person to note who's in the courtroom and why.

"This is highly unusual, your honor." Eileen Stannard, one of the lawyers for Children Services - the one assigned to this case - isn't anyone's favorite. She and Stanley Willis, the biggest dog there ever was in Juvenile Court, have their own little "mutual admiration society": they hated each other on sight. Things haven't improved and likely never will, especially since Willis once offered to stick his hand up her ass and grab her brain, drag it down between her legs and bounce it on the desk like a tennis ball. When I grow up I want to be Stanley Willis.

"I object. Mr. Compton has no reason to be here. The child has a guardian *ad litem*, and the guardian *ad litem* has a very able lawyer to represent her."

Saying that must have about killed her, since the lawyer for the guardian is none other than Stanley T. Willis, Esquire, my personal hero.

"Mr. Willis, how say you?"

"Thank you, your honor." Willis is so rich he could buy Ohio and have the plumbing updated, but he is always absolutely respectful of the magistrates and he is always prepared. "The guardian, your honor, wishes to hear from Mr. Compton."

"Mr. Compton, would you care to explain yourself?"

"Yes, your honor. I spoke with my client at the close of last week and inquired as to his desires. In answer to my question as to whether he wished to retain me as his counsel, he responded audibly in a fashion which I took to be in the affirmative."

"You are saying that Benjamin said he wanted you to be his lawyer?"

"That's how I took it, your honor."

"I object! I object! The child is not verbal!"

"Miss Stannard, you cannot object to the child hiring a lawyer." The magistrate, Edwina Tompkins, is as unflappable as anyone I have ever met. "However, Mr. Compton, it does seem unusual that a child of Benjamin's age would be able to, ah, comprehend the nature of the proceedings."

"Unusual, yes. But when I asked him if he wanted me to be his lawyer, Benjamin said, and I quote, 'Ah, wah.' He then grasped my hand, er, finger, and we shook on it. I took it that I was hired, since he smiled at me."

"I see."

I was willing to bet she didn't, but I thought maybe I should keep quiet for a while.

"Were there any witnesses to this transaction, Mr. Compton?"

"Yes, your honor. An individual known as Charlene Evangeline Sweda was present, and is here today to testify in support of my representation, should the court so desire." I learned to talk that way by listening to Stanley Willis. "Further, I have Dr. Giancarlo Gambesi of the Child Abuse Center here as a witness on Master Randolph's motion that the caption of the complaint be amended to reflect that he is alleged to be an abused child."

"You can't let him do that! This is the most bizarre crap I've ever heard!"

"Watch it, Miss Stannard. It's called 'contempt of court' and it isn't just for litigants." Magistrate Tompkins turned back to me, and I could see it in her eyes: what trap was I setting for the ever agitated Miss Stannard? "Mr. Compton? Perhaps we'll hear from your witness now."

"Thank you, you honor."

I went to the courtroom door and waved, and Charlene waltzed through the door, paused at the witness stand to be sworn and then sat, the image of demure respect.

"May we have your name, now that you have been sworn?" No way was I going to suggest to the court that Charlene was a woman.

"Charlene Evangeline Sweda." Absolutely true. He'd had it legally changed.

"Are you acquainted with a child known as Benjamin Edward Randolph?"

"Yes."

"How so?"

"We're friends."

"I object!"

"Miss Stannard, you will have the opportunity to cross-examine the witness."

"But this is silly!"

"Continue, Mr. Compton."

"Yes, your honor. Miss Sweda, did you have a conversation recently with Master Benjamin Randolph?"

"Now, you know I did." When Charlene is in the moment, he can be insufferable. All he had to say was "yes," and he was off and running like every other witness on the planet, unable to utter a single monosyllabic word, whether "yes" or "no."

"He took your hand. Well, your finger, at any rate. He said he wanted you to be his lawyer."

"Exactly what did he say, in your presence?"

"He said, 'Ah, wah,' and then he smiled and shook your, ah, finger."

"I see. When was this?"

"Last Friday."

"Did you have a conversation with Master Randolph prior to that to which you just testified?"

"Yes, on Thursday last, the day before that conversation."

"What was the content of that conversation, if you please?"

"I asked him whether anyone had penetrated him anally, and he replied in the affirmative." Charlene looked directly at the magistrate and continued, "He said, quote, 'Ah, wah. Boo.'"

"Ah, ha!" Stannard was on her feet, waving her hands. "Ah, ha! That is an entirely inappropriate question! Just asking it conditions the child to give the answer which the questioner expects, and there is no evidence at all that this person is in any way qualified to deal with child sexual abuse!"

Checkmate.

Stanley Willis rose, bowed to the court and said, "It seems that Mr. Compton has proved his case. If the agency believes that the child can understand such a question and be swayed in his answer, then surely he can understand what it means to hire a lawyer."

Stannard choked.

"The court agrees. Thank you, Miss Sweda. You may step down. Your next witness, Mr. Compton."

Charlene rose and left the stand, moved to the door and held it for the doctor, who then testified that he was licensed as an MD, that he had examined Benjamin and that there were anal striae which in his professional opinion could have been caused only by penetration, whether with a finger or some other object.

If you thought Stannard was through stepping on herself, you were wrong.

"If it please the court, this is all well and good, but this is our complaint and it is captioned, 'Benjamin Edward Randolph, an alleged neglected and dependent child.' There is nothing in the caption to show that the child is abused, and there is no need to amend the complaint. The agency investigated and with all due respect to the doctor, the allegations of abuse were found to be 'unsubstantiated.' There is no need and the court cannot order us to amend our complaint."

"Mr. Compton, rebuttal?"

"Thank you, your honor. To quote from paragraph six of the complaint, 'Mother states that her father sexually abused her and she has seen him with his hands in the child's training pants for no reason.' True, there is nothing at the top of the complaint alleging the child to be abused, but the contents of that paragraph constitute an allegation of abuse, and a child alleged to be abused is entitled to a lawyer, according to the Juvenile Rules.

"When the court advises parents of their rights, reference is routinely made to, and I quote, 'The allegations of the complaint.' I have a copy of the transcript where this court so advised the mother in this case, should you want to see it. I haven't offered it as an exhibit as I didn't see the need."

"Nor do I. Motion granted. The complaint is amended to show that the child is alleged to be an abused child. I believe we have a trial date. We're adjourned."

Damn, it worked. Now what do I do?

"How far do you plan to go with this?" Willis is always direct.

"Just as far as I can, Mr. Willis."

"Then what?"

"Yes, then what?" Stannard was off and running, and for the next ten minutes all I heard was her invective, larded with words like "irresponsible, inappropriate, unprofessional, short-sighted," and my personal favorite, "twaddle." By the time she wound down, Willis was gone, Charlene was smirking from across the floor and I had a ringing headache and no patience.

"It's like this, Eileen. Someone, likely the grandpa, shoved something, likely his finger, up my client's ass. He lives with the woman you guys think should have my client, the kid. I can't say, because we didn't talk about it, but I'm willing to bet Benjamin isn't looking forward to a prepubescent prostate check. So get it straight: find another place for the kid to live."

* * *

Back when Charlene moved to Toledo, my law practice was marginal. What was a good month then is a marginal day now, in money terms, and I still have trouble thinking about myself as being able to pick up a check - any check, anywhere, any time. But Charlene doesn't have any such trouble. He dresses well, he eats well and he lives well. He drives a good - not flashy - car and he lives in a good apartment in a good neighborhood. There is nothing about him that belies his persona: a youngish woman of substance, tasteful and well-bred, looking to marry well or not at all, comfortable with herself. Being with Charlene has improved my manners a whole bunch.

Yeah, I'm still a yutz sometimes. But I have learned to hold chairs and doors, and to stand so that I'm not looking up her - his skirt when he sits down, especially in the driver's seat. Although, I'm tempted. Charlene has his clothes tailored so that he always looks like a hot woman with a smallish butt and slightly broad shoulders, and I can tell you, the sight of his thighs in stockings as his skirt rides up still makes me sweat.

There was one time, about three years ago, that I held his

overcoat as we went to dinner. In his heels we were eye to eye, and with his hair and those eyes, well, I almost forgot myself. Or better said, I almost forgot he wasn't a woman. Actually, I forgot the hell out of it and reached out to smooth his hair. Talk about feeling uncomfortable. But he laughed and said, in his real voice, "I'm ok with it, and you should be too."

Sure. Easy for him to say. He's the one wearing custom-made silk and satin thongs and things, and I'm the one looking at him like a horny teenager with a crush on the music teacher. Which is one of those things you say which is entirely innocent until you realize who you said it to. Turns out, Charlene's first woman was his music teacher. She was thirty-three, he was sixteen. It was her idea, and her pregnancy. It was his burden. He was born with a stubborn streak of unrelenting morality, which is why he is so very good at his work.

He never seeks publicity.

He leaves no signature when he works.

Whenever harm follows in his wake, the evidence points to misadventure, to natural causes, to willful absence, to anything but foul play. And if perchance someone should suspect otherwise, he is ready to sell himself - meaning his male self - to the cops. Once, when they were closing in, he raped himself - dressed as Charlene, not as Dwight, of course - and tied himself with his stockings so that the cops who came to serve the arrest warrant on whatever fake name he was using called for the paramedics and then added a rape charge against the non-existent man. No, I don't know and no, I don't want to know the details. Who would? What I know is that the composite photo the cops came up with matched a guy shot dead by the cops in another city, probably Cincinnati, maybe Cleveland. Cases closed, no innocent persons implicated. But that's not where I was going with this. Charlene scores with more women than any other man I know.

You'd think I'd get the leftovers, but no. Once they're his, it's like with any other guy-guy relationship. His women are his, and when I said flat out I didn't get it, he laughed. He's got this rich, throaty chuckle that a movie star would envy, full of sex and heat and womanhood, and when he laughs like that, even the women are aroused. He focuses on a woman, gets to know her and then beds her.

"How? Tell me how," you cry.

Easy. According to Charlene, Toledo is the capital city of available, willing women. This is the place, he maintains, to be a single, attractive man. Then, with the sorrowful, pitying look that a woman gives a man when she explains such mundane matters as the Meaning of Life, he lectured me.

"How many women can you screw at one time?"

Me, I started thinking about juggling calendars and keeping names with faces.

Charlene said, "One, if you're lucky. None, if you keep thinking what you're thinking."

"How do you know what I'm thinking?"

Again the look, and he pointed at his crotch. "Don't let the underwear fool you. I'm a guy, remember?"

"Oh, yeah."

Charlene started, "It's takes about twenty minutes to do a woman. Add time to hold her and appreciate her so she doesn't feel like meat, it takes an hour. Add dinner, you've got at least two hours. You have to work, and that takes at least ten hours a day. One date, one woman, one day. Unless you have that supposed male fantasy thing about two women, and unless you have more money than I know about," he looked around, his disdain obvious, "you're going to be limited to about one woman a week."

I felt so macho.

"And that would be a really good week, considering what I'm seeing here."

So much for my self-image. We were sitting on my couch, feet up on the coffee table, two guys in their underwear having a beer. Of course, Charlene's underwear was custom-made silk and satin, and mine was Jockey cotton.

He had his ankles crossed, perfect ankles covered in white nylon, elegant legs in sheer white stockings, a white satin garter belt and a white satin G-string which made his package look decidedly womanly. These days, everybody has a pierced navel. Charlene, always on the cutting edge of style, wore a diamond navel stud with an emerald teardrop pendant, and this was years ago. His bra showed his breasts to best advantage, and right there it got creepy. I can deal with the shoes - those sandals that are all straps and spike heels, black or white or red, even - and stockings, but he has these falsies which are complete with nipples, and there I draw the line.

If he just sat there in his undies, ok. Hair, eyes, lips all done, even. But those falsies are too much. It's like being up high and feeling this urge to shove whoever I'm with off the building, to drive off the bridge, to jump off it and fly, whatever. People who aren't afraid of heights have no idea, and people who don't know that Charlene is the hottest looking woman I have ever seen. I look at him and I think, wow! I want to do *her* in the worst way. Never mind that she's my cousin, she must want it too or she wouldn't dress like that around me.

She's my cousin.

There isn't anything I can think of that comes close to watching a grown-up straight man dressing himself in pantyhose. The knowledge that this man could kill me without hardly moving, let alone taking a deep breath, does nothing to normalize the view, if you follow me. Because, you see, he puts on the falsies and his bra, then his G-string and then his stockings and garter belt. Or his pantyhose, depending on his wardrobe choice *du jour.* And no, I haven't a clue how a woman does it, which should be obvious to all, since I'm talking about watching my cousin dress. You think this would be going on if there was a woman in my life?

Anyway, we were sitting there drinking beer, two guys in our underwear, and he was lecturing me about my attitude toward women and life. He was using his Dwight voice, just a guy talking to another guy, and then so subtly that I missed the change, he became Charlene. Softly reproving, teasing, gently admonishing. He stood, walked to the kitchen and brought more beer, turned down the lights and came back to the couch. Every movement I saw, every step, every bend, every turn was womanly. When he sat again, it was as a woman, with his left leg tucked under him, then brought his right leg up so that he was facing me, a woman talking to a friend.

He said that I had these qualities, that I wasn't a bad fellow, just not well socialized and shallow, but that he would help me. He said that men and women think differently, that we view things differently, that neither was right or wrong. He stroked my hair with his left hand, let his finger play with my ear as he complimented me on being a really nice guy at heart, and said how lucky any woman would be to have me as her friend.

Charlene's nails are naturally strong and smooth, and always manicured and polished. Soft, womanly fingertips pulled gently over a man's shoulder and down onto his chest, a little dragging of the fingernails over his skin, a slight rubbing of his nipple, and he forgets that men are supposed to be tough and on top, pounding home while the woman decides what color to paint the ceiling.

A warm, mature hand caresses a man's jaw, trails down onto his throat, soothes. A woman's finger traces his lips, moves up his cheek and under his eye, across his nose. Her voice is true and honest as she confesses that he has her off-guard, that she isn't like this usually, that she is afraid she will offend him.

The fresh beer bottles are on the coffee table and she takes his empty bottle, places it beside the fresh bottles and then turns again to compliment him and to deprecate herself. He is so self-possessed, so self-assured that he has no need to speak, no need to interrupt her and she compliments him, tells him that his taciturn masculinity is so ... so pleasing and ... irresistible. Her thumb is under his chin, lifting and turning him toward her, and her fingers are keeping his eyes half-open, half-shut so that he sees her hair falling just so, across her eye and touching the corner of her mouth as she smiles shyly, a woman assured and yet only hopeful.

A soft downward movement of her hand and he closes his eyes, drifts along as she cajoles, as she compliments and praises him. She shifts herself and he feels her heat against him, feels her hand along his jaw and her thumb at his chin, at his lips.

"Danny."

"Hmm?"

He feels her weight against his thigh, feels her heat through the satin of her covering as it rests on his thigh.

She touches his lips with her finger and he reaches for her hand to hold it against his lips and kiss it as she folds her fingers over his, then moves against him so that her breasts are against his chest. She holds his hand and brings it to her breast, opening the fingers and holding it against herself as she stays so close to him that her breath is on his cheek as his hand lies upon her breast, gently kneading it.

Falsie, for crying out loud! Falsie! It felt just like the real thing, at least to my inexperienced hand, with this half-erect nipple. Somehow, he glues them on in the morning, and he says they'll stay on in the shower, although why is way the hell over my head. He says that they absorb his body heat and feel just like a real breast, and I'm here to tell you, he ain't kidding.

It registered that I was about to make it with my cousin, a man to boot, and I came out of it and sat up fast, my eyes bulging.

Charlene sat back and almost killed himself laughing. "Danrod, you have got to learn that flesh is flesh, and what makes a woman worth the time it takes to bed her is what is in her heart."

TWO

Dan-rod.

I hate being called Dan-rod, because it reminds me that although I have my JD, which is the same as a Ph.D. except that I can make a living with it, and Charlene has only a high school diploma, he is way better educated than I am. Dan-rod comes from *Penrod*, which Booth Tarkington wrote about a hundred years ago and which is to some people a minor classic, and of which I would never have heard except that Charlene audited some graduate level classes in American literature. Charlene says I could understand why he calls me Dan-rod if I'd just read the book, which he found somewhere and brought to me. No, I'm not going to read it. I'm just that stubborn and besides, why would I care?

It was bad enough that I was sitting there in the half-dark while my cousin rubbed himself on me and had me ready to mount up and ride, but the son-of-a-bitch didn't have the decency to reciprocate, if you know what I mean. So I asked him about it and he just laughed at me, and said that I should remember that not only his professional success but also his life depended on his ability to be a woman.

Sure. Have the surgery, then.

But Charlene pointed out that his success also depended on his masculinity, and the loss of his manhood would soften him - I choked on that line - and reduce his physical strength and ability.

What about the way his male hormones make his beard grow?

No problem. Between modern chemicals and laser therapy, it's all under control. Add the skillful use of high quality cosmetics and careful behavior conditioning, and no one can tell he isn't a woman, especially since he has those high grade falsies and - I left this out before - butt falsies to match.

No part of my life had prepared me for any of this.

For that matter, no part of my life had prepared me for the Randolph case. I have cruised through life avoiding all sorts of serious matters, including just about everything related to law. And now, thanks to Charlene's machinations I am holding a child's life in my hands. Worse, I have the opportunity to make a complete fool of myself right there in front of Stanley Willis.

Family. Every chance they get, they sue you, screw you or send you to jail. But who else do you have? I've tried finding out how Charlene came to exist, and what happened to Dwight. Charlene alludes, but Charlene does not admit.

One summer night, we were standing down by the river and the lights were reflecting just like in a movie. The wind was light, teasing his hair and lifting the hem of his skirt, threatening to show his stocking tops. He was looking very Marilyn Monroe in *The Seven Year Itch*, except softer; prettier. No kidding, he is the hottest, prettiest woman I have ever seen. Anyway, I was feeling like I was on a real date with a real girl, and he must have been feeling something, too. He put his arm around my waist, girl style, and we stood there watching the lights dance on the water, and then he laid his head on my shoulder, then turned to snuggle against me with his nose in my ear. I was pretty confused until I realized that there were people watching us.

I said, "I'll get you for this, Charlene," and he just laughed. That throaty, womanly laugh carried along the water and the other people looked at us, and I knew they were jealous of our easy-going love.

Charlene was just staying in character, allaying suspicion. He reached down and took my hand, and we walked along the river front, lovers on a summer night, and he told me a story of love and passion, of credulousness and rapacious greed, and death.

A fellow once fell in love with a pretty woman. He was deeply, trustingly and unquestioningly in love. She returned his love and they promised each other Forever After, and they had their private jokes and their secrets.

They were about the same size and build, and the man was unsure of himself because he wasn't a football player or a wrestler, and he knew she respected masculine physicality. But she told him how she had found true love with him, that women look for excitement and fun when they are young and foolish, but they look for love and loyalty and real, true manhood when they choose a mate for life.

He believed her.

He let her dress him in her clothes, and he let her play the man, ravishing him with herself and her toys, and he let her have her way and win arguments. He loved her so, and he would die for her, and he would work as hard as he had to so that she would have her dream house.

It wasn't much of a job that he had, but it was a job and it allowed him to please her, and she was his world. He had saved his money and built his pension, and when he met her and they had married, he took everything he had and used it to build her dream house, and to give her Forever After.

She promised that she would do likewise. Instead, she slept with her boss. She had a right to be happy, she said. After all, her boss had lettered in football and basketball, and a woman wants to feel safe when she is with a man. She filed for divorce.

In a divorce, there are such things as temporary orders. She got the apartment, he paid the rent. She got the new car, which they had bought through his credit union. He paid for it. She needed temporary alimony, to get her through the tough times of readjustment to her straitened finances. He paid the construction loan.

He lived in his van.

She slept with her boss in the apartment; in motels; in his big, new house.

The dream house sat there, half-built. The construction loan ran out and the bank wouldn't approve more money, so the work stopped.

She complained to her lawyer who filed to have him held in contempt and punished accordingly.

He ate little for he had little to spend on food. He had no money for dry cleaning and no easy way to launder his clothes. He had to ask for help from coworkers. They let him use their washing machines, and sometimes they fed him.

She called him at work one day to say that maybe they should try to work it out. She said that she had told her lawyer to file for reconciliation, and she wanted him to tell his lawyer to go along with it.

He still loved her and so he agreed.

Then he found out that "reconciliation" meant that the case was delayed for six months, and then she said she had no intention of going through with the counseling that was to rehabilitate the marriage. The temporary orders continued, of course, for as the court said, if she hadn't a husband she should have his money.

She called him at work and laughed at him, and said he should get used to it. Her boss liked what he got and so he paid her lawyer to stick it to him.

He snapped.

He lured her to the mall and struck her from behind, tied her hands and gagged her, stuffed her in the trunk.

He planned to take her to the half-built house and nail her to the rafters, and leave her there to die. He had nothing left, neither self-respect nor sanity.

He would leave her there and eventually the cops would find him in his van and take him away. Eventually.

But vengeance belongs to God, and what goes around comes around.

Two delinquents car-jacked him.

The cops solve about twenty per cent of crimes committed by strangers. This time, there were witnesses. No one saw enough to argue that his wife was in the car. In fact, all anyone saw was the two delinquents drag him out of the car and beat him, get in and drive away. One witness swore he saw the woman in the passenger seat.

Five states away and nine days later, the highway patrol found the car. The delinquents tried to run. A high speed chase, an artless driver, a grinding, flaming crash.

Sorry, sir. Your wife is dead. Sorry, sir.

No one else was sorry, including her boss. She had been stealing him blind.

So that was it. He got the apartment back, and all her clothes and shoes. He got the insurance and the half-built dream house. He got her bank accounts and the money she had stolen from her boss.

He thought about going to school, decided not.

He thought about traveling, decided not.

He thought about changing jobs, decided not.

And then he understood what he had to do.

He sold the half-built house to a contractor, and so he cleared his name and credit with the bank. He traded in the van, using the insurance money from the wrecked car to pay the difference. He surrendered the apartment, and left the furniture behind.

He kept her clothes.

He changed his name.

He went to the college and hung around, made friends. He learned to tease and cajole, and he watched.

He watched women. He watched how they dressed and walked, how they handled books and papers and cafeteria trays.

He watched men, and how they reacted to women.

He practiced walking and talking, smiling and flirting. He listened to his own voice and he learned to modulate it until it was his own and yet a woman's voice.

He took up martial arts and learned to defend himself.

He bought a treadmill and learned to run in high heels.

There was more to the story, but that was what he told me, leaning on the railing and looking out at the river and watching the lights twinkle.

Then he stood up straight and nodded at the river, turned to me and said, "She broke his heart and he still loved her. His anger grew until it consumed him, and although he loved her, maybe because he still loved her as he always had, he could have nailed her to those rafters and let her die."

I waited for the rest of it, but that was all there was.

He turned back to the river, his hands on the railing, and then looked sideways at me. The wind lifted his hair and ruffled his skirt, and he reached for my hand. He gave me a wise and gentle look, and it was the most womanly look I have ever seen. He stood upright and then led me along the river, lovers on a summer night, silent, lost in thought.

Can I say that Charlene is the man in the story? No, and neither can I say he isn't. I can't even say the story is true, although my professional experience tells me that it more likely is than isn't. What I can say is that something happened that turned Dwight into Charlene and, knowing both of them, Dwight and Charlene, whatever happened was dramatic and drastic.

At home, alone, I thought about it, the lovely irony of a gentle fellow who suffered the usual childhood bullying by the usual suspects and who became a contract killer because he suffered indecent abuse at the hands of a predatory woman. I'm sure there was a moral lesson in there, knowing Charlene as I do, but first I had a little too much to drink and then I went to bed, for it had been a long day.

* * *

"Mr. Compton, Mr. Willis will see you now."

Willis' secretary, Joyce Roberts, has been with him for years. No one screws with her, for doing so is the same as screwing with Willis, only worse. It's more like a traditional Southern family thing, just like when I got in trouble in school and got a beating, then went home and got another from my mother, and then another from my father. The teacher was never wrong, and there was no appeal: screw up and die.

Willis and Joyce are exceedingly protective of each other, and no one questions it because everyone is at least a little jealous of their friendship. He respects her absolutely, trusts her with his life and his wallet. She knows exactly what she knows and what she doesn't, and she knows a hell of a lot more than she doesn't. As much as any lawyer on this earth, Willis has achieved the mythical status of Perry Mason, meaning that he has Della Street for his secretary: elegant, absolutely loyal, entirely competent, and she brings him coffee.

Like I said, when I grow up I want to be Stanley Willis.

"Mr. Compton, be comfortable." Willis waved at the chairs in front of his desk, then sat in his recliner. He's the only lawyer I know whose furniture is custom upholstered to match the carpet, and everyone knows Joyce took care of that, too.

I sat, and Mrs. Roberts asked if I wanted coffee, and yes, I call her "Mrs. Roberts." It's how I was raised and besides, facing Stanley Willis in the court room is one thing; pissing him off by failing to show his secretary proper respect is another. Suicidal ideation does *not* run in my family.

"What's your purpose in amending the complaint?" Willis is always direct. "What will you get, besides status as his lawyer?"

"I really don't know."

"Excuse me?"

What was I to say? That my cousin, the cross-dressing, but not transvestite, contract killer said he wanted me to do something for the kid, that he wanted me to make sure that he didn't have to live with his grandmother? But lying to Willis would surpass stupidity, and so I told the truth. "I really don't know what I'll get out of this, but to be honest, it seemed like the right thing to do." *And because I am in love with the woman who my cousin isn't.*

"At least you're honest about it." Willis nodded, and then tapped the legal pad on his desk. "I took the liberty of making some notes, in case you and I can come to an agreement."

I nodded. What else could I do? I had just figured out that I was in love with a woman who did not exist, although I had held hands with her. My head started to hurt, and I considered asking for aspirin to go with the coffee.

"It seems to me that his desires can be presumed, so that his lack of verbal skills will not be too great a disability." Some people claim that Willis can read the IRS code and make it sound logical. I was starting to believe they were right. "What child, when asked, would say that he wanted to be sexually abused, much less in his own home?"

Why didn't I think of that?

"Also, there is the question of the child witnessing the abuse of his mother at the hands of one of his proposed custodians."

Do what? Sometimes, my Southern DNA asserts itself.

"As we know, the grandfather was abusive towards the child's mother." Willis nodded, confirming his own point. "I doubt that any child, when asked, will say that he wants to watch his mother being abused, even a child with a reason to want her dead."

I was willing to bet Willis didn't know too much about Southern families, but then I thought about Charlene, who has more right than anyone I know to curse his mother. I doubt even he would want to watch her suffer, given the story he had told me that night, down by the river. I decided that Willis was smarter than I had guessed, and I had guessed he was about the smartest man I know.

"What do you think?" Willis looked at me over the rim of his coffee mug.

"I think you're right." I felt like I was back in law school, only this time the instructor actually knew something about lawyering, and didn't need a guide dog to find the courthouse. "How do we use that?"

"You're his lawyer. Figure it out."

Sure, Stan. You're such a help. "I guess, if he goes with the grandparents then he is going to be exposed to abuse, and if he isn't going to be abused himself, his mother is likely to be." I shrugged, because I was making it up as I went along and I had run out of inspiration. And bullshit, for that matter.

"That is the point, of course." Dry humor always impresses me, except when I am the butt. "Perhaps you can put your resources to work checking out the grandparents and their proclivities." He sipped from his mug, kept it in front of his face, went on. "I was thinking that a good private detective, sent to examine their past and to inquire in their neighborhood, might find something of merit. At the very least, it might give us some insight as to their motivation."

"Motivation?" It was out before I thought.

"Why do they want custody of your client?" He raised his eyebrows, as quizzical as a law school prof who really does know the answer.

Beats me.

It hadn't occurred to me to wonder about that.

Willis looked at his watch, put down his coffee mug and stood, offered his hand. "Thank you for coming by. If you get anything from your private detective which you feel that you can share, I would appreciate hearing from you."

I stood and reached to shake his hand, clumsy as a teenager meeting his date's father, and tried to look cool and self-possessed. "Thank you for seeing me."

Mrs. Roberts was in the doorway, ready to escort me back to the reception area. Because she is so nice, and because I had no one else to ask, "If you don't mind, maybe you could explain to me why we were so formal. We kept calling each other 'Mr.' and every other lawyer I know uses first names, no matter what."

"Anything else, Mr. Compton?" Her smile was kind and I felt a little better.

"Probably."

"Perhaps he wants you to earn your spurs." She offered her hand, and I decided that whatever it took, I was going to earn those spurs just so I could show them to her.

"Thanks. Er, thank you. I'll let you know what I find out."

* * *

I spent the next two hours standing by the river, trying to recapture the way I felt that summer night when I stood there with Charlene. Yeah, I know. You can't go home again.

I have this one quirk which makes me crazy: I'm too nice. People say things and I hear them. I hear the nuances and the implications, and I ignore them. I guess it comes from having the hell beat out of me all the time as a kid, and maybe my family life wasn't much better than Charlene's. Maybe, if he hadn't married that woman, or if he hadn't been born so pretty, or if he hadn't been born in the South, maybe Dwight would have been a normal CPA and not the man he is. Maybe.

But in my heart, I know that he is who he is and what he is, and I know that he treats me differently from everyone else. That knowledge makes me just a little bit edgy about this whole Randolph thing, and I am so very glad I stuck up for him, all those years ago.

It's like Willis said, look for the motivation. Maybe it's nothing more than some latter-day Baptist thing: "Where trouble calls or danger, be never wanting there." Yes, we both went to Sunday school. I can still quote the Bible and I can still sing the seventh verse of *Amazing Grace*, which you thought had only four, right?

I stood there in the afternoon sun, trying to feel the same way I felt that night, and feeling nothing except disappointed and foolish. I watched the boats and the circling gulls, and I looked at the traffic on the Cherry Street Bridge, which was renamed years ago to honor Dr. Martin Luther King, Jr.

It is a handsome bridge of cast concrete, a drawbridge owned and operated by the city and which actually works. Sometimes, before all the development along the river front, I would look down at it from my office window and pretend I was looking down at the George Washington Bridge in the city. I'd stand at my office window and watch the occasional tow truck, amber warning lights flashing, cruise over the bridge and pretend I was back in Manhattan in my sister's apartment, watching the traffic on the G-W-B and those tow trucks became escort vehicles for the hazardous cargo carriers. But that was a few long years ago, and now my office is in one of those new, tall buildings that block the view I used to have. Like they say, you can't go home again. So I stood there by the river and looked at the Craig Bridge carrying the interstate in the background and the haze over Lake Erie beyond that.

"I thought I'd find you here."

Sometimes I wonder whether he kills that way, an amazingly pretty woman materializing beside them, disconcerting them, disarming them and then giving them the shiv.

"I think you need a vacation."

"Very funny. You just euchred me into the worst case I have ever handled, I have no idea what I am supposed to be doing and you think I need a vacation." I'd have decked him, but explaining it to the cops would be worse than the beating he'd give me if I tried. I tried looking at him and venting my anger, but being in love with him - her - him, made it impossible. He's just too pretty and too charming.

He put that womanly hand on my face and smiled, "I've made reservations for us in Atlantic City. You and Charlie are going gambling and whoring." He smiled. "Lighten up. This time you'll be the tall, rugged guy who scores while his soft, pretty buddy sits around and wishes he were tough and ugly like you."

"Sure."

He dropped his hand to my waist, held me close and let his Chanel perfume drive me crazy. "Or do you want me to go as Charlene, and show you a really good time?"

"Does it show?"

Again that womanly, throaty laugh and again, the envy of bystanders. "Like a zit on prom night."

"What am I going to do about it?"

"Live with it, die with it. It's up to you." He moved closer to me, which I wouldn't have thought possible, and with his free hand he waved at the East Side, the part of Toledo on the other side of the Maumee River. "When you were in your old office and you were looking out at the bridge, you could pretend you were in Manhattan."

I frowned, because I had forgotten that I had mentioned that to him.

He smiled and shook his head. "I remember everything. It's how I stay alive." He rubbed my back, just like a girlfriend comforting her tired fellow. "But now that you have that fancy office and the better view, you cannot have that fantasy. It's like sitting in the front row and watching the dancers sweat. The reality overcomes the image."

THREE

Charlene was right: I needed a vacation and Atlantic City was just the place. We drank, we gambled, we scored. Charlie had girlfriends, and he threw one or two of them at me. Want to feel insignificant? Try going to Atlantic City with a shorter man with long hair and a pretty face, and watch while he scores four to one, and he spots you that one.

The trip started with a bang. Not only is he legally Charlene Evangeline Sweda, he has a complete identity as Charles Edward Sweda, her loving and devoted brother - or husband, as the situation dictates. The luggage monogram - C E S - works either way, and he has a whole line worked out about that happy coincidence.

He went first through the check-in and security scans, and by the time he was done, he was buddies with all of them. Me, they gave the fish-eye. So Charlie, ever the good ole boy, explained to them that I am a stuffy corporate lawyer who is afraid to fly, and he was taking me out there to the gambling tables so I could learn how it felt not to have every second planned. I thought about busting him out and teaching him a thing or two about human kindness and consideration, but since he was dressed as a man and since his suitcase carried only man-stuff, I figured I'd come off as something between a sub-moron and insane. So, I grinned and bore it, and as we took our seats in first class I remembered that a sub-moron would be an idiot, and I felt so much better that I hadn't said anything.

The stewardess flirted with Charlie. Me, she called "sir."

The desk clerk fawned over Charlie. Apparently he is a high roller out there.

The pit boss - I think that's what he's called - greeted Charlie like a long lost brother, asked him if he had come to play or just for the shows. Charlie said, a little of both and asked for some chips, gave the guy a knowing look and nodded at me like I was the little brother he had to babysit. I got a complimentary bucket of nickels and directions to the slots.

I lost the whole bucket. Charlie made back his money plus about thirty-five hundred.

I sulked, Charlie laughed. It went like that for the whole four days we were there.

Coming home, another stewardess flirted with Charlie, and called me "sir."

All things considered, it was the most fun I have ever had.

* * *

Back in Toledo, I still had no idea what to do about the Randolph case. Charlene was unsympathetic.

"Ask."

"Excuse me?"

"Ask. Questions."

"What questions?"

"*Which* questions, Cousin." He was a girl again, soft brown hair lightly curled, dinner make-up in place, stylish - meaning ugly - shoes and seamed stockings, and a black business suit over a white silk blouse.

"You have a date?" I've learned not to be surprised by what he does and what he says, but sometimes he can catch me off guard, like now.

"Yes, but she doesn't know it yet." He winked. "She thinks it's just another negotiation."

"Negotiation?"

"Don't worry, Cousin. This is purely pleasure, no business involved." Another wink, then a demure, womanly smile. "At least, not the kind of business you're worried about."

"Really." I aimed for dry sarcasm, but my voice wavered and I sounded like a strangled duck.

Charlene raised his eyebrows. "My, aren't we Puritanical tonight."

"Huh?"

"Your jealousy is showing, Cousin. I have a date with a woman, who I will soon bed. I shall explain, eventually, that I am still

a man, that I have not yet been able to commit to the surgery, that I ...
I feel so ... so ... and she will take it from there."

"You're going to seduce her." A statement, not a question.
Anything to prolong the conversation and distract myself from the
Randolph case.

"Hardly, darling boy. She is going to seduce *me*." He tossed
his head, fluffed his hair, then grinned at me. Two steps closer, those
eyes and that sultry, womanly look, and the explanation. "She is the
executive vice-president of wherever she works." A little shrug. "She
wants me just as you do, all demure and womanly. Once she learns
that I am still physically a man, her passion will take over. She will
protest to me that it will give me the chance to see that I truly am a
woman yearning to be free, that my desires are to be a woman with
women. But inside, she will be thinking that I am her breathing dildo,
that I am safe because I am really a woman, that she will avenge herself
on men and faint-hearted Lesbians who will not declare themselves;
any of those and all, for what I know." He smiled, and I remembered
him as Dwight, happy and carefree before the bullies beat him and
made him tentative. "Hell if I know what will go through her mind, but
I know what will go through her low brain."

A bawdy wink and he was gone, and as he walked away I
recalled what he had said about being hot. "Most mid-western women
walk like a cross between a plow horse and Marshall Dillon. Once I
learned to walk like a woman, I had it made."

If *I* could just learn to walk like a man.

I went back to the office and read the Randolph file again, and
tried to figure out why Charlene was so interested in an otherwise
anonymous child. I also tried to figure out what I was supposed to be
doing as that child's lawyer, but Charlene's motives seemed a
shallower pond for fathoming. Sometimes when I'm facing a difficult
decision, I make up questionable metaphors.

The logical place to start was the complaint that Children
Services filed. The alleged father was Charles E. Davis, whereabouts
unknown to the Children Services. The mother was Lisa Randolph,
with an address on the East Side. According to the complaint, the
mother was unemployed and liked to drink and party - no, it wasn't

stated so clearly, but my trained eye had no trouble reading between the lines. Except for the part about grandpa putting his hands in Benny's training pants, it was tame stuff. I was where I had started, wondering why this one kid attracted Charlene's attention.

Unless.

Nobody's perfect. Sure, the cops haven't ever arrested him, but there was that one time that they were on his trail, which I already mentioned. So, could there be this one time he wasn't so careful when he was Charlie instead of Charlene? That would explain it all. Benny's father wasn't really Mr. Davis, and there hadn't been any genetic testing so he hadn't been ruled out. And if Charlie Sweda left a little love muffin as a souvenir, wouldn't Charlene be there to protect him? Considering that there weren't a lot of referrals listed in the complaint, maybe Charlie thought little Benny was in good hands. It all fit.

Crap.

I could just see it, the three of us in an apartment. Charlene, the hot woman who is really the father, pretending to be the mother. Me, the kid's uncle, acting like his father. The kid, smart and handsome, getting into everything and having the ability to talk his way out of any kind of trouble. So much for my love life, which admittedly I don't really have anyway, but at least I have my dreams.

Double crap.

Not only do I have the opportunity to humiliate myself with Stanley Willis. I can risk my life in front of the client's father, Charlene-Charlie Evangeline-Edward Sweda, murderer.

Crap and crap and crap again.

Willis will see that I am a putz, Charlene will kill me. I am likely to die without ever having had true love.

Crap.

Ok, once again from the top. According to the caseworker, Benny was dependent, meaning that his parents couldn't take care of him, and neglected, meaning that his parents *wouldn't* take care of him. His mother was a drug-dependent party whore who lived on the East Side and legally, Benny didn't have a father. Exactly why the caseworker thought Mr. Davis was Benny's father wasn't stated in the complaint, but usually it was the mother who said so. Since she was the one person who was at both the conception and the birth, she was the logical place to start. Not that mothers always get it right. I've had cases where the mother names four, five, even six guys before she gets it right. What's really strange is that the prostitutes get it right more than the party whores. Go figure.

Anyway, Charles Davis was supposed to be Benny's father, but Lisa Randolph hadn't bothered to prove it yet, so she couldn't get child support from him and neither could the state, not that it mattered. Nobody had a clue where to find him and the last time he had a job, he was fired for not showing up.

Although.

I had handled another case where the complaint said pretty much the same thing about the father's whereabouts being unknown, but at trial he walked in and raised hell about paying child support and talking to the caseworker - the same one assigned to this case. He went on about trying to visit with his kid, who he said he had lived with, along with the mother, until she had him arrested for domestic violence. The cops hauled him off to jail and she and their child moved to a shelter while he was in custody. Of course, he got out right away - she picked him up outside the jail just after midnight, when he was released - and the case was eventually dismissed because she wouldn't appear for trial. Somehow, I don't think that this is quite the same situation, but I'm still not convinced that the caseworker has turned every stone. Or even most of them, knowing this particular worker.

How stupid am I?

Charlene and Willis both told me to my face what to do, and I just didn't get it. Well, I have it now, so I reached for the speed dial and called the private eye we keep on retainer to give him the low-down, and to send him out to watch the grandparents. I felt like Mickey Spillane working out a new job for Mike Hammer.

That done, I went back to the complaint. Most likely, CSB wanted Benny out of foster care because of the cost. As long as there was an arguably suitable relative, why not save the money? Some day, someone will rat out CSB, which keeps at least a full year's expenses in the bank "for emergencies." How many people do you know who can afford to keep a whole year's gross income in the bank "for emergencies"? I suppose that since it's tax money, a few tens of millions in the bank is no big deal.

Right.

Anyway, I figured that CSB decided to send Benny to his granny and save the foster care money, and somehow Charlene found out and was pissed. The rest of it, as much as I know, I already told you. Which brings us back to the complaint, and what I think I will accomplish as Benny's lawyer, trying to keep him from living with his grandparents. Obviously, Willis has an idea about that, never mind what Charlene is up to, and there is no way that Charlene and Willis have been working together on this. So, that means Willis is thinking that if I give him the information I'll get from the private dick, then he can work with it. That means, Willis wants me in the case so I can be his bird dog, no matter what I think I'm doing as Benny's lawyer. There's an ego boost. So, I sat back and closed my eyes, figuring that Willis wasn't likely to tolerate a semi-competent lawyer representing the kid, no matter what resources I might bring to the table. And then, Eureka!

Assuming I didn't embarrass myself and unintentionally make Stannard's case for her, the witnesses which I might find through the private eye would be disclosed to Willis, and he would pursue those leads to make sure that there weren't other witnesses, and he would cross-examine my witnesses, and I would cross-examine his witnesses, and we'd both cross-examine the grandparents.

Well, I'll be damned. Maybe Willis doesn't think I'm a total idiot, after all.

I felt so much better that I decided to give myself the night off, and go play with my trains. After all, I had done what I could until the reports came in, and knowing Lefty Martinez's Detective Agency, I'd be seeing the first of those reports in the next two days. Did I mention that I bought a house?

Charlene finally embarrassed me into it, pointing out that tax advantages came with real estate, that women are more favorably impressed by men who own houses instead of renting tacky apartments and, the clincher, that I'd have a room for my trains. I'm not so sure he approves of my hobby, but he's kind enough to pretend and so I reciprocate, and pretend that I bought the place for the tax advantages and to entice women, and not just so I'd have a train room.

It's a respectable hobby, fraught with danger and requiring self-discipline, organization, mental acuity and at least some physical competence. No kidding, I've hurt myself worse playing trains than most people have with guns. There's hot solder and spinning drills; fumes; saws and knives in every size, shape and dimension; paint, ladders and solvents; and enough electricity to stun an elephant. Want to hear about the time I learned about galvano-electric shock?

Anyway, I actually *play* with my trains. I am not a collector, and I don't worry about prototypical management practices, which means I don't give a rat's ass how real trains run. I build little houses and not so little factories, and I create scenes which relieve the stresses that come from representing perverts who would rather beat their children to death than put them out for adoption and give them a chance to have decent lives. I vent my anger and my disgust, and maybe that's why Charlene thinks that I'm emotionally disturbed.

Sorry.

Presently, I am building a factory complex which on the outside looks like any other scale model of a four story brick building. It started out as a brewery, but it's big enough for what I have in mind, so I got some one-way glass and sheet plastic, and with the help of some surplus computer cable and miniature light bulbs, I am creating a mannequin factory.

Those people who think that a model railroad should have a purpose besides going in circles around a Christmas tree should be happy. Making mannequins requires plaster and lumber, and God-only-knows what else, and then there are the finished dummies to ship out. Box cars, flat cars; coal hoppers for the power house, if I build one; covered hoppers for the incoming bulk plaster. Of course for me, the real attraction is modeling the interior, using the one-way glass and small mirrors to make it look like I really created a working factory. And how do I represent the mannequins? Thanks for asking. Would you believe that the Europeans - if you think guys here take their model trains seriously, cruise Europe some day - sell scale models of naked women, just for people who play with trains?

And Charlene thinks *I'm* disturbed.

Oh, well. When I was a kid, the big deal was if the power was on, the train moved and stayed on the track. Back then, even I could take things apart and understand what I was looking at, and put them back together and have them work. Now, everything is so sophisticated that it takes a surgeon's patience to take things apart, and a jeweler's workbench to work on the mechanism.

On top of which, you can buy almost everything built-up and ready to go, and some of the engines include computer modules so that you can run them into each other, head on, just like the big guys. Trust me, playing with trains is not for lazy, dull-minded sissies.

Of course, having a house isn't for sissies either, between updating the plumbing and replacing the roof, cleaning the gutters and worrying about lightning strikes and wind damage. And tornadoes and earthquakes and unusually heavy rains and flooded streets and backed up sewers. Why the hell did I buy this place?

Oh, well. Too late now.

Besides having a train room and tax advantages, I have a garage with an opener, and by "opener" I mean an integrated security system which not only opens the door, it turns on the lights and television, and powers up a designated outlet in case I want to hook up a blender and have a sissy drink waiting for me when I clear the door. I tried that once. The top blew off the blender and it took two hours to clean up the mess, which pretty much put me off sissy drinks unless there's a bartender handy. I guess I'll leave it with the television and the lights.

I checked the mail and as usual, the bulk was just that, Bulk Mail. I do not open Bulk Mail. Trash and recycle, sure; open, never. And of course, the bills.

I get a perverse pleasure from bills. Not from the bills themselves, but from the ability to pay them on the day they come, no questions asked, no juggling of payment dates, no worrying about exorbitant credit card interest rates. For that, I am every day grateful to Charlene. There was a time, not too long ago, that every month was an adventure in creative finance. Now, the firm deposits an embarrassing amount on the first of every month and then the mortgage and similar expenses are magically paid. I could have the credit cards and incidental bills handled that way too, but the monthly ritual brings me satisfaction and lets me pretend that I have some control over my life.

Control is something which I usually don't feel like I have, especially with Charlene there to point out my shortcomings and sign me up as Benny's lawyer, and things like that.

Things like, Charlene decorated the place. Besides a killer sense of style, he knows furnishings. He also knows how to get everything wholesale. When I started to rebel and demand that he keep his claws off the project, he smiled and raised his hands in mock surrender, crossed his arms and waited. And waited. Finally, having made my point, I let him have some input.

As Charlene said later, after I had fully expounded my theories on decorating, had recited every principle and maxim of line and color which I knew, and stated a detailed analysis of the appropriate way to redo the place, it had been a most interesting seven minutes. He then took over, and I admit he knew exactly what to do, and how to get it done. Wholesale.

Bitch. Or prick. Either fits.

The whole place looks like Frank Lloyd Wright developed a personality to go with his genius. Charlene called in the best carpenter slash contractor he could find, gave him instructions and told me to get out of the way. Three weeks and two days later, they let me back in and I had to admit, I'd have just screwed it up. But I still have this image of Charlene posing in those four inch heels, batting his eyes at this guy and saying, "I'm so pleased you took us on, but could I suggest ...?"

Pleased, yes. Suggesting? Not even a little bit.

So now I have a solid house with a screened back porch, a semi-formal living room, a kitchen that would make Marriott drool, and carpet so thick you could sleep on it, with a pile so deep you could maybe lose a small dog in it. The living room ceiling is stained and varnished pine, and there are laminated beams to hold it up, stained and varnished to match. There wouldn't have been room to do that, as I understand it, but the prior owner had insisted on a sunken living room with a ten and half foot ceiling. The walls are antique white, which has a slight greenish cast, as Charlene explained it, and that subtly compliments the hunter green leather furniture. There is an area rug in front of the fireplace, and if I had been asked first, I would have said that an area rug on top of carpeting is overkill. I would have been wrong, unless I had tried to do it myself. And there is the master bathroom.

It's all black and green marble, and the faucets are brushed stainless steel. Me, I would have tackied it up with gold plated stuff, or cheaped out with chrome, but Charlene kept my hands off and it worked out fine. Now if I just had a tasteful woman of substance to appreciate it and to compliment me on my choice of decorators.

Sure.

I thought that my favorite room would be the train room, or maybe the den. Which, by the way, is about as cozy and masculine a room as I could dream up. More stained pine and leather, burgundy this time, and brass. You'd think that the hunter green in the living room would make it look like a hunting lodge, but actually it all fits. The den, on the other hand, has that L L Bean look, as though I have just returned from a hard day of relaxing in a trout stream, my favorite fly rod in hand and needing the perfect place to record my latest trophy, a huge rainbow which I released because I respected the fight he showed.

Right.

One, I am not about to wrap my hands around a trout. Two, this is Toledo, Ohio, about as far from Montana as I can get and not be in Manhattan. Hmm. Apparently, I have been in the vodka already. Maybe this is not a night for trains after all and besides, I cannot get Benny What's-His-Name out of my head.

Crap.

FOUR

Any man who isn't aroused by the sight of a pretty woman in a G-string and a garter belt is either too old to care, too young to understand, or gay. This woman was pretty, though not exceptionally so. Pretty still, even when seen from behind in the half-light of morning. She was youngish, with good skin, a slim waist and a womanly behind divided by a well-made silk G-string. The garter belt was also well-made and yes, you're right. I know way too much about lingerie, thanks to spending so much time with Charlene. Too bad I know so little about women, including this one's name and why she was in my house.

"Who the hell are you?"

She jumped about six feet, spun and gasped.

"Sorry." Actually, I was. I pretty much always say the wrong thing and then spend the rest of the night trying to apologize. Of course, this time it was way early in the morning and I had no interest in the woman outside of her presence in my house, and the fact that she was half-naked. It finally occurred to me that her breasts were bare, that they were small and nicely shaped, and that she seemed to wear G-strings and garter belts as a matter of course.

There's a point. Women are always dressing themselves in oversized, worn out clothes, complete with sensible underwear and shoes, and perhaps with a dab of cold cream - certainly not mascara - then complaining that men don't look at them, sport hard-ons and say, "Oh, darling! How beautiful you are!" Wanna guess why?

It's like this. The average woman wears a thong because she wants to outdo other average women, not because she wants to get lucky. So, when I came unbidden upon a total stranger in my house, a total stranger whose bottom was shapely and minimally clothed in a G-string, naturally my curiosity was awakened. Not fully aroused, just awakened.

"I, ah, I came with ..." She pointed to the guest room, and I figured my cousin, be it Charlene or Charlie, was in there asleep.

"Charlie?" I figured, as distracted as she was right then, I'd go with Charlie. In case it was Charlene who had brought her, "Charlie" was easier to slough into "Charlene" than vice-versa.

"Yes. Charlie."

Swell. I finally get a woman in my house who knows how to dress to impress, and she already belongs to Charlie. No chance here.

"Known him long?" Pathetic, I know, but what the hell.

"No." She blushed and her face turned almost purple. "I met him last night at the poker game."

"Oh?"

"That's why I'm here."

"Of course." What was I supposed to say? "I suppose he won you?"

"Sort of. Actually, I'm collateral."

Yeah, right. I'm a lawyer, and I know lots about "collateral," including that as a word it is both a noun and an adjective. Nothing I know about the word has anything to do with a half-naked woman in my house in the early morning, with the possible exception of "security for a loan."

"What were you, table stakes?"

"No, just collateral." She kept looking around, as though she had lost something.

"What are you looking for?"

"My dress."

"Ah. Did you have it when you came in last night?" See why I'm so popular with the ladies?

"I think so." She looked confused. Genuinely, pathetically confused. She turned around, searching for her dress, and I saw that what I had thought was a birthmark was really a badly drawn tattoo.

"Maybe I can help?" Eventually, after I have my coffee, I make contact with reality. That I was able to concentrate at all was a tribute to my increasing maturity. Or perhaps, just an indication that I was waking up.

"Please." She cut her eyes toward the guest room, and I gathered that she had seen Charlie in full cry, or Charlene at his worst, if you prefer.

Yes, I know: you can't decide if you want me to call him Charlie or Charlene, and refer to him or her. Sorry, but that's your issue, not mine. Right now, I have a pretty woman looking at me like I'm not the least interesting person she has ever met, and she already knows Charlie. For me, this is scoring big.

"Rough night?"

"Oh, no." The implication registered. "No! He was very nice."

"Are you missing a bra, too?"

"No, I ... I didn't wear one."

I held up my hand. "Stay here. I'll find your dress."

I'd had too much vodka to be playing with my trains, so I had given up and gone to bed. I slept hard, and when the alarm rang I flung myself around the bed as though there was a fire and the smoke alarm was ringing instead of the clock. I had forced myself out of bed, more because Benny Randolph was haunting my sleep than because I had to. My secretary, Lydia, runs things better than I do, and as long as I show up occasionally and pretend to oversee things, everyone works hard and the money flows in. Nobody ever said anything about a pretty woman, half-naked, showing up in my house. But there she was, and Charlie was still asleep, which made me think I had half a chance.

I found her dress on the floor of the guest room and brought it to her.

"Thank you."

She looked down at herself as I held the dress for her, then raised her arms and let the dress slide down over them, and onto her shoulders. "Why are you being so nice to me?"

"Uh, it's too early to be myself?" I'm so smooth, no doubt I intimidate women with my *savoir-faire*. A little self-denigration, and right away they see the sterling fellow lurking within.

"I mean, you two treat me so well." She shrugged, amazed at our kindness. "The others, well, treated me like I was their property."

Could it be the tattoo? "You said something about being collateral?"

"What?"

I pointed to her bottom. "The tattoo?"

She frowned, "How do you know about that?"

I turned her around and patted her butt, then helped her smooth her dress over herself. It came to the bottom of her butt, just below the crease where it joined her thighs. "It's sort of obvious, if you know where to look."

"Oh, that." She smiled, "That's not really a tattoo. Charlie is going to take me in today and have me tattooed for real."

"Ah."

She smiled apologetically, and I had no idea why she'd apologize to a stranger that his cousin was having her tattooed.

"My husband likes to play poker, but he isn't very good at it."

"Well, that explains it." No, it didn't, but I really didn't care. I wanted my coffee and I wanted to get away from the woman before she started to make sense.

She nodded, "It was pretty embarrassing the first time it happened, and I still feel kind of awkward when I go home with whoever won the pot, but your cousin didn't try anything with me and you're being, well, really nice, too."

I cannot tell you how my self-image soared that a strange woman whose husband apparently thought of her as a poker chip considered me to be as nice as my cousin, the cross-dressing hit man.

"I don't mean to be rude, but I haven't had my coffee yet and I have to get downtown to the office."

"I can cook, if you'd like breakfast."

"Don't worry about it. I'm used to taking care of myself." That's because the last woman who said that to me set the house on fire, and the one before that tried to poison me. Guess which was my mother.

"Oh, sorry. I just thought, well, the other men expected me to do things around the house."

That's when I realized that she still hadn't told me her name and that I really didn't care. "It was nice meeting you, but I have to get ready to go." I nodded toward the guest room. "He's usually better behaved in daylight."

"Is there anything you want me to do while you're at work?"

Yeah. Get out. "Nope, not really. Just don't steal the silverware."

She looked somewhere between confused and hurt.

"I know all the cops. It's really just cheap stainless and I'll be embarrassed when they catch you and bring it back. They think I'm rich, or at least that my taste isn't in my mouth."

"Huh?"

Apparently, the girl had no Southern DNA whatsoever. Just about everybody born south of the Mason-Dixon line knows that, "Her taste is in her mouth," usually means she's a step above White Trash. "Make yourself at home. Charlie will tell you what to do. I assume the poker game will be going on again tonight and he'll be taking you back and trying to recover his cash. Meanwhile, enjoy."

"Oh, I get it." Apparently, the light had dawned. "You're a funny guy." She had a pretty smile, I'll say that much for her. "How do you like your coffee? Weak, strong or medium?"

"Medium, I guess."

"How about your eggs?" Persistent, too.

"No eggs. I hate eggs unless they're in waffles or pancakes, or maybe French toast."

"Go shower and dress. I'll find the kitchen." Suddenly, she was a woman.

"Ok." No need to fight over having my own way. Which by the way they don't teach in law school. You'd be amazed at how many lawyers don't know enough to shut the hell up when they're winning. And yes, the longer they talk, the greater the risk they'll prove the other side was right all along, or maybe make the judge mad enough that he doesn't care. I know, I talk a lot. But there's a reason to what I say and do.

I learned a long time ago to talk until people get numb. Then, just when they dismiss me as a long-winded yutz, I close in for the kill. Meaning, of course, I shut up. The silence unnerves them and they start to chatter and pretty soon the judge likes me a whole lot better. Pretty soon, I look a lot smarter than the opposition. I know: tricky bastard. It was either that or learn lawyering, and like I said at the beginning, I'm not that good a lawyer.

* * *

I do my best thinking in the shower. Like Willis said, look for the motive. Exactly what Charlene was up to this time wasn't clear, but maybe he was collecting a family, building one from people he liked. Those God gave him weren't worth cremation, and stranger things have happened. Hell, bizarre things happen every day of my life, and I am so accustomed to them that what surprises me isn't what happens so much as that what happens doesn't surprise me. Follow?

So why couldn't I figure out Charlene's motive? Or motives, in case his reasons for me to save little Benny Randolph were different from his reasons for bringing this unnamed woman into my house.

But Charlie's motives - or Charlene's - weren't as important just then as finding out if this woman could make decent coffee. I dried off and dressed, and went to find out if my long-held belief holds water: any woman is more comfortable in any kitchen that any man, his own included. Plus, I was getting hungry just because there was a possibility that I might have a real breakfast before I hit the road.

Turned out, she could cook.

At least she could make microwave bacon, decent pancakes and coffee. I thought that was pretty good, considering that it was her first time doing any of that stuff in my house, and she was wearing evening clothes, including her shoes.

I didn't mention her shoes before, right? I hate to repeat myself, not because I dislike the sound of my voice, but because I don't want to appear senile. Anyway, she was wearing simple black leather high heeled pumps. Thanks to Charlene, I knew that. Who cooks in those things? I have trouble walking in standard shoes and this woman was whipping around the kitchen - my kitchen - like a ballerina on stage.

"Sit down. I'll bring it to you."

I looked around and saw that she had set the table, complete with place mats and napkins. So I sat and drank the orange juice which she had set out. I also noticed that she was actually a pretty woman with very nice legs, and the appearance of a pleasant disposition.

"Thanks."

She put the plate down with a firm hand, sure of herself but not bitchy.

"This is really fine."

"You haven't tasted it yet." She brought the syrup, which she had warmed, and poured the coffee. "Do you want milk or half and half? You have both in the fridge."

"Half and half."

She brought the cream, and sat down with her own plate, looked at mine and frowned, "When did you eat last?"

"Dinner." I hated to take the time to answer, but she had asked so nicely.

"Was it a light dinner, perhaps?"

"Not really."

"Would you like more?"

"Sure." I nodded, and reached for my coffee cup. "But you eat first."

She pointed to the stove. "There's more. I just left it on the stove to stay warm."

"Oh?" My plate and I went to bond with the stove.

"I would have gotten it for you." There was a hint of hurt in her voice, or maybe insecurity, as though she wasn't keeping up with her duties.

"Don't be silly. I can do some things for myself."

She looked at the pile on my plate and the nearly empty plate on the stove which, realizing that I should show some consideration, I brought to her. "Here. Before I eat it all, you should take this."

She looked at the remainder and said, "But that won't leave anything for Charlie."

"Screw Charlie."

"I beg your pardon?"

"You cooked, he slept, it's my house. He wants food, he can get up like the rest of us, come to the table on time. You want to make more, I won't stop you. But right now, eat while it's hot."

Apparently, no one had ever spoken to her quite like that. I say that because she got this funny look. But she took the plate and helped herself, and together we finished what she had cooked. Being basically a selfish, self-centered and insensitive guy, I suddenly saw opportunity knocking. "So, Charlie took you as security for a poker debt?"

She flushed, and I mean purple. "Yes."

"Your clothes are expensive, but you know how to cook."

"My husband has a good job with a good income." She looked away from me while she answered. "We weren't always poor."

"Let me guess. You stay home while he goes to work, and now his gambling is out of control. No cash, the credit cards are maxed out and the bank is on your ass about the mortgage."

She nodded, still looking away.

"So your husband, the gambling addict, loans you out so his buddies will let him stay in the game."

She nodded, and then looked at me.

"How about I pay Charlie the thousand dollars that drawing on your butt says you're worth, and then you stay here for a while and cook? You have someplace better to be?"

"They already thought of that. One of the boys, Ed, said he'd pay the money. But they couldn't figure out who he'd pay. Willie - that's my husband - owed Arnie the money. But if Ed gave Arnie the money, then I'd go with Ed until Willie came up with the cash, and what would change? If Ed gave the money to Willie, he'd just gamble it away, and then what? He'd owe both Ed and Arnie, and I'd still be the collateral, and I'm not worth two grand. At least, that's what they all said after they passed me around."

She looked down at her plate, and I felt so very, very masculine. Proud of myself, too.

"Why did you let your husband turn you out as a whore?"

The flush changed and I could see the words forming in her brain: *I am not a whore.* But we both knew that her husband had traded her for money, and that had included sexual services. That made her a whore no matter how she looked at it.

On the other hand, I have spent a few years reading people and I had the idea that she was somewhere between being an amiable slut and a wife and mother. So I asked her, "How old is your daughter?"

Her jaw fell, and her mouth worked silently. Finally she recovered herself and asked, "How do you know about my daughter?"

"Wild guess." I didn't see a need to mention that I had noticed the slight belly fat, a subtle hint that she had a child, and that her behavior bespoke a woman of the mother-protects-child syndrome, a self-proclaimed self-sacrificer who lies down in the path of the monster so that her child will be protected from abuse and perversion, sheltered from the excesses of the other parent. I had seen it too many times, the men and women who subject themselves to abuse so that they can all pretend to live in a normal, healthy family and the children can grow up well-adjusted.

It's a load of crap.

The children already know what the parents are up to, they know which parent is strong and which is weak, and they don't respect either. Guessing that her child was a daughter was purely instinct: too many years of reading perverts, I guess.

"Does she know about Willie's gambling, and what's written on your bottom?"

"No! No." The change in her voice meant she was beaten; I waited. "I thought if he saw what he was doing to me, he'd be worried about how it would affect her. I thought he'd get help and she'd never have to know." She shook her head, and I had the feeling she was past crying.

Novelists write about "a sinking feeling," and "cold certainty" and such like. Me, I knew exactly where this was going, mostly because of those years I spent navigating Juvenile Court before Charlene made me rich. What people do to their children and with them is amazing. As a society we bemoan the plight of abused and neglected children, then we pay lawyers to protect them at half the rate we pay people to build cars and sweep streets. We hire prosecuting attorneys to say, "Nope. Can't prosecute without a confession. Too tough. Juries won't convict."

What they don't say out loud is, "Besides, children can't vote."

"How old is she?"

"Seventeen." She smiled, "She's really pretty and popular. And she's smart, not like her mother. Straight "A's" on every report card."

It felt good to see her smile, and it felt good to smile back. "You can stay here as long as you want. No sex, and you don't have to clean if you don't want to. We'll evict Charlie and your daughter can come here too."

"Why are you being so nice? I'm a total stranger." *And a whore.*

The eyes always give them away. "I like your pancakes."

Naturally, Charlie showed up just then.

"There's pancakes?"

"Sorry, Cousin. Kitchen's closed." I stood up and yawned. "I have to go. You kids play nice while I'm at work."

"I'll fix pancakes for you." She stood up too, and walked to the cupboard to get Charlie a coffee cup. "Do you want juice?"

"Sure. Thanks, Mitzi."

Mitzi?

"You're welcome." She went back to cooking, every move sure and confident.

Mitzi?

But as Mark Twain once wrote, this warn't no time to swap knives. I had to get downtown and act like a lawyer, and supervise the underlings before they figured out they didn't need me and started out on their own, leaving me destitute.

"Mitzi?" I couldn't help myself.

She turned around, a natural response to having her name called. "Yes?"

"That's your name?"

"Yes."

"Oh. You hadn't told me your name."

She smiled, "Mitzi Lynn Watson, at your service, sir."

Boy, was she prophetic when she said that. It also explained why she seemed like an amiable slut.

Why people name their children as they do is way over my head. Well, no. It's not. People get these weird ideas, some because they want their children to have unique names, some because it's an exercise in transferred egotism, some because they have no idea how other children will twist their children's names into tools of torture; and some because they are on drugs when they give birth and give names.

"What's you daughter's name, if I can ask?"

"Patricia." She smiled, proud of her child. "Not Patty, or Patsy, or Trish: Patricia. She's very firm about it."

Charlie just happened to catch my eye right then. Remember the part about the sinking feeling?

"Want to do me a favor, Danny?" Charlie can be as innocent looking as a baby when he tries. Now, he was all open-faced honesty. "It's my turn to host the poker party and you know how Sis is about cigar smoke."

"Not really."

He gave me a look. "Not really what?"

"Not really do I want to do you a favor. I can see what's coming. That's what the Holiday Inn is for. Go get a hospitality room."

Charlie cut his eyes toward Mitzi.

I read, *Do it for her,* in his look.

Why? I can give looks too.

"Here? Hold it here?" Mitzi paused her work on Charlie's breakfast and turned to join the conversation. "I can take care of setting it up if you want to do it here."

"Swell!" Charlie wasn't about to let my wants and needs interfere with whatever he had going on, and knowing him it wasn't likely that he would involve me in any of his work. I let him win. "Thanks, Danny."

Mitzi went back to making Charlie's breakfast, and spoke to us over her shoulder. "Let me know if you want anything special, otherwise I'll just do the usual."

I started to ask what the usual might be but, since I didn't care, I decided not to. "Do whatever you think everybody will like."

"You trust me, huh?" She looked up and smiled. It touched her eyes and I could see her heart, and I knew this was going to be a lot more complicated than I had planned.

"It's cheap silverware, remember?"

Charlene - I mean, Charlie gave me a flat look of appraisal, like guys give each other when they see somebody about to screw up.

I nodded to the doorway, because I knew he'd have something to say.

Mitzi watched us leave the kitchen and called out, "Breakfast will be ready in about three minutes, so don't get carried away."

"No problem. I'll do the talking." Charlie waited till she turned around, then rounded on me. "What are you thinking, Cousin?"

"That's there's more to her potential than there is to her. That you're up to something, but I doubt it's work. That tattooing her is a really bad idea."

He nodded, "Just keep on thinking all of that, Cousin, and we'll both be fine."

"I was also thinking that maybe I should pay you the thousand that she says her husband owes you."

"Her idea?"

"Nope. In fact, she said the boys thought about it, gave up on the idea and passed her around."

He nodded. "Sometimes, even beer swilling, poker playing macho pigs get it right."

"Should I ask what you're up to?"

First that mischievous Charlene smile, then a look of smoldering passion. He touched my cheek and said, "Be a good boy and run along, make a lot of money and protect our children. *Ciao, bello.*"

He turned around and then, sure that Mitzi wasn't looking, walked into the kitchen with that insolent Charlene walk, leaving me standing there feeling foolish.

Just that suddenly he had become Charlene and I knew I was in love with a woman who didn't exist, and I was trying to protect a woman who existed but who would never be the woman she could be, and that was nowhere close to the woman that I had projected onto both Charlene and Mitzi.

I hadn't finished dressing, let alone left for work, and already I had a headache. But there was nothing I could do, so I went back to my room and found my tie and jacket, and then I wandered to the office and pretended that I was interested in my cases, and especially that of Benny Randolph.

FIVE

My secretary is hot. Maybe not so bright as Joyce Roberts, maybe not so interested in her boss's welfare, but hot. Truly smoking hot. Next to Charlene, she's an old shoe, which causes me to wonder whether it's true that no one knows what a man wants like another man.

Lydia, my secretary, has no interest in me. I'm the boss and I am boring. Not "Ho-hum, that's nice dear," boring, but "Drag me from my chair and put a bullet in my brain," boring, as though she were sitting through a dramatic reading of the IRS Code. No lie, in the midst of dictation - at which she is very, very good - she once put down her pad, yawned and stretched and told me that, "You need a life. You're good-looking, you're smart, you're rich. But you are, God help you, the most boring man I have ever met."

"I'm not trying to be exciting here, I'm trying to win the case."

"And I don't want to be an accessory to manslaughter if some poor son-of-a-bitch dies of boredom while he's reading this letter."

"Would you sleep with me?"

"Sadly, Danny, that's just what it would be: sleep." She stood up. "I know what you want to say, so I'll just go write the letter and you can punch it up. Or down, if you prefer."

I signed it just as she typed it, in case you were wondering.

Anyway, her legs go right up to her ass - and she refuses to let me say that. She is smart and pretty, and keeps me in business, and if she could just figure out why Charlene stuck me with the Benny Randolph case, she'd be perfect. But I can't tell her that Charlene is a guy and I can't tell her that I think Charlene is his father, and I'm willing to bet that if she meets Mitzi she'll be even less charitable to her than Charlene is.

"Good morning, Mr. Compton."

Double crap. "Good morning, Lydia. How much trouble am I in this time?"

"No trouble at all, Mr. Compton. Here are your messages, and

Mr. Martinez is waiting in your office to go over the Randolph reports."

"You know what's in those reports, don't you?"

"I may have an idea."

"I'm going to have to work, aren't I?"

"All day long, Mr. Compton. Shall I bring you coffee?"

"Sure, and send someone out for bagels and cream cheese."

"On your desk."

"Martinez likes lox with his bagels."

"Yes, he does."

Sometimes, there's nothing else to say. I walked the eight steps from her desk to my office door thinking that if there were any justice in this life, I'd be wearing blue jeans and sweatshirts and working at Hydramatic or Jeep, and Lydia would date me and find me interesting, especially if I didn't try to talk and say interesting things. Just so long as I could keep my mouth shut and say, "Yes, dear," at the right times, and not stress because she was working downtown with a bunch of suits, I'd have it made. But no, I had to go to law school and then I had to be a lawyer, and then I had to open the door and let Charlene come back into my life.

Thanks, Mom. Thanks for the brutal, sadistic upbringing, and thanks for your unbending will that I be something better than a happy, unimportant man with a steady income and a pretty wife. Thanks for never losing sight of your goal that I be something of which you could approve, no matter what it cost me personally. But all that's done and you're in Hell, and no doubt loving it.

I had a flash of Satan calling Saint Peter on the Hot Line, claiming that she was in the wrong place and demanding that Peter get her on the Heaven-bound escalator pronto. "She's a saint! A saint, I tell you!" And Peter, knowing better, hissing into the phone like there's a bad connection, yelling, "What? What?"

The imagery cheered me enough to open the door and meet with Lefty Martinez, the private dick we keep on retainer.

Lefty Martinez isn't a lefty and no, I don't know where he got the nickname. He's not quite six feet tall, which means I have an inch or so on him, and he has that jet black hair and slightly Hispanic complexion which makes him both forgettable when seen in public and so popular with the women that I have trouble figuring out how he gets his work done. He's also the best, most thorough PI around these parts, and his reports reflect his FBI training: complete, accurate, expensive.

"Morning, Counselor."

"Lefty."

"There's more stuff out there, but this should give you a good idea of the situation." He handed me the package of reports, records and photos.

"Thanks. How's your bagel?"

"Perfect, as always. If you ever get tired of Miss Efficiency out there, let me know. I'll take her on in a heartbeat."

"You'll lose."

"What?" Lefty looked up over his bagel, eyebrows raised, puzzled.

"If you take her on, you'll lose." I had his report in one hand, my coffee mug in the other. "Hands down."

"Oh, I get it." Lefty chuckled, nodded. "You're probably right."

He sipped and chewed while I read the report and went through the records and photos he had attached. So much for the grandparents getting custody of Benny Randolph. But his report still didn't give me a clue as to why Charlene should give a rat's ass about this otherwise anonymous little boy, cherubic though he is.

"Anything you didn't put in here?"

"What I like about you, Counselor, is that you pick up on the subtleties." He nodded, pleased, and continued. "What's not in there is that the Children Services people are pretty steamed at you and Willis right now. Stannard says - this is strictly on the Q-T, of course - that there are ways for her to lose this case, and then the agency can back away and let the grandparents and the mother litigate the custody themselves. She seems to think that the court won't pay Willis to stay on as the guardian's lawyer. Tight budget and all that."

"Then she's dumber than I thought. Willis could buy Ohio, if he wanted to. What the county pays him for an hour - assuming he even bills the court, which I doubt - would buy his lunch. And you and

I both know, Willis doesn't need anybody to buy his lunch."

"I figured you'd enjoy that one." He leaned forward, emphasizing the intimacy of the conversation. "What's really got a burr up her ass is that stunt you pulled, getting yourself recognized as the kid's lawyer. She's planning on teaching you a lesson."

"Let me get this straight. Eileen Stannard thinks that she can throw the case, then Willis will quit because the county won't pay him and - what - all of this is important to me personally?" I sat back, picked up my coffee mug and pondered the irony. The only reason I was in this case at all was that Charlene said so, and if there was any reason that I was concerned about winning, it was that I want Charlene happy and not trying to kill me. "What the hell lesson is she going to teach me, besides not arguing with the agency?"

"My source hasn't told me." He smiled, and I could just see him close to his source, smiling that boyishly wicked, woman-getting smile. "But I expect I'll be hearing more soon."

"And I'll know as soon as you know, right?"

"You'll know real soon after I know. How's that?"

"That'll be swell."

"Gotta go." He stood and stretched. "Thanks for breakfast, but duty calls."

I stood up to shake his hand. "Your source is reliable?"

"Counselor, few things make a person more, ah, reliable than the chance to save a child, make a buck and get lucky, all rolled into one fine, moral bit of civil disobedience."

"The report doesn't say anything about where the father is. You got any thoughts on that?"

Lefty smiled and said, "I sort of think the guy is dead. See, I got a line on another source, a guy who knows a guy. The thing is, all these guys think they're hooked up. You know what I mean, right?" He rubbed his fingers against his thumb. Yeah, I knew what he meant: *cash.* "Anyway, when I find out for sure, I'll send along another report."

"Along with the bill?"

"Always, Counselor. Always."

He walked to the door and paused with his hand on the door

knob. "Tell your cousin hello for me and give her my best, ok?"

"Sure, Lefty." *And while I'm at it, I'll tell her - him - that I think you should look into Mitzi Lynn Watson and her daughter, Patricia. Of course, then you'll find out that she is married to some lump who lost her in a poker game, most recently to my cousin's alter ego, Charlie, who I'm betting you don't know exists. Sure, Lefty.*

I sat down and Lydia walked through the door, picked up my coffee mug, went to refill it and brought it back, all without being asked, all without a word being spoken. She headed for the door, still silent.

"Lydia? Hold on, ok?"

She stopped and turned, returned and sat down, crossed her legs and folded her arms across her chest. "Bad news?"

"Not really."

"Woman trouble?"

"Why do you ask?" She can be scary, the way she homes in on things before I say them.

"You have that look, like you're five and mommy just told you that your puppy had to go live in the country with grandpa, and you didn't have a chance to say good-bye."

"How long have you worked for me?" Although usually, it feels the other way around.

"Going on four years, since right after you opened the doors." Her foot started swinging, a sure sign I was headed into trouble. What I did this time, who could guess? She stared right at me. "Something on your mind, you should say it. Otherwise, I have work to do."

A smart man knows that when a woman crosses her arms to talk to him, crosses her legs, it means something. Sometimes, it means she thinks he's trying to get in her pants, sometimes it means she wants him to try. Sometimes, it means she's comfortable that way. Go figure.

"You're the best friend I've got. You're the best friend I've ever had."

She turned away and smiled, and her foot stopped swinging. She wasn't smiling when she turned back to face me. "So, who is she?"

"Why would a woman let her husband use her as collateral in a poker game?"

"It certainly isn't because she is overburdened with self-image. Who is this person? Do I know her? What's her name?"

"Her name is Mitzi Lynn Watson, she says, and she has a daughter named Patricia."

Lydia always makes me feel good. Usually it's just because I like being around her, but this time it was because for once I hadn't bored her. I know because of what she said next.

"Mitzi? You're kidding, right? Mitzi Lynn?"

"Watson."

"Mitzi Lynn *Anything*." She laughed, and my toes curled. I just love it when Lydia laughs. "Just when I think you are hopelessly boring, you come along and surprise me." She shook her head, uncrossed her arms and stood. "You stay right there. I'm going for my coffee and then you are going to tell me all about Mitzi Lynn and her daughter, Patricia." She shook her head again and said, "My, oh, my. Daniel Rodney, you sure can get yourself into things."

* * *

What I know about poker is, you play it with cards and chips, and say things like, "See, raise and call." In what order and for what purpose, I cannot say. Apparently, poker cannot be played without boxes of cheap cigars, cases of beer and pounds of salami. Also liverwurst, pastrami and corned beef.

Mitzi was at home with the crowd, Charlie plus five overage post-adolescents including her husband, all of them by turns sullen and boisterous. What I noticed was that Mitzi's husband was pretty much always the almost winner, while the other guys took winning by turns. I had the feeling that there had been a shift in the membership, and he wasn't truly within the circle of players. Since I know next to nothing about the game and the players, Charlie excepted, I stayed out of the way and watched.

I watched them play and watched how they treated Mitzi. They weren't outright nasty or rude to her, but they pretty clearly thought of her as community property, subject to common usage. What came to mind was the story I once heard about a retirement village. It was a gated community, and most of the residents were fixed so that a golf cart was too expensive, a luxury, and so they were sometimes restricted in their travel around the community. But one of the younger residents, being good with his hands, came up with a solution. The community bought a bunch of old bicycles and he refurbished them. Since it was a gated community, they put in some bicycle racks and whoever needed a ride took a bike and left it when he got where he was going. Maybe Charlie should have "Schwinn" tattooed on Mitzi's tush next to the poker chip.

"What are you smiling at, Dan-rod?"

"Remember the old joke about the man who bought his wife a bicycle so she could pedal her ass all over town?"

"I worry about you sometimes, Cousin." He dropped onto the couch beside me, put his feet up on the coffee table and make a large dent in the contents of the beer bottle.

"Is this half-time, or a timeout, or did y'all run out of money?"

The doorbell rang, and I never really found out why the recess. Mitzi's daughter was standing at the door and no, I have no idea how she found out where to go, nor how to get there.

Crap.

"Patricia! Why are you here?" Mitzi was truly concerned.

"Patty-baby! Come give your daddy a big hug."

Patricia - never Patty-baby - gave her father an icy "Hello, Father," and looked at her mother with the casual dislike of a society matron in the company of a bag lady. "I need money for school and I need this signed for the class trip."

Personally, since it was the middle of summer, the last thing that came to mind was that a seventeen year old girl would be in school, considering that she had all "A's" on her report card. But she was obviously seventeen going on forty, and maybe she was on the advanced track and this was some kind of honors program.

"Sure, sweetheart. Come on over and let me see that."

"I'll take care of it." Mitzi swooped in, took the paper and read it, questioned Patricia.

Patricia gave the right answers, apparently, because Mitzi signed the paper, then said to her husband, "Willie, give her some money."

"You signed it, you give it to her." He fingered his chips, looked around the table and, asked, "We gonna play poker or what?"

The other guys shrugged and looked at each other, called out to Charlie that if he was in or out, he should say so.

"Out." He raised his hand and beckoned for Patricia to come to him. "How much do you need, kid?"

Patricia stalked over to him, as sullen in her movements as she had been answering her mother.

Mitzi started to object but Charlie waved her off. "Well?"

"Forty dollars."

Charlie and I traded looks, knowing that we had the same thought: forty dollars, same as in town.

See, the old priest is reassigned to the convent and his duties include hearing the confessions of the nuns. He keeps hearing "blow job" over and over, and being an old man, has no idea what they're talking about. So he goes to Mother Superior and he asks her, "Mother Superior, what's a blow job?" And she answers, "Forty dollars, Father. Same as in town."

Charlie reached in his pocket and pulled out a small roll, thumbed two twenties and handed them to her. "Well?"

"Well, what?"

"Do you know who I am?"

"No."

"But you're taking money from me."

Patricia shrugged. "My parents are here and they aren't complaining. So?"

Charlie looked up at her and his words made my skin crawl. "I am going to introduce you to my sister. She is going to teach you how to behave. You will do exactly as she tells you." He waved her away. "Have fun on the trip. Be safe."

"So now Charlene is your sister?"

Charlie gave me one of his looks, the kind which reminds me that these questions about his identities are mine alone, and which make me feel foolish.

"Dear boy, the girl needs Auntie Charlene to help her grow up, to help her find herself, to help her reach her potential." He raised himself, looked over the back of the couch at Mitzi and Willie and sighed in disgust. "Certainly, neither of those two can do her much good."

"But you will keep her on the straight and narrow?"

Eyes rolling, he emptied his beer and waved at Mitzi to bring another. "Face it, Cousin. I am the most disciplined person you know. Moving from Charlie to Charlene requires absolute focus. Living as Charlene requires a clarity of purpose never required of people like you."

"You mean, normal?"

Mitzi arrived with fresh beer and so prevented his answer.

"You two look serious." She smiled at Charlie. "Afraid you'll never lose me back to Willie?"

Charlie flashed her one of his charming, self-denigrating smiles. "I'm growing accustomed to your face." He patted her rump, looked over the sofa as though interested in the progress of the game in his absence. "Who's winning you now?"

She looked over at the table, then down at him. "You're still holding title, it looks like."

He looked up and met her eyes. I felt like a fifth wheel, an accident witness, a guy who belches in an elevator. "My sister is coming back to town in a few days. I know it's not my business, but maybe she could play favorite auntie to your daughter. Patricia, is it?" He nodded over the couch toward Willie. "Maybe another woman can give her a positive view of how you are trying to protect her."

Mitzi took the deepest breath I have seen a woman take.

And another.

For a woman who didn't need a bra, she had an impressive rack.

"Excuse me." I stood up, looked at Charlie. "You want another beer? Mitzi? Can I bring you something?"

She sighed, "No, I'm fine."

Charlie lifted his eyebrow just enough that I knew to leave them alone.

I drifted toward the poker game, more interested in Willie and his friends than in the game. Sure, some people watch poker games the way other people watch chess matches. Me, I don't watch much of anything, including football. I used to watch the Super Bowl - for the commercials - but it took too long, so I quit. Lydia, who really gets into pro football, pointed out that I could tape the game and fast forward through everything but the commercials. Then she shook her head, looked away and smiled just like today when I told her that she is my best friend. Thinking about that conversation was a lot more pleasant than watching six guys, all going to fat and baldness, argue over cardboard. Besides, it was getting late.

I went back to the couch, but Charlie and Mitzi weren't there. *Crap. I can see where this is going.*

All I needed was for Willie to look around, see that his wife was missing and so was Charlie, and put two and two together. But Willie was way into the game and Charlie and Mitzi were being quiet, wherever they were, so I went prowling. They were in the kitchen, washing dishes.

Actually, Mitzi was washing the dishes and my cousin, the cross-dressing but not a transvestite hit man was drying them and putting them away. Just then, Willie missed his wife.

"Mitzi, what are you up to?"

"We're doing the dishes."

Willie turned in his chair, leaned around so that he could call into the kitchen for Charlie to get back into the game. "Hey, you! Moneybags! Come on out here and give me a chance to win my wife back."

Charlie strolled out of the kitchen, drying his hands on the dish towel. "I don't know, Willie. I'm feeling pretty lucky tonight."

"Come on, give me a chance to get even."

"Yeah, Charlie. Be a sport." Arnie seemed to delight in Willie's troubles.

Charlie raised his hands, pretending surrender. "Ok, ok, I'm in."

I considered watching them, just to see how bad it would get.

But truthfully, I was tired and my thoughts kept drifting back to Lydia. "You guys, don't kill each other, ok? And Charlie, if you lose the maid, you have to clean up this mess yourself, so don't get careless." I waved. "Night, all."

I got a chorus of grunts and "Yeah, night."

I was already history to those guys, so I headed back to the kitchen to finish things with Mitzi, who was about to become a fixture.

"Charlie is going to clean Willie's clock. You'll be staying tonight, and for a while after that. I've got a feeling things are going to sound worse than you can imagine, but that's all. Charlie likes you, I can tell, and he is serious about helping your daughter. And no, he doesn't 'like little girls,' ok?"

"I think so." She was tentative, mostly because she didn't want me to realize just how much she wanted to be in bed with my cousin.

"Goodnight, Mitzi."

"Goodnight, Mr. Compton."

I had already turned away from her, so she didn't see me frowning. But respect is never unwelcome, and I think she was aiming for distance - trying to keep me from expecting something she wanted to save for Charlie, follow? So I nodded, and kept walking.

In my dreams, Lydia had a very deep tan and she kept laughing. But she wasn't laughing at me, and so I slept through to the alarm, and woke up smiling.

SIX

No, Charlie didn't lose Mitzi and no, he didn't go home for the night. I found that out when I woke up and headed to the bathroom. The door to the guest room was open just enough that I could them in there, together, I could see that Charlie was, shall we say, in full glory, and Mitzi was helping, ah, glorify him. Happily, they didn't notice me and happily, I could right away tell that I am least a little more "glorious" than Charlie.

I have many times seen him suiting up as a woman, and the most distracting, dizzying thing I can think of is to watch a physically competent - he's a hired killer, remember? - otherwise entirely straight man carefully smoothing his stockings and adjusting his seams, then stepping into four inch heels, and checking his dress in the mirror. If one more time he asks me, "Does this make me look fat?", I'll strangle him with his own pantyhose. But I digress.

All those times were forgiven as soon as I realized that in the heat of passion there is more to me than to him. Yes, sir, I felt cheered and happy, and a little smug. I felt so good I decided to give myself a few extra minutes in the shower, glorying in my manhood. Then I remembered that Charlie gets "glorified" a hell of a lot more than I do, which sort of took the top off any celebrating. Plus, Charlie and Mitzi were still occupied *in gloria flagrante* when I was ready to leave, and that eliminated any chance of pancakes. Unhappy, unfed and unlikely to enjoy the morning, I went to my office to sulk, and to wish evil on Benny Randolph's mother, his grandmother and Eileen Stannard, in equal parts.

"Good morning, Lydia." She wasn't at her desk, but was squatting to look in the credenza which sat along the wall which in turn faced my office door. That put her back to me as I passed her desk, and so she looked over her shoulder to say, "Good morning, Danny," in that sweet, resonant contralto that makes my knees weak and my mind wander.

The stilettos and stockings did nothing for my composure and the garter belt and thong about sent me over the edge. Never mind how I knew. Obviously, Charlene taught me what to look for.

"Uh, ah, you, ah." It's the smoothness that gets them. "You have plans, maybe have to leave early?"

"No." She smiled and looked away; the smile was gone when she looked back. "I just felt like dressing up today."

Which included putting on her makeup and doing her hair and her nails - all twenty of them.

Then she stood, and it was like watching a plant grow out of the soil on nature television, shown in time-lapse photography. She stood and straightened, turned toward me in one fluid movement, and I thought I'd drool on myself. It registered that she was braless and wholly comfortable with me knowing that. I could feel my face burning and my knees shaking.

"Is the coffee ready?" That was the hardest thing I ever had to say, up until then, and if I say my voice was steady, then it was. God, I hoped it was.

"Already on your desk." She smiled, and I mean it touched her eyes and I thought I'd wet myself. I swear, she brushed herself against me as she went to sit at her desk, and for the life of me, I could not fathom why she had been digging in the credenza: her hands were empty. "Also bagels." She wagged her finger. "But no lox. Mr. Martinez isn't coming in today."

"Thank you. I'll, ah. I'll be in my office."

"I'll hold your calls till you've finished." She winked, "Breakfast, I mean," then sat with special attention to her posture.

Pretending nonchalance, I went inside my office and sat at my desk. Coffee as promised, and bagels and cream cheese. A plate, a place mat and a real knife, just like home. Or home, if there were a woman there to care for me, or even Mitzi, if she were awake and functioning. Maybe. Maybe not. Mitzi was awake and functioning when I left home, and I still left hungry.

Either Lydia was psychic or something was going on which was way beyond my poor, masculine intellect. Except that Lydia has been with me for four years, which we just covered, as you will recall, I'd be thinking she was coming on to me. But I know Lydia, and she does what she wants when she wants, and she has a life. Mitzi, on the other hand, has what men give her.

If Lydia wanted to spend time with me she'd say so. But Lydia has interesting friends, people with whom she parties. She is wildly popular, which is no wonder considering how she looks and how she acts. By that I mean, she is sure of herself and she never tries to make herself look better by making others look bad, and she is thoughtful. I had the bagels and cream cheese to prove it.

A favor! She wants a favor! I suppose it's possible, but she knows all she has to do is ask. She'd have to be brick stupid to miss how I feel about her, and there is nothing stupid about her. Besides, as Charlene once said, a neon sign would be more subtle. So what, then?

Crap.

I had no business thinking about this now. Lefty Martinez gave me enough to think about yesterday, and even if my appetite has to take a back seat to Charlie's, that's no reason to ignore my obligation to Benny Randolph. I opened Lefty's envelope of reports and went to it, reading everything at least twice, sifting and sorting; gleaning; learning; thinking about the way Lydia looked when she smiled.

There was no help for it. I couldn't go forward and I couldn't go back. I couldn't admit that I was in love, that I had been in love since the second I laid eyes on her. I paid her more than I had to, keeping her dependent on me, and I wouldn't say so to her because that would hurt her.

Right.

Lydia is the toughest person I know, Charlene included. She has her goals, which she pursues; her friends, of whom she is protective and to whom she is nurturing; and her ideals, which she never forsakes. Life comes at her and she accepts it, embraces it, rejoices in it. But then, she had real parents who raised her and who love her, and who give her strength. I'd envy her, be at least a little jealous of her, but every time I think of her I smile.

Like now.

There she is in my doorway, tapping files against her palm, acting as though I have nothing in this world to do except to wait on her whimsies. Here I am, looking up at her and wishing I had the stones to make her behave. But actually, I don't care what she does so long as she does it here, and she knows it.

"Yes?"

"My lunch date just canceled and I was wondering if you'd go with me. I checked your calendar and you're free. All the little boys and girls have their cases under control and if you get busy with that file and make your witness notes, you can leave at eleven-thirty. So, is it a date?"

Everything she said was true, and if I'd had the courage I'd have asked her myself, instead of waiting for her to take the initiative. Except, I wasn't so much her date as a last-minute fill in. Given my high level of self-respect and my exalted position in the community, I of course said, "Ok."

"Good. I'll remind you so we can get out of here on time. If we go early, we'll get served faster."

And she was gone.

* * *

After lunch, I was back at my desk pretending to work on Benny Randolph's case, and thinking that there is no justice. To the world, Benny Randolph is just another anonymous child caught in the swirl of the Toilet of Life. All that separates him from thousands of other anonymous children is that he somehow caught the attention of Charlene, who in turn is the cousin of a lawyer who makes up bad metaphors when he is distracted by love. Actually, I was remembering the looks that all the other men gave Lydia, and the looks the women gave me. Their jealousy, meaning the men, warmed my heart and their lustful, appraising looks, meaning the women .... Now that I think about it, they did nothing for me.

Crap.

According to Lefty Martinez, who had resurfaced long enough to fax an estimate of the cost for the real interviews, Benny's father was dead. Lawyers talk like that. For normal people, Lefty sent me a fax because he needed an answer pronto, and he had a live one. So I faxed back, "Go for it, just don't sell your children." Then he faxed back the details, and now we are maybe going to set up a deposition, right after I get the affidavits of Lefty's sources. Maybe not.

Here's the thing. If Benny's father is really dead, and if I can come up with a way to make it work, there's a nasty thought brewing in the back of my head about beating Eileen Stannard into the ground like a tent peg. When I decide it has at least some chance of working, I'll let you in on it. Meanwhile, I am going to sit here and think about how Lydia looks when she dresses up, and pretend that she wanted to have lunch with me and the part about the last minute cancellation was just a ruse.

"Miss Sweda is here to see you."

Well, swell. "Send her in."

But Lydia walked her to the door, held it while Charlene sauntered into the office, and then announced unnecessarily, "Miss Sweda, sir."

Charlene turned on her, smiling like a madam in an upscale whorehouse - no, I have never been in an upscale whorehouse - and looked her up and down, then held Lydia's eyes until her nipples showed through her blouse and her cheeks were burning. "Thank you, dear. Be a darling and bring us coffee, won't you?"

Lydia looked at me and I nodded, and I felt just a little sorry for her but I didn't know why. It was her job, after all, to do exactly that. So I winked, too, and she straightened, and right then I realized that her shoulders had sagged just a bit when Charlene dismissed her as just the help.

"Miss Sweda likes her coffee black, with sugar."

"Yes, I know." Lydia's pride was intact and she was in control again.

Charlene raised his eyebrows. "Pretty, in an obvious way. Don't you agree?"

I stayed silent.

Charlene dropped the fake culture. "Ok, Cousin." That was our duress word: cousin. Whenever one of us used it, whatever followed was the truth. We were bound by family obligation and honor, such as it may be. The Yankees among us may not understand, but among old time Southern families there remains that elusive entity, honor. It was *honor* that sent Pickett's men, and Pettigrew's and Trimble's up Cemetery Ridge at Gettysburg. It was *honor* that kept Lee's men from going into the hills after Appomattox.

Of course, some say that it was *honor* that started the "recent unpleasantness," as it is still sometimes called in the South. Some call it the War of Northern Aggression, and others say it was pure, mean stubbornness. But I have digressed.

"You're in love with her."

"Charlene, sometimes you are insufferable."

"Oh, darling boy, I am always insufferable." A bawdy wink and Charlene advanced on me the way a woman advances on a man she finds tasty, and I have to admit that I felt a stirring which any woman would envy, Lydia included, given different circumstances. I had no trouble picturing myself deep inside Charlene, her legs holding me close as she offered throaty exhortations, "Give it to me! Give it to me!"

He offered! *Him!*

"What do you want, Charlene?"

"What do I always want? Money an' sex, of course."

When Charlene finds it advantageous, or when he's being especially annoying, he lapses into his Georgian drawl and trust me, few can resist him. Women go weak and men bow. Y'all ain't seen it til y'all have seen a Yankee man take off his hat an' bow.

"Miss Sweda?" Lydia stood at Charlene's elbow, tray in hand and offering coffee.

"Thank you, dear."

"Charlene, be nice."

He smirked, but not so that Lydia saw. "Thank you, Lydia."

His honeyed contralto still made me shiver even though I was long past that night when he reintroduced himself, this time as a woman.

Lydia, mollified, placed my mug on my desk and went to the door, paused to ask, "Will there be anything else, Mr. Compton?"

"No, Lydia. Thank you."

Charlene looked over his shoulder, made sure we were alone and then, "Lefty tells me he's figured out that Benny's father is dead."

"Imagine that." I sipped my coffee, not at all surprised that Lefty would call Charlene and let him - her - know that he had it figured out.

Charlene stared at me over the rim of his mug.

I stared back.

"Well?"

"Well, what?" I could play this game all day.

Charlene stood, an elegant woman unfolding, and set his mug on my desk, then walked around to stand beside me. "You're so tense."

He laid his elegant woman's hands on my shoulders and then began massaging them, strong fingers finding places that ached, easing knots and soothing pains. "Don't be cross with me, Danny."

Never underestimate a woman's ability to insinuate herself in every aspect of your life, even if she is really a man.

One hand massaged, one hand loosened my tie.

Both hands massaged.

One hand opened shirt buttons, the other caressed my neck.

Both hands massaged, and I leaned back, relaxed and happy.

I swear, the son-of-a-bitch has developed a woman's radar to go with the wardrobe. Just as Lydia knocked and opened the door to announce Lefty Martinez' arrival, Charlene leaned down, lips to lips, and winked at me. Of course, Lydia didn't see the wink and the lack of contact, and Charlene was standing discreetly, calmly smoothing my shirt in a cousinly fashion when Lefty cleared the door.

Lefty chuckled.

Lydia closed the door forcefully.

"Miss Sweda. Counselor." Lefty, smooth as ever, eased up to my desk and deposited an envelope.

I picked it up, pulled out the contents and saw the bill, which was substantial, the transcribed statement, taken by telephone, of one Carl Sinclair and a copy of a death certificate for Charles E. Davis. Gee, I was stunned. "You'll send along the certified copy of the death certificate when you get it, naturally."

"Naturally." Lefty grinned and nodded. "Already on the bill, if you care to look."

"I already looked. I'm being pedantic."

Lefty chuckled, "Aren't you always?" Then he shook his head and asked, "Is this what you need, and do you really think it will work?"

"Will *what* work?" Charlene was as impatient as any woman I've ever met.

"The counselor has a plan." Lefty actually seemed pleased to be a part of it, so pleased that he was becoming proprietary. "If it works, it'll be a pip."

Charlene's eyes narrowed and I could see his intention: get it out of me.

"Anything else, Lefty?" I doubted he had anything else to say. Lefty is anything but reticent, and he knows enough about legal procedure that I don't have to draw him pictures.

Charlene looked to Lefty, ready to take him drinking. But I caught Lefty's eye, and winked. Lefty turned to Charlene to ask, "Will you excuse us? I have to talk about another client."

Charlene went out with a walk that had Lefty's eyes bulging, and let me know that if I'd been smart, I'd have let them leave together and let her - I mean, Charlene - pump him dry. Yeah, go ahead and read into that whatever you want. But no, I had to be the winner. I had to prove that mine's bigger, which I already knew it was, and why did I bother?

Lefty regained his composure. "Wow! Like my old man would say, *muy guapa!*"

"If you want, go out there and let her take you drinking, and for what the hell I care, go ahead and fill her in on the details." It had registered that there was another way to get done what I planned, and Charlene could likely expedite it.

"You sure?" He was frowning, because no matter what lust was growing in his heart, "client confidence" was ringing loud and clear in his head.

"I'm sure." I nodded. "As long as I don't know about it, Charlene will be a big help getting this plan to come to fruition. Plus," I shrugged, "my client won't ever hear about anything you two talk about, right? No way little Benny is going to pick up the phone and call the Bar Association to say 'Ah, wah, boo.' Right?"

Lefty smiled and nodded, and the smile kept growing wider. "You should have been a general." Still nodding, grinning like a kid on Christmas morning, he headed for the door and Charlene. "Maybe in a past life, you were."

He left the door open, and I sat there staring at the wall outside my door for nearly a whole minute before Lydia came in, shut the door and leaned against it, her arms crossed over her chest. She looked somewhere between unhappy and worried, and I knew a lecture was coming, but not for what.

"You know better than to sleep with a client."

Now, I knew for what. "I'm not sleeping with a client. For that matter, I'm not sleeping with anybody."

"You're a grownup and you'll do whatever you want. Just don't try to tell me I didn't see what I saw."

I couldn't answer her. Too much to say, too little time to frame the answer.

"Danny?"

"I'll behave." It was all I knew to say. "I promise."

"You better. I like this job."

I could feel it in my chest, the pressure which comes when I'm about to take a risk: win it all, lose everything. "If I were going to misbehave, it would be with you."

She snorted, "Who's asking you to? I get plenty of sleep as it is."

But her stare softened and she didn't offer to leave.

"Thanks for going to lunch with me." Yes, I know. Actually, I went with her. I figured maybe I could get back some control. I was wrong.

"You went with me, remember?"

"I remember every second, Lydia." Absolutely true. I remember every second with Lydia. I remember how I felt the first time I saw her, and how I had to force myself not to crawl across my desk to get at her.

"Good. Then you remember that I said we have work to do." She dropped her hand to the doorknob. "Next time, you're buying lunch."

"Keep me out of trouble and I'll buy you dinner."

She turned away, fighting the smile. "Will it count as overtime?"

"If you stay awake." She was in the doorway, and every line and shadow was perfect. It was one of those moments, a flash of reality perceived in an instant and kept in memory against the darkening days of old age. As she closed the door behind her she smiled, and I could see she wasn't fighting it.

I leaned back and closed my eyes, grinning. At least once more I would see her outside the office, and she liked the idea, too. *Slowly,* I reminded myself. *Go slowly and be aloof.*

Yeah, right. I'd be lucky if I managed not to stand on my desk and howl like a wolf. Still grinning at her exit, I relived lunch: every glance, every gesture, every nuance. If I could just get Benny Randolph out of my head.

* * *

Usually, Lydia tells me she is leaving for the day and says, "Good night, Danny." Usually, but not today. Except that I was disappointed that I didn't see her as she was leaving, I considered it a good sign. She had done enough smiling around me and she was keeping control. And if you think I was that logical about it, you're fooling yourself as much as I am. I went home cranky, and the sight of Mitzi did nothing to cheer me.

True, she brought me a lovely vodka and tonic, generously garnished with lime. True, she knelt to untie my shoes and to replace them with my slippers. True, she looked really good in the French maid outfit, which suddenly registered with me.

"Mitzi?"

"Yes, Mr. Compton?"

"New clothes?"

"Yes, sir. Miss Sweda bought them this afternoon."

"Turn around, let me see the whole thing."

She pirouetted slowly, careful not to trip on the deep pile

carpet. Facing me, but not making eye contact, she lifted the skirt hem to show off the garter belt and G-string. She was keeping some distance between herself and her master, but not so much distance that she couldn't change beds if she had to.

"Excellent. Has Miss Sweda met Patricia?"

"Yes, sir. They're out shopping now. Miss Sweda asks that you meet them for dinner at eight. She left a note for you."

"May I have the note?"

"Yes, sir. But she said I was to wait until after you had a chance to finish your first drink." She curtsied. "I am to bring it with your second drink."

Why is she curtsying now? "I rarely have a drink before I drive, and never two."

"I am supposed to drive you, sir."

"Dressed like that?" Somehow, riding up to a restaurant in Toledo, Ohio, in a chauffeured automobile, especially an automobile chauffeured by a pretty woman in a ruffled skirt so short that her butt cheeks were visible between her hem and her stocking tops, seemed foolish.

"Oh, no. I have a different skirt for driving."

"That will be fine." I emptied the glass and handed it to her. "Bring me the note and that drink, please."

She curtsied again and complied, and went to change her clothes. She hadn't mentioned that the driving skirt included a change of hosiery and shoes: from ruffles to a miniskirt, from a garter belt and stockings to fishnet tights, and from high heels to *really* high heels, six inches tall and made of black patent leather.

Someday, I will let Charlene seduce me. I will let it go and go, and then in the heat of passion I will slowly and gently, yet with the intensity of imperative lust, slide his stockings down his elegant legs. I will gaze into his eyes and sigh, and then I will wrap those sheer nylons around his neck and strangle him.

But first, dinner.

SEVEN

Mitzi looked pretty hot dressed as a chauffeur, much hotter than she did as the maid. Maybe it was the cap, maybe it was the fishnets, or maybe I just don't like ruffled skirts. Maybe a lot of things, including that as a chauffeur she was less of a servant, and maybe I was put off by all those "sirs" that she was throwing around. Maybe I felt more comfortable in the car, away from the house which I had bought at Charlene's insistence and which he had decorated, and in which he had lodged Mitzi, who was now serving as the maid.

But more likely, it was that Charlene wasn't due back in town for a few days, according to Charlie, and now she was here and taking over my home life as well as my professional life. I mean, *he* was here and taking over, et cetera. We have got to decide on a convention here. Is Charlene "he" or is Charlene "she"? Or should it change to differentiate between them?

First, Charlie says that Charlene will be back "in a few days," and then Charlene shows up the next day. You try living this life and see what it gets you. I'm betting on apoplexy.

With Charlene in town, Charlie wasn't likely to be around for a bit. Knowing Charlene, putting Mitzi in that maid's outfit and giving her those instructions was his way of keeping Charlie's hand on Mitzi until "he" could come back and do it himself. Putting her in the driver's clothes, as compared to the maid's outfit, was somehow supposed to draw a line between the two stations. But what? And then it hit me: live like a woman, act like a woman, think like a woman, feel like a woman. Charlene's behavior made sense, once I put it in those terms.

You see, I think like a man. If a woman cooks and cleans, does the laundry and puts out, I'm happy. If she does any of those things once in a while, I'm not going to complain too much, in case she quits entirely. But women - *real* women, anyway - don't see it that way. *Real* women expect *other* women to get up in the morning, get the kids off to school, go to work, do the marketing, cook dinner, do the laundry, clean the house, take the cat and dog to the vet, get the oil changed and make sure the bills are paid. Single mothers even more so.

The guy is happy if she lets him watch TV while she cooks dinner and then puts out afterwards. If she owns a garter belt and wears it to bed, he'll buy her a car. If she wears it to dinner, he'll buy her a car *lot*.

That point always seems to elude women. Dress better, work less, put out. Everybody wins. But I've digressed again.

Charlene has taught himself to think like a woman, and by inference he has come to feel like a woman. Whatever his plan is, unless he explains it I likely won't figure it out. Even if he explains it, the odds are that it will go over my head. But here goes, anyway.

Charlene is a man, but everyone thinks he is a woman. Charlie doesn't exist except as Charlene's alter ego. Mitzi and Patricia think he's real, Patricia because he gave her money and Mitzi because he's so "glorious." Me, I think he's a pain in the ass: I'm the one who has to keep it straight.

Whenever I talk about Charlene, it's like he's a she. Whenever I talk about Charlie, it's like he's real. Two guys: one real, one fake. Which is which? Like I said, we need a convention, a way to refer to them which doesn't confuse things more than they are. Therefore, from now on, Charlene is "she" and Charlie is "he", and if you get confused, well, welcome to my world. It gets worse.

Whenever Mitzi or Patricia is around, Charlie is Charlene's brother.

But at the airport, he's Charlene's husband, and when we get to Atlantic City he's single.

As Pooh once said, "Oh, bother!"

Anyway, back to Charlene's plan. First, find the motive. Charlene wants to play favorite auntie to Patricia, but why? Does she see in her some special light which she intends to bring to its full brightness? Or does she intend her to take over the family business, so to speak. Whichever, she has to separate mother and daughter so that she can get control over both. Find the gap, drive the wedge, split the pair.

But if Willie is the gap, then Mitzi's poor self-image is the wedge. So?

Right then I ran out of ideas, so I sat up and looked around, and then I noticed that Mitzi was a competent driver. I have always thought that riding in the back seat without a front passenger is somewhat pretentious, although as a person of wealth and influence I suppose I should be occupying my mind with more than the details of mundane travel over a familiar route to a known destination for a specified purpose. Ten minutes in the back seat and already I'm pretentious, and I have become a person of wealth and influence.

Yeah, right.

Riding up front in my own Town Car while a liveried driver handled the wheel would make me look stupid, which would be worse than looking pretentious, so I bit the bullet. Than I realized that I had it wrong. Willie didn't count, and I was the wedge. Was Mitzi's poor self-image the gap?

My Town Car wasn't built as a limo, which means there is no partition to separate the wealthy, influential people from the insignificant, though hot, chauffeur. So, I hadn't brought along a puppy cup, just in case. I mean, I didn't bring a drink along because that would be an open alcoholic container in a motor vehicle on a public highway. Of course, I hadn't heard of puppy cups until Charlene came along to broaden my horizons. Since I had no idea that Mitzi was a competent driver, and because I am conservative by nature - meaning a paranoid, anal-retentive tight-ass - I decided to be good. Besides, I was hungry and I was already feeling the first two drinks. Mitzi was a competent bartender with a fine, steady hand, as the Irish might say. For the rest of you, she wasn't skimpy with the vodka. So I sat empty-handed, enjoyed the ride and wondered what Charlene had in mind for dinner.

I should have seen it coming.

We made quite a little scene arriving at the restaurant. Mitzi wheeled up to the door and as the valet walked over to offer his services, Mitzi dismissed him with a casual wave, somewhat more condescendingly than I thought necessary, but she let him open the door for her and hold it while she sashayed around to open the right rear door for me. I couldn't see, obviously, but I didn't have to. As she opened the door, she bent enough to make her skirt ride up and show a hint of butt cheek.

As I stepped out of the car, she straightened, curtsied and said, "Very good, sir," as though I had given instructions, which you know I hadn't. Right away, I got the idea that Charlene had laid down the law and had given her specific instructions about how to dress and speak. With her lack of self-esteem, being forced to wander around in clothes which accentuated - hell, put on display - her legs, her butt and her bust gave her the thrill of a lifetime. She could do almost anything that would draw attention to herself and she would be obeying instructions. Just as long as Charlene didn't get angry with her, she could do anything she wanted.

A blind man in New Jersey could see it coming; I didn't.

Everyone who saw her, stared. Mitzi was enjoying the attention. I, however, was not. I was especially not enjoying the fact that Lydia was waiting to get inside the restaurant with her friends, and every one of them was staring at me.

Rumor has it that the nylon in pantyhose has a higher tensile strength than steel. Thus, it will be perfect for the hanging: Charlene is going to *die*.

"Daniel."

"Lydia."

"Mitzi, I presume?" Frost formed in the summer air.

"Yes."

"She's older than I expected." Icicles.

"Nice seeing you."

Did you ever have to say something and not have the faintest idea what? But you had to say something and so you did, and as it was coming out of your mouth you were thinking *Stupid! Stupid! Stupid!* But you couldn't stop and out it came, and as much as you had to say something, that was the one thing you should have never said, but you said it anyway?

Of course, now I can say I know what Lydia looks like when she is angry.

Although, angry may not be the right word for a woman who

was so wrathful that she couldn't speak. Her friends took it pretty well, though. So, having entertained them and with Lydia verging on a stroke, I went inside to the hostess stand, and asked for my table - Charlene's note said the table would be under my name.

The hostess smiled and said my party was there waiting for me, picked up the menu and offered to lead me to my table. I had been to that restaurant more than a few times, and this was the first time the hostess had shown more than minimal interest. Of course, this was the first time I had shown up with a chauffeur in spike heels and a miniskirt, clearly visible to her as she waited at her stand.

She held my chair and let her hand rest against my upper arm as she asked for my drink order, neither of which had happened before. Then she handed me the menu and managed lingering contact between our hands, and she put an impressive amount of swing into her hips as she walked away.

Charlene was the epitome of the *grande dame,* and graciously acknowledged the arrival of the master. "Daniel."

"Charlene."

"I see you have made another conquest." Charlene nodded at the retreating hostess. She turned to Patricia. "You recall meeting Mr. Compton, don't you, Patricia?"

Patricia was her sullen self; Charlene's disapproval showed. "He looks familiar." She shrugged, dismissing both Charlene and me. "I don't know, I meet a lot of old people." She busied herself with the menu, ignoring us.

Charlene's eyes narrowed and I had the feeling that her patience was wearing as thin as my own, but she kept her composure.

The hostess led Lydia's party into the dining room and managed to smile at me while she was showing them to their table. Their table was across the room, too far away for us to overhear or be overheard. Lydia seated herself so that we could see each other, and I wondered if she could read lips at that distance.

The hostess went back to her station by way of our table, and managed to brush against me on the way. She put out her hand to steady herself and to apologize, and then bent to ask if my drink had arrived - obviously, it hadn't. Tsking, she hurried off to see to it for me.

We weren't so far away that I couldn't see Lydia's expression, and for the only time in memory I was glad of the distance between us.

The best part of the evening was behind me.

"What is *en brochette*? Why can't they just say what it is?"

The talented lawyers who work for me can read a complex contract faster than Patricia read the menu, and without the snide remarks. I know that adolescent boys often go through a stage where everything is "Damn," as in, "I can't cut my damn' meat because my damn' knife is too damn' dull, damn it." At least, when I was an adolescent, back before cell phones and such like were the way of teenaged life, it was a common thing. Since my experience with adolescent females is limited to the time spent with Patricia, I can't truly say that condescending, conceited speech is likewise a generational rite of passage. Perhaps the age difference and the fact that I am childless make me not so tolerant of what might be normal behavior.

"If they don't know what it is, how can they cook it?"

Or, Patricia is a snotty kid who needs her ass whipped.

Whatever, I had trouble conceiving of Charlene finding pleasure in the company of an entitled whelp who's only asset was her prettiness, and that was off-limits. At least, to my eyes it was off-limits. Maybe Charlene held a different view. Or maybe, Charlene saw a replay of the dead woman that I took to be her - his wife, the woman who had sent her - him over the edge.

Go back to the idea that I don't think like Charlene. I may not be able to conjure *his* plan. If *he* is truly the man in the story, I can't empathize with *him*. No matter what I have suffered, I have never been at the point of murder. Although, Patricia was pushing me far closer than I would have imagined possible.

But Charlene sat serenely, smiling tolerantly as Patricia offered such urbane comments as, "Who ever heard of fixing fish like that?" And, "Gross. Snails." And my own favorite, "I don't know why people get upset about veal. Cows are stupid."

But I was sitting where I could see Lydia, and she wasn't ignoring me. She wasn't blowing me kisses, either, but at least she was looking at me. Right then I was willing to believe that, like bad publicity, there is no such thing as bad attention. I let myself believe that things weren't so bad as I thought, that I should relax and enjoy the view of Lydia, outlined against the downtown skyline.

Cheer up, I told myself. *Things could be worse.*

Then, just like that day at Pete's Gas Station, things got worse. Ever so much worse. You see, Pete was this typical old-time garage owner. He ran the corner gas station and fixed all the cars in the neighborhood, which had changed around him and his station. But he never changed, and he knew cars. All through law school he kept mine running, and I never got a bill I couldn't pay. When I graduated and got to be a lawyer, it was time to repay the favor. Once or twice, I spread my wings and saved him a dollar or two.

It was a friendly place, where the mail man felt so much at home that he poured his own coffee without asking, where the old guys from the neighborhood came to stand and watch the traffic whipping past at speeds that once they had only felt on the train. Pete moved around them without even thinking about it, because they were always there and they were always standing in the same places, each man with his favorite spot.

One of them one day brought in one of those quaint little signs, the kind that come in plastic frames, ready to hang. This one said, "Everybody told me to cheer up. Things could be worse. So I cheered up and sure enough, things got worse." Seems this guy's wife found it at the dollar store and brought it home for him to take to Pete, which he did, and they had a good laugh at it the way old guys will, and Pete hung the thing on the wall.

A little while after that I went there for gas. The mail man brought in the mail and Pete stopped what he was doing long enough to open the envelope from his gasoline supplier. He said, "Son-of-bitch," and stalked over to the wall, yanked the sign down and threw it in the trash and stalked outside to pump more gas. Being nosey, I picked up the letter. They had canceled his lease.

The hostess brought me my drink, kept her hand on my shoulder and bent solicitously to inquire if everything was all right. Suddenly animated, she laughed at everything I said and, truthfully, I'm not that entertaining.

Lydia stared daggers, and though some were for the hostess, most were for me alone. I would be a long time living this down. And then, it got *worse*.

The hostess rumpled my hair and walked away, and it hit me that we were sitting there like the average Middle American family: mother, father and snotty teenaged daughter. As that was sinking in, Charlene cut her eyes at the retreating hostess and turned just enough that Lydia had to be able to see her mouthing, "Touch her and I'll cut out your heart."

Having nothing left to lose, I called the waitress and sent a bottle of Dom Perignon to Lydia's table, with a note. "I can't misbehave with you all the way over there."

Lydia ignored the gift, but her friends did not. The blonde on her left pulled the bottle from the chilling stand and checked the label. I could see her nod her approval as she showed the bottle to the others, and the redhead on Lydia's left read the note and passed it to the others. The little brunette turned in her chair, caught my eye and gave me a thumbs up. Her friends, at least, were starting to like me.

Patricia watched the whole thing and then said, "Old people are so lame."

I started to backhand the little slut but Charlene caught my hand and said, making sure that Lydia could read her lips, "Now, darling. She's just going through a phase."

Like I said, the best part of the evening was behind me.

Way behind me, as it developed. If I hadn't been so wrapped up in my Lydia woes when I came home, I might have been smart enough to ask Mitzi how it came to be that Charlene had bought her a maid suit and chauffeur's togs. But I was, and so I wasn't in the slightest prepared for the ride to Wang Ho's boutique.

I had been off-guard all evening, first because Charlene had shown up before she was supposed to. The little scene at the office had eliminated any possibility that I would think that Charlene had been at my house to chat with Mitzi, let alone that she would have had time to go gallivanting to Wang Ho's boutique, on the edge of Detroit, to outfit Mitzi. Add to that Mitzi's statement that they were out shopping, and who would have thought?

I should have, of course. Where else but Wang Ho's would Charlene have gone to outfit Mitzi as a genuine fantasy French maid, let alone on the spur of the moment? Wang Ho has been supplying Charlene with her personal clothing for longer than I care to imagine, and putting a real woman in women's clothing can't be any challenge to him at all.

So, after we had watched Lydia and her buddies leave, after Patricia had offended the hostess, the waitress, the busboy and the people at three nearby tables, we left. We went to the front door and there was Mitzi, waiting at the rear door of my Town Car to curtsy us into the back seat. All of us, her insipid, annoying daughter included. I had been foolish enough to think that I might be allowed to go home and sleep. No chance of that, as it turned out. Oh, no.

I had thought that Charlene drove herself and Patricia to the restaurant. Nope. Charlene hired a limo - she disdains the Toledo cabbies and their vehicles. Whatever, she and Patricia rode to the restaurant and waited for us, and the rest of that you already know.

Anyway, Mitzi held the doors and curtsied, and Patricia sat between Charlene and me and commented the whole way on the lameness of my car - it wasn't a limo, and who would be seen getting out of anything but a limo? I mean, like, really? And then there was my overage chauffeur who should know that women of a certain age should learn how to dress. She moved on to how I should get a real chauffeur and a real limo, otherwise people would be making fun of me and thinking that I am not a very good lawyer, which they already probably do because I am such a lame dresser, you know? Charlene looked out the left window and I looked out the right, and finally I tuned out Patricia as she droned on and on.

From the restaurant, Wang Ho's is about an hour north into Michigan, and as Mitzi wheeled us along I thought about what she might have said, had I asked her, about her becoming my slave. Yes, slave. What else would you call her? She isn't paid, she can't leave and she has nothing except what she is given. How do I know this already? You really want to know?

Without anyone saying anything to me about it, I can guess

what Charlene did and said. First, she visited Mitzi at my house, found her as she knew she would in her cocktail dress, tidying up. Maybe she was wearing my robe, but I doubt it. Anyway, Charlene would sit her down and give her a choice between slavery and something more drastic. Either way, Charlene would get her daughter and raise her. So, having no real choice, Mitzi signed up. She would dress, speak and do as she was told, and hope that Charlie would come back and rescue her from his family.

As if I needed confirmation of my speculation - which I didn't - Mitzi drove straight to Wang Ho's without Charlene telling her anything more than, "Wang Ho's and don't waste time on the way."

Mitzi did as she was told, and I have to admit that I wasn't worried about her driving. In fact, had Patricia shut her mouth I could have dozed comfortably. But Patricia's mouth moved as fast as the Town Car, and although I could let my mind wander enough to conjecture about Charlene's visit with Mitzi, her whiny, nasal voice was just sharp enough to make sleep impossible. On the good side, I rarely get to ride as a passenger and enjoy the scenery, so I made the best of it until, finally, we pulled up at Wang Ho's door.

Mitzi stopped near the front door as casually as though this were a regular stop for her, and not the second time in her life she had been there. Engine running, she got out and held the door for Charlene and then for Patricia, who ignored her with the haughtiness of the newly rich. If Mitzi felt the tooth of the serpent in Patricia's behavior, she didn't show it. She came around behind the car and held the door for me, curtsied and returned to the driver's door, parked with the easy skill of a practiced driver.

The parking lot held several late model autos, but none of them reeked of wealth. I took it that some of Wang Ho's regulars were there for alterations, maybe some late shoppers looking for an impulse bargain. It was too late in the year for parents to be seeking prom clothes, and too early for the charity ball season and so that left the regulars, like us. Although I was willing to bet that there wasn't anyone who was quite like Charlene, let alone our whole collection of misfits.

I looked around as we walked the few steps from my car to the door, noting the complete lack of noteworthiness. Wang Ho's was an old warehouse, three stories tall, that had once been painted gray. Where the paint was still clinging to the bricks, it had faded to a dirty white. The paint was peeling off the window frames and the down spouts were rusting and rickety looking, and the bottom ladder had fallen off the fire escape so long ago that it had rusted to nothingness where it lay. The light fixtures by the door were loose, one to the point that it hung off the building by the wires and the other so that it had spun around and pointed down rather than up. The rubber welcome mat was missing parts so that standing on it required careful foot placement and a good sense of balance.

We stood at Wang Ho's door and waited for Mitzi to open it for us, and I felt fairly silly standing there while a woman weighing just over a hundred pounds struggled to open a door weighing thrice herself. But I knew that Charlene had laid down the law, and I saw no reason to give her frown lines by treating Mitzi as anything but a servant.

I had been inside Wang Ho's a few times before, brought there by Charlene to give a man's perspective on her latest purchase. Talk about feeling silly! Charlene made it clear to Wang that I was her straight, stuffy cousin, brought along to give my opinion because she wanted something sedate for a special occasion. She also made it clear that I was the stiffest, most "sedate" man she knew, and on those occasions I had come to terms with the idea that I would never be more to Lydia than her ever-so-boring boss. But now that Mitzi had entered my life, Lydia had developed an interest, so I decided to enjoy whatever show Charlene was intending to put on. I looked around the lobby of the boutique, and wondered how I had missed the studied tackiness of the place on those prior visits.

The place was a study in dinge. Yes, I know. I could have said it was dingy and let it go at that. But truthfully, the place was so intentionally dingy that saying so like that didn't do it justice. Plus, I looked it up and it's a word, so enjoy. The furniture was old, as though Wang Ho had gone to a used furniture store and looked for dressers and breakfronts and chairs, all of which would show his customers that they were paying so little for his wares that he could hardly afford to live.

The floor was cracked linoleum near the door and worn, stained carpet within. The walls were painted white, with old, wrinkled photos of God-knows-who in chipped, peeling frames. The ceiling showed water stains from an old leak and if there was a theme to the furnishings, it sure as hell escaped me.

Patricia looked around, tossed her head and remarked that she hoped we'd be through before the place was condemned. "Like, if there's a fire, maybe there'll be a reward or something."

Charlene's eyes narrowed but she held her tongue, for Wang Ho was coming out to greet us, bowing and shuffling along. "Hello, missy. Good see you come back."

Tonight, in the company of Charlene and two women, I had figured I might rise in Wang Ho's estimation. Nope. He looked at me like I had come in with a delivery. Clearly, except that I was there with Charlene, I would have been left standing in the lobby while the others were attended to in the show room.

"Oh, look. A gnome." Patricia wrinkled her nose and rolled her eyes.

Wang Ho is a small Asian of unknown ethnicity. Some say Chinese, some say Korean, some say Vietnamese. I don't know and I don't care. What I know is that he has made Charlene's clothing for years, and he isn't surprised by anything he sees. So, when Charlene swept in with the three of us in tow, he simply bowed, nodded, parted the curtains and showed us to the fitting room.

"Wang, darling!" Charlene waved an expansive hand at us. "You know my cousin, of course, and you clothed his," he paused for dramatic effect, "driver." She held her hand, palm up, to introduce, "Patricia, a young friend of mine who needs your clever touch." She sighed, "We spent the whole day shopping and found nothing - simply *nothing* suitable." She sighed again, saying that, "Toledo is a lovely town and I cherish every moment there, but sometimes the shopkeepers are so desperately provincial."

"Ah. So." Wang nodded in sympathetic empathy, offered Charlene a small bow and said, "You come, missy. I show you nice stuff. We talk-talk."

They bowed to each other, and Wang started toward the door

marked, "Private."

Charlene beckoned, "Come along, Daniel," and led me into the inner sanctum, tangible proof that I had arrived. Where, exactly, I wasn't sure, but I knew I had arrived.

"Wang, darling. It's so good of you to see us privately. You know I depend upon you totally, that I trust you implicitly to guide me. You are my sartorial guru."

With the door closed, Wang stood up straight, looked Charlene in the eye and said, "Can it, Chuck."

Charlene dropped the hoity feminine persona. "I need a drink, Wanger."

Wang pulled out a bottle of excellent Scotch and three glasses, set them on his desk and dropped into his chair. He looked at Charlene, nodded toward me and asked, in clear, though Brooklyn-inflected English, "Who's the stiff?"

Charlene sprawled in one of the desk chairs, hiked her skirt and crossed her ankles on top of Wang's desk. "My cousin, my lawyer. You've met him."

"I take it he knows?" Wang poured, then slid the glasses across his desk.

Charlene waved at me, and I leaned over and took the glasses. I handed one to Charlene. She inhaled deeply and sighed happily; sipped. "Daniel, the girl is beginning to try my patience."

"One more crack about what a hole she's in ..." Wang sipped his Scotch. He didn't finish the sentence, not that he had to.

EIGHT

In vino veritas, for sure. We spent almost half an hour in Wang Ho's office, sipping his fine Scotch and bonding. We weren't worried about making the women wait, what with one being property and the other being snotty, so we enjoyed ourselves and said just about nothing. Wang kept the bottle, held it up to inquire as to refills. Charlene and I raised our glasses to accept. An occasional sigh of satisfaction, a casual inspection of a glass and its contents: guy stuff. But eventually, we had to get back to the purpose at hand.

Charlene stood and stretched, and then went up on her tiptoes and reached for the ceiling. Talk about gorgeous! She bent backwards, still on her toes, and yawned, then rolled her shoulders. When she reached under her skirt to adjust her G-string, well, so much for the fantasy.

"Damn, Wang. This one rides up on me."

"Let me check that for you." Wang slouched around his desk and Charlene turned her rump toward him and lifted her skirt hem.

I have no idea what happened, but Charlene's eyes widened and she slapped his hand away. "Maybe you should send Mei Ling to do that."

"Be real. Her hands are rough and calloused, not soft like mine."

"And warmer too, as I recall." Charlene moved away from Wang and adjusted herself, frowning. "How did your hands get that cold drinking whiskey neat?"

But she still had her skirt hiked up and like I said, *in vino veritas*. So I ran my hand over her bare buttocks, which I would never have done except that we were all a little drunk, and snapped the suspender of her garter belt. Besides, Wang had gone first.

Charlene started, shrugged, said to Wang, "Daniel's hands are pleasantly warm." She looked over shoulder and gave me a bawdy wink.

I squeezed her rump and said, "Warm hands, cold heart, big

dick."

Wang said, "Ah, jeez, get a room," and shook his head. He held the door as Charlene swept past him and touched his cheek with one perfectly manicured finger, then he nodded to me. "Out."

He followed us back to the show room, once again in character as the longsuffering clothier, muttering incomprehensibly.

Wang Ho was a smart man, obviously, and he had a genius for merchandising. As rundown as the outside was, and as dingy and tacky as the lobby was, the show room was elegant. The ceiling was high, with the lighting recessed to mimic skylights in full sun and supported by Doric columns. The walls were white and immaculate, interrupted by alcoves which held cabinets and shelves. The alcoves were separated from the main room by velvet drapes which complimented the Oriental carpets strewn about the floor in a tasteful, casual manner. Large, live ferns and fig trees stood on stands and in urns which matched the columns, a fountain burbled and gurgled in the background, and all things considered, anyone in that room had to feel like a Roman senator being served by Asian slaves brought back by Caesar's legions.

A carpeted dais with a full-length, extra wide, three panel mirror behind it, took up the front wall, faced by two comfortable arm chairs for the customers. The lighting for the dais was indirect, shielded from both sides by a valance. Each chair had its own lamp and drink table, with pens and pads for notes, coasters for drinks and a call button for service. Any woman going from the common area to the showroom had to feel that she had been admitted to the inner sanctum, that she was being treated like royalty, and Patricia was no exception. She admired herself in the mirrors, oblivious, while Mitzi stood behind and between the customers' chairs, also admiring herself but pretending that she was only waiting for us to return.

In vino veritas.

Charlene stood between Wang and me as we watched the tableau: two women, each conscious of the other yet interested only in herself. That the one was the mother of the other, naturally her superior yet socially her subordinate, provoked some sort of atavistic response. Each of us felt it, each of us acknowledged it.

Wang sighed.

Charlene dropped her hand to my crotch and gave me a slow, womanly fondle.

I didn't stop her.

Charlene has wonderful hands and in the dark of the hallway, half in the bag from the vodka at dinner and the Scotch in Wang's office, I didn't care at all that the woman of my dreams was a figment, that the woman holding me was a man in drag and my cousin to boot. Wang knows she's a man, and that was my conflict, to be blunt. But Wang couldn't see what she was doing, and right then I didn't care. So we stood there in the darkened doorway, silently watching the two women preen, and I felt like Huck Finn when the Duke and Dauphin came on board.

What I mean is this. Huck and Jim were floating along on the raft, enjoying life and taking it easy. They had a carefree routine which suited them just fine, and then Huck found a canoe and went searching for some berries. Along came these two con men, running from a posse, and Huck would have paddled himself away from there - anytime he saw someone running, he figured they were after him and Jim. But these fellows begged him to save their lives - said they hadn't done anything and were being chased for it. Once they were on the raft, they took over and it wasn't long before Huck and Jim knew they were frauds and not the royalty they claimed to be. And sure enough, they caused all sorts of problems.

Charlene and I had been floating along nicely, thank you, and then Charlie played poker with Willie, and brought Mitzi and Patricia into our lives. There's a comparison in there somewhere, but the liquor was beginning to affect me, and it addled my thoughts. What was for sure was that until Mitzi and Patricia stood there admiring themselves, there was no way that circumstances would have come together and I would have let Charlene grope me.

Mitzi looked pretty hot in her chauffeur's togs, with her cap tucked under her arm and her breasts visible through the white silk blouse. Patricia, on the other hand, looked practically dowdy in her knee length skirt and mid-high heels. Mitzi, who had taken her turn on the dais in the morning, knew her place and kept to it. Patricia obviously considered herself the center of attention and saw no reason to speak to Mitzi. After all, Patricia was a sought-after guest and Mitzi was only a servant.

The whole thing bothered me, at least a little bit. I was drunk enough to enjoy Charlene's attention, drunk enough to take Mitzi into another room and consummate our friendship, so to speak; but not so drunk that I could approve of Patricia's all too easy acceptance of her own superiority over her mother. Granted, I don't like Patricia, and no matter how you dress it up, to me she's still a snotty, bitchy twit. And maybe that's part of it, too. What on earth Charlene saw in her that had us in Wang Ho's, swilling Scotch and trading sidelong looks while two women, a mother and a daughter, faced off, escaped me. But I didn't have much time to think about all that, because Patricia couldn't help being herself, and the fight was on.

Patricia faced the central mirror and checked herself full-on. "Bring me something to drink."

"I will not." Mitzi straightened, indignant.

"You will, too." Patricia spun on her heel, crossed the dais and stepped down onto the sales floor. She stood in front of and between the chairs and faced her mother, arms akimbo. "Or else!"

"I don't answer to you."

"You answer to everybody!"

Wang's people were sticking their heads in to see what the commotion was about, and Wang was muttering something in Brooklyn-tinged English about crazy Anglo women, don't know how to act.

Patricia stepped forward so that she was between the chairs, inches from Mitzi's face. "You slut!"

"Patricia! Behave yourself!"

Imperious as ever, Charlene stalked crossed the floor, glared at them and dropped into the closer chair, crossed her knees and adjusted her skirt. Her left hand fluffed her hair and her right drummed on the table. I decided that I was an important customer, being with Charlene and all, so I took offense when Patricia spun in front of me and took the second chair.

Patricia looked up at me and sniffed something about how

boorishly I had been brought up, not to know that a gentleman always yields the chair to a lady.

Wang scurried around shouting polysyllabic commands to his staff, clapping his hands and gesturing, chasing them away.

Restored by the conference in Wang Ho's office, Charlene returned to the task which she had set for herself: humanizing Patricia. "Mr. Compton and I are here to assist you in choosing an appropriate wardrobe. I will sit here," she waved her hand, "and he will sit there."

Never mind what Patricia said in reply. It was ungracious in the extreme.

Yes, I was brought up to offer my chair to a lady. If you can see any way that a smug, snotty, foul-mouthed teenager qualifies in that regard, fine. But I was up close and personal with her and there was nothing of a lady about her. On top of which, it was also a part of my upbringing that children defer to adults, no exceptions, period.

"Patricia, darling, perhaps you don't understand." Charlene was back in character as the favorite aunt, patiently redirecting Patricia's adolescent energy, gently molding her character, guiding her.

"I understand, all right. I'm in a rundown discount house in the middle of nowhere, waiting for an old foreigner to shuffle out here and show me some out of date crap, and I'm supposed to feel grateful that old people let me ride in a car with them." She crossed her arms and pouted. "I have friends, you know, and I could be with them right now, having a life."

It was sort of like watching a train wreck. I didn't cause it, I couldn't stop it, and I didn't want to look away. Yet, I felt uncomfortable watching it happen. I knew Charlene was about to drop the axe, and I was looking forward to the execution. I figured Mitzi was feeling about the same way, for her own reasons.

She stood there watching too, keeping her respectful chauffeur's pose as she watched her daughter misbehave herself into a trap. She was beaten, whether by her husband's gambling, or by her own lack of character, or just by life in general. Not that it mattered. Beaten, she had given herself into servitude, at least in part to protect her undeserving daughter. Servile, she was her daughter's inferior. Inferior, she could enjoy Patricia's comeuppance.

Two great men emerged from the American Civil War, Lee and Lincoln. I know it sounds like a non sequitur, but it's not. The alcohol has relaxed me and relieved my inhibitions, and I'm feeling chatty. Be patient, and I'll connect all the dots for you. There are stories about both men, and those stories reflect their characters and their backgrounds. Never mind the rest of it. Just focus on two bits of Lincoln trivia.

When I was a kid, I had a framed quote from Lincoln hanging on my bedroom wall. "I like to see a man proud of the place in which he lives. I like to see a man live so that his place can be proud of him." At least, I think that's what it said. It was a long time ago and I haven't seen that plaque in decades. Plus, I think I am the only one in my circle who ever heard of it, unless maybe I already told them.

Whatever, Patricia had no pride in herself or her place, and her behavior was so bad that no one would claim her except that they had to. That left Mitzi, her mother, and Charlene, her self-appointed mentor. Me, I'd happily hang her by her thumbs and let the flies and gnats have at her.

The other story goes this way. Lincoln once said something about how if we see a widow struggling along, and she slips and falls on the ice, we hurry out to help her up, and gather her packages and make sure she's all right. But if a rich woman goes sprawling on the same patch of ice, we're all secretly pleased. We might go help her up and be solicitous, but inside we're laughing ourselves silly.

Mitzi had tried; she had failed. She had already felt the whip-like cut of Patricia's tongue, and already she knew that to Patricia she was nothing more than a servant. She would have been less than human if she hadn't enjoyed watching Patricia climb the scaffold and put the noose around her own neck.

Even half-drunk, I began to see a glimmer of Charlene's plot, and her motivation. Since I owned Mitzi, I decided to exercise my prerogatives. After all, it's never too early to establish discipline and control. I turned to Charlene, pointed to the call button and asked, "Doesn't Wang keep a bottle in one of those cabinets?"

Charlene brightened and said, "What an excellent idea." She snapped her fingers and pointed at one of the cabinets as she spoke to

Mitzi. "You. Girl. Drinks."

Mitzi followed Charlene's pointing finger to the cabinet, then looked at me, wary and confused. Just as I thought, she wasn't clear who had control when both Charlene and I were present.

So, I took over and asked Charlene, who pursed her lips before she answered, what she'd like to drink. The point was made and she accepted it, and asked for Scotch. I dropped her a slow wink, turned my attention to Mitzi and instructed her to bring Miss Sweda a Scotch, and the usual for me.

"I'll have a gin and tonic." No please nor thank you, no concern for her mother's feelings, and no one had asked Patricia if she wanted a drink. Being that she was seventeen, maybe that was intentional.

"Darling, perhaps you should wait a few years before you cultivate such adult tastes."

Patricia dismissed Charlene with a sniff and a toss of her hair.

Half drunk and totally bored, I gave Patricia my best fisheye. "Kid, you're too young to drink, and too snotty for me to bend the rules." I waved my fingers in Mitzi's direction, then pointed at Patricia. "She can have tonic, she can have a twist. No alcohol, no caffeine."

Patricia sniffed, "I'd rather die."

"Suit yourself." I looked to Mitzi, raised my hand in a silent, *Go to it.*

Whether Charlene knew what I was up to, I couldn't say and I didn't care.

Mitzi opened the cabinet, found it to be well stocked and mixed the drinks. She brought them to us on the small silver tray which Wang Ho kept there for that purpose, and as she was about to return the tray I took it from her and motioned for her to stay.

"Sir?"

I circled my finger and she pirouetted, puzzled.

"Mr. Wang, if you don't mind?"

Wang paused, bowed. "Ah, so?"

"The fishnets are very nice, but I think I prefer something more formal. Seams, perhaps." I gestured, to show some appreciation for his work. "Tights, of course."

"Ah, so." He nodded his understanding. "I bring."

I gave Mitzi the tray, pointed to the cabinet. "Put this away and take off your tights."

She blushed right up to her hairline, and I would have felt sorry for her if I were sober, maybe, or a better person. But I wasn't and I'm not, so I caught her eyes and held them, and I frowned at her daughter. It was subtle move, but she took the hint. I know because she straightened just a little bit and a very tiny smile tugged at her mouth.

She returned the tray to the cabinet and braced herself against it, stepped out of one shoe and then the other, rolled her tights down over her legs and kicked them aside. I could guess that Wang Ho had given her the full treatment, whatever that might be, when he had dressed her. I was willing to bet that Patricia was about to find out how much fun it was to piss off Charlene.

Wang returned with the seamed tights, offered them for my approval and then held them out to Mitzi.

Patricia took in all this with feral interest, the younger woman watching the older fall prey to the hunters, leaving her the winner.

Wrong.

Mitzi dressed herself without getting naked, which Patricia had clearly expected.

And then Wang Ho, given permission by Charlene, made himself happy at Patricia's expense.

Suddenly, Patricia went from human to mannequin. Wang Ho's staff appeared with armloads of clothes, stripped her naked and lifted her bodily up and onto the dais. She stood there in shock, her jaw around her ankles, while they dressed her, then stepped back bowing for Wang Ho and Charlene to appraise.

Nods, head shakes, shrugs.

Notes.

More clothes.

More notes.

Wang Ho's staff spun Patricia like a top.

Mitzi stood behind our chairs, ready to do our bidding.

Charlene reached backwards to hand her glass to Mitzi.

"Again, please."

Mitzi curtsied as she took her glass, and that was about enough.

"Mitzi, I know you had your instructions from Miss Sweda, but now you have them from me. Knock off the curtsies. I'm getting seasick watching you bob up and down like a cork. Got it?"

"Yes, Mr. Compton." She half-curtsied in reflex, caught herself and straightened.

"Here. Fill mine, too."

She took my glass and thankfully, didn't curtsy. "Certainly, sir."

Charlene gave me one of her studious looks and asked, "Daniel, did you just act like a man?"

"Can it, Chuck." I pointed to Patricia. "Watch the show."

Charlene sat back, bemused, and waved at Wang to continue.

Patricia was now wearing a thong and high heels, and Wang was shaking his head, frowning and saying, "Too much hairy."

Mitzi interrupted her bartending to stare, openmouthed, and moved her eyes to look at me and I knew I was right: she'd had the treatment. I was right, too, that she could still feel maternal about her child who in turn felt nothing for her mother's predicament.

Wang's staff hustled Patricia off the little dais and into the back area, and I decided I really needed the john. Curiously, the can was in the same direction as Wang's staff had led Patricia, not that I cared.

I could hear her protesting her treatment. "What do you think you are doing? Let go of me! Take your hands off me! Let me up! I'll have you know that my father is a very important man and he will have all of you deported!"

Underlying her complaining was a chorus of Oriental vocalizing, none of which I understood.

She was still at it when I came back from the bathroom. I wandered back to the showroom and enjoyed not fighting for my seat.

Charlene leaned over, patted my arm and asked, "Better now?"

Mitzi brought me a fresh drink, and Charlene and I traded the occasional *bon mot*. We emptied our glasses again and sent Mitzi for refills. When her back was turned, feeling scampish, I ran my hand under Charlene's skirt and gave her a friendly squeeze, withdrew my hand and resumed my proper demeanor.

Startled, Charlene couldn't react with uncousinly affection before Mitzi brought the drinks and took her position behind us.

And then, as though on cue there were three long quavering yells - or screams, if you prefer, then barely audible whimpering, and then silence. I guess waxing hurts a lot.

Mitzi took it well. She didn't flinch when Patricia screamed, she didn't look away when Wang Ho's staff brought her back, dragging and shoving her along with her arms trapped by her side to show the results of their work. Again, they picked her up and put her on the dais, and once again, they busied themselves dressing her.

Charlene made her choices without asking Patricia, or Mitzi's permission.

Wang waved and the head staffer offered Patricia a small mirror so that she could see herself as they dressed her again, this time limiting themselves to the items which Charlene had selected. Each time, they started with bare skin and added lingerie, then shoes and finally skirts and blouses. Each change of clothes required another return to bare skin, and fresh lingerie, and Patricia used the intervals to admire herself, especially when she was nude.

I checked with Charlene, and we had the same unspoken opinion: exhibitionist bitch in training. Given the opportunity, Patricia would use Mitzi without conscience.

Mitzi, on the other hand, clung to the maternal instincts which had landed her in virtual slavery. Reflected in the mirror, her face showed concern at the rough treatment, and pride in her daughter's physical beauty - which brings up another point. Remind me later to talk about how women claim to be big on inner beauty, but won't accept it when a man recognizes that a woman is truly beautiful only when her heart is pure. Back to Mitzi.

No matter that she had been enslaved by my cousin. No matter that I had participated in the humiliation of herself and her daughter. She recognized that I had taken on the role of her master and her protector, if not that of her lover. She clung, too, to the hope that Charlie would return to free her, to release her from her bondage to his family, which he had himself created.

Fat chance, Mitzi.

But I was feeling generous, and I saw that I could ease her situation and not lose face. I signaled to Wang, and he stepped closer. I pointed to Mitzi and asked him if he had a private fitting room. He nodded, puzzled, and I asked him, "Will you please take her in there and fit her with something she can cook in, sleep in and wear to the grocery store?"

"Ah, so?" Clearly, Wang wasn't sure what I wanted.

"Find her some shoes, maybe three or four inch heels. She should look good, like she does now. But get her something loose and comfortable, and something she can wear to bed." I shrugged, "A gown or two, or pajamas. A robe. Some bedroom slippers."

"Ah! So!" He brightened and offered, "I bring you nice-nice, you look."

"Don't bring me anything." I waved him away. "I'm enjoying this show right here, and you know more about this than I do. Take her, dress her, bring her back."

"Ah!" Wang bowed, pointed Mitzi on the way and said, "So!"

Mitzi walked away with enough swing and sway in her step to make me a little seasick, so I looked back at the dais and her semi-naked daughter. For the first time that I could remember, a young, well-built, naked woman was of no interest to me. That could have been, I suppose, because we were in Wang Ho's showroom and Patricia was nothing more than a dress form. More likely, I was for the first time ever hopeful, for Lydia was paying attention to me as a man.

Suddenly, I was bored.

Charlene stood and walked to the liquor cabinet with a slink and sway that made Mitzi look like what she was, a nearly middle-aged woman with a nice body for her age. She paused at the cabinet and offered me a sultry, enticing look, redolent of passion and heat.

Lydia who?

I felt that same tearing, tugging lust which had permeated our relationship throughout the past five years. With the loosening effects of the evening's drinking and the not so subtle conditioning of watching Patricia admire herself as she posed in front of us, I cannot say that I would have turned her down, no matter what.

Charlene knows just how to pose.

Just then, Wang returned, directed his attention to us and I could see him roll his eyes. He sighed and said to me, "Nice lady pick clothes. She very happy, you such nice fella." To Charlene, "Missy got minute? Talk-talk?"

"Crap. Just when I had you on the ropes." This was Charlie speaking, and then Charlene's honeyed contralto returned. "Certainly, Mr. Wang." She put her lips on my ear and whispered, "I may be a while, darling. Mr. Wang can be so attentive to details."

She ran her hand through my hair, dragged her nails along my neck, pursed her lips and blew gentle kisses, and followed Wang back to his office.

I helped myself to Wang's vodka, went back to my chair and waited.

Even without Wang and Charlene, the staff dressed and undressed Patricia, made notes, packed boxes.

Mitzi returned with one of Wang's staff following her, arms loaded with boxes. She took her position behind my chair, watched as I emptied my glass and then took it from me without being asked. As she bent forward to reach for the glass, she held her mouth close to my ear.

"Thank you."

* * *

The trip home to T-town was way different from the trip north to Detroit. Patricia had a new found love for herself, Mitzi was in a better mood, and Charlene was as distracted as I have ever seen her.

Now that Patricia had seen herself in short, tight dresses and real high heels, she had a new view of herself and her importance in life. The constant complaints of the upbound trip were replaced with unending adolescent drivel and an interminable replay of the evening, as though we hadn't suffered through it with her.

I tuned out Patricia's self-important, adolescent drivel and watched Mitzi as she wheeled us through the night. I decided her driving was smoother than earlier, that she had made a decision about something and that she was feeling more secure than she had in a while.

With Patricia between us, Charlene and I weren't in a position to talk, not that she wanted to, and that was fine with me. Just as Mitzi had made a decision, and just as Lydia suddenly found me interesting, Charlene was in love.

Sometimes I know things, and I'm not talking about precognition here, just one of those instantaneous flashes when intuition and instinct collide head-on, then merge into certain knowledge, all without a shred of evidence. Man or woman, no one is more attractive to us than someone who is attractive to someone else. It all fit.

Lydia suddenly found me interesting, at least in part because Mitzi had come along, perhaps in part because Charlene had gone out of her way to make her jealous. Mitzi knew about Lydia, I was sure, because Lydia and her pals were about as obvious as teenagers greeting a rock star.

Charlene had immersed herself in womanhood. Dress like a woman, act like a woman, think and feel like a woman, react like a woman. Other women found me attractive, and suddenly the game was turned. Instead of torturing me, she was torturing herself.

So to each of them, suddenly I was an attractive man. Mitzi had some new clothes which she chose herself, showing that her position was secure. Lydia had just seen Mitzi's butt and her friends had helped her empty a bottle of Dom. I was at my personal zenith, and as long as I kept my mouth shut and didn't do anything stupid, I was guaranteed to succeed. Not being stupid, I closed my eyes and dozed.

Mitzi took us to Charlene's apartment and parked, and I dozed while she carried the boxes of Patricia's new clothes inside. Not my job, not my problem.

She came back, not at all offended that I hadn't moved, and drove us home. I was so comfortable that I made her unfasten my seatbelt - I was too drunk and lazy to be bothered, and said so, and then as she bent inside to release the seat belt I ran my hand over her butt and gave it a friendly, appreciative squeeze.

"Now, Mr. Compton." Mitzi didn't refuse the attention.

Instead she reached in and helped me stand. "What would my husband say?"

"Never mind your husband. What would Lydia say?"

NINE

"Mr. Compton?"

Vodka usually does not give me a hangover. Although, mixing it with Scotch was not, in hindsight, too smart. I woke in a fog, yet content.

"Sir, it's time for you to get up."

"Swell." Something was different, yet comfortably, pleasantly the same. I usually sleep on the right side of the bed, but this time I kept Mitzi on the right, between me and the alarm clock. Being the servant, it's her place to get up first and take care of her master.

Mitzi? "Mitzi?"

"Sir?"

Slowly, seen through the clearing fog of incautious male bonding, the night returned. I had kept her with me through the night, a living, breathing body pillow to keep me warm and comfortable, a man's idea of cuddling: no obligation to be tender or considerate.

"Get back in bed and be quiet." I had figured out that Mitzi was standing beside the bed and bending over me, wearing nothing but her driving legs - her seamed tights.

"Yes, sir, but you will be late for work."

"Didn't I just buy you more clothes?"

"Yes, sir. But when we came inside last night, I didn't have time to go back to the car and bring them in." She adjusted my pillow, forcing me to move.

"Did you get up last night, maybe go to the bathroom?"

"Yes, sir." She turned slightly to her left, and her profile was so very pleasant, so easy on the eyes. She handed me my morning coffee.

I closed my eyes and sat there, inhaling the aroma of fresh coffee brought to me by a pretty woman who wore nothing but sheer, seamed pantyhose, every part and detail of her on view. I willed my eyes to open and thanked her, this pretty woman with a little bit of belly fat and such sad, grateful eyes. A small courtesy extended, a beaming smile in return.

"How bad was I last night?" She wore last night's sheer pantyhose - there's a word I loathe, along with panty, panty girdle and panties, and no, I don't have a another word to suggest in its place. They were still in good shape, no runs, no ladders, so I figured I hadn't assaulted her in the traditional sense, at least.

"You weren't bad, Mr. Compton. Just lonely."

That explained some of it. Slave or servant, she had a safe place and she wanted to protect it. By returning to my bed she had obeyed my instructions; by keeping on her pantyhose, she had defined our boundaries. The coffee in bed was her way of thanking me for the new clothes. Bringing it to me half-naked was her way of imposing on me an obligation to keep her safe. The sheer nylon of her tights was the only barrier between us and I could have ripped it off her with no effort at all. I could have done whatever I wished and she would have accepted it just as she had accepted similar treatment from the other men. But I had accepted our relationship as she had defined it. As long she was in my service, she decided who touched her and how.

"What would you like for breakfast?"

A simple question asked by an unassuming woman who, I already knew, could cook. Slowly, certainly, grew the conviction that just as if I had brought a puppy home from the pound, I had adopted her, and right then I knew just how Jefferson Davis felt when they elected him president of the Confederate States. It wasn't my idea, it wasn't my desire. It was my duty, imposed by years of training and generations of honor.

Crap.

"Mitzi?"

"Yes, sir?"

I looked her in the eye, held her steady. There was a tiny bit of apprehension showing in her eyes, as though she was about to be sent back to the pound. "If you're going to stay here and run this place, you need to know what I don't like: no eggs; no butter on the waffles, pancakes or toast. Whole milk if we have cereal. Orange juice or grapefruit juice. No pineapple juice. It gives me gas this early in the morning."

"Yes, sir." She brightened and stood up straight and squared her shoulders.

My own word, "early", rang in my ears. "What time is it?"

"Six forty, sir."

"For crying out loud, Mitzi. This is an hour before I usually get up."

"If you get up now, you can have your coffee, then shower, dress and have your breakfast."

Logical women always flummox me, maybe because I know so few of them. Two, to be exact; three, counting Charlene. I got up.

Not a good move, since I went to sleep *au naturel.*

To her credit, Mitzi remained unfazed. "Perhaps you should finish your coffee while I lay out your clothes for the day."

An excellent idea. "Thank you, Mitzi." I sat back down and covered myself, enjoyed my coffee and waited while she laid out my suit, shirt, socks and shoes. I quite enjoyed myself, lying there like the lord of the manor while my man - in this case, woman - moved about, handling those tiresome, mundane details which start every day. I especially enjoyed watching a pretty woman, nearly nude, move with easy grace and casual confidence, clearly comfortable in her own skin. When she finished, she brought my robe and held it so that I could get up and into it without embarrassing myself again.

I tied the belt and turned, ready to go to the bathroom and shower, ready to face the day. Mitzi was leaving, purpose in her stride and not even a hint of a plow horse or a television marshal.

The next time I saw her, she was fully dressed in her new work clothes, and I had to admit that between them, Mitzi and Wang Ho had done me proud. From the floor up, I saw black leather pumps with three inch heels, sheer black nylons, a skirt hemmed nearly to the knee, a white blouse covered by a full apron - who wears aprons? When she turned, I saw a kick pleat with a bit of black lace visible. She was wearing a slip.

The table was set, coffee and juice were waiting, and the electric frying pan was heated and ready for the batter: pancakes. There is nothing better in the morning than the mixed smells of bacon, coffee and pancakes. Except the bacon, coffee and pancakes themselves, served with warm maple syrup.

And of course, someone to serve all that, so that I didn't have to move once I sat.

"Your paper, Mr. Compton."

"Thank you, Mitzi." I tore into breakfast like a child unwrapping his Christmas presents, and kept at it until I had to come up for air.

"Mitzi?"

"Sir?"

"How are we fixed for food?"

"Oh." Obviously caught off guard, she blushed. "I should make a list, in case you want me to make dinner."

"That will be fine. Here." I reached for my wallet and found some cash. "Can you make do with this?"

Mitzi took the cash, counted it and wrote the amount on the note pad I keep by the phone. "This is enough to feed an army, Mr. Compton."

"You haven't seen me eat, especially if your dinners are like your breakfasts."

This time, the blush came with a smile.

"You can drive me to work, then go shopping for whatever you need. I don't like liver."

"Who does?"

I nodded wisely, and tried not to laugh out loud. Bad for discipline, you know, to fraternize with the help. "We'll be fine, Mitzi. Just fine."

"Shall I bring the car around, sir?"

"Around where?"

"It's a form of speech, sir." She raised her arm to indicate the garage, the driveway and the street but I interrupted her.

"Where did you learn to speak like that?"

She blushed again, and tried to answer. But she was at a loss and she was uncomfortable, and I didn't really care. Wherever she had learned it, Charlene had put it to use, and no doubt had backed up her instructions with a promise of pain that overrode any hesitation, any resistance that Mitzi might have shown. I'd have felt sorry for her except for one thing. Charlene was right: she could have left him.

"However you choose to do it, get the car ready. Drive me to the office, then do the shopping. Figure out a budget for the kitchen, and for whatever you need for yourself."

"Very good, sir." She took the car keys and her purse from the breakfront, removed the apron and moved to the garage door, paused to ask, "Should I change into my chauffeur's clothing, sir?"

"What do you think?"

She frowned, nodded, and put down her purse and the keys. "I should change."

Watching Charlene dress up as a woman was disorienting, but it was nothing compared to watching a very pretty, very hot woman trot across the floor, disappear down the hall, and then reappear within three minutes in her chauffeur's uniform. Talk about a phoenix.

She opened the garage door, purse in hand and chauffeur's cap crooked in her arm. I went to the car and waited while she came to hold the passenger door for me, and realized that I was beginning to enjoy having a person - a factotum, if you will. I settled in and read the paper while Mitzi drove downtown, and found the experience entirely pleasant.

Mitzi rolled up to the front door and stopped. Every day for years I have driven myself downtown, parked at my reserved space in the garage, and walked to the building through the walkways and tunnels which keep me out of the elements. But today, there I was in full view of the world, with a female chauffeur holding the door for me. A female chauffeur with great legs, a great figure and a pretty face, wearing shoes with six inch spikes for heels.

Happily, she remembered not to curtsy.

"What time shall I come for you, sir?"

"Six, I think. I'll call if I need you earlier."

"Very good, sir."

You know, of course, that Lydia was standing there for the whole thing.

"Daniel."

"Lydia."

As Mitzi pulled away, Lydia stalked to the door and yanked it open. "Mr. Compton, sir, if you please."

Memories of Charlene's reaction drifted past, and I figured, what the hell. If it works with one, it'll work with the other. "Shorter skirts, higher heels."

I went through the door and let her follow me to the elevator. As she stepped up beside me, I pointed to the call button. "Up, please."

She stabbed at the button, crossed her arms over her chest and faced away from me, tapping her foot. When the elevator doors opened, she stepped back and bowed me inside with such definite deferment that the rest of the passengers paused before coming in with us, and when we reached our floor she pressed the "Door Open" button and held it so that I could leave without risking the indignity of being caught in the doors, then set a brisk pace so that she could beat me to the office door and hold that, too.

This was going to be one long mother of a day, for sure.

* * *

I figured I would be lucky to live through the day without blood loss or frostbite. Actually, Lydia went out of her way to be offensively solicitous. My coffee cup was never empty and my calls were carefully screened to eliminate cranks. Since I didn't have my car, she ordered a take-out deli lunch and made sure that we found a pleasant place by the river, shaded by the sycamores and away from the vagrants, the joggers and the kids.

She made sure she knew that Mitzi was scheduled to be waiting at the door at six, and then had us down there five minutes early, so that we wouldn't be blocking rush hour traffic by making the driver wait. Naturally, Mitzi was already there, standing beside the rear door and ready to open it for me. Right then, I had a flash: Mitzi and Lydia going at each other in a giant tub of Jell-o.

Mitzi opened the door, Lydia smiled at her through clenched teeth and declined the offered ride to her car. And, *crap*.

"Daniel, darling! And the lovely Lydia! How pleasant is this?"

Charlene's skirt showed enough thigh to start a riot, Mitzi looked wary and Lydia nearly hissed as she said, "See you in the morning, *Daniel*."

"Lydia, darling! Do come with us to dinner! Now that we know we have the same tastes in restaurants, it will be so fun!"

"No. Thank you." She spun on her heel and left in anger, always a bad decision for a woman whose walk is being watched and graded.

Charlene clucked, "She is such a pretty girl, yet she walks like an angry man chasing a horse."

Mitzi and I traded shrugs. Apparently, we had both missed that comparison. I slid inside the car and Mitzi closed the door, walked around to the driver's side and took her seat behind the wheel, then drove us back to the restaurant.

Funny how things change. Last night, Lydia was jealous of Mitzi and Charlene and showing her interest in yours truly. Mitzi was a timid woman and Charlene, who was not a woman at all, very nearly had her way with me. Now, Lydia was throwing a tantrum because she saw me with women whose existence is neither a secret nor a threat to her position. Mitzi is behaving in a confident manner, and now that I think about it, she might find herself on the payroll. And Charlene, who started all this, has annoyed me to the point that, if I thought I could get away with it, I'd beat the hell out of the son-of-a-bitch.

Years of watching Lydia, never dreaming I'd truly have a chance with her, have conditioned me to accept the idea that she would spin around and storm off when offered dinner with my cousin and a ride in my chauffeured automobile. Years of loss and near-success, of near-failure and minor triumph have brought me a sense of futility, so that faced with a last minute opportunity to have dinner with the woman of my dreams, all I could do was watch her stomp off in jealous pique, asking myself inane questions. So what if my driver has legs almost as good as Lydia's? So what if her job description requires her to dress to excess? For me, right then, the highpoint of my expectations was a really good dinner brought to me by a woman for whom I hold no physical interest.

"Daniel, you are so quiet."

"Charlene, I was planning on a quiet, restful dinner at home, featuring Mitzi's best efforts in the kitchen. What's up?"

"Now, Daniel. Don't be cross with me."

"I'm not cross, Charlene. I'm pissed." I looked up at the rearview. "Mitzi?"

"Yes, sir?" Likewise, she used the rearview for eye contact.

"What had you done about dinner before you were hijacked by Miss Sweda?"

"Not much, sir. I bought a roast and vegetables, which will keep till tomorrow just fine."

I turned on my cousin. "Charlene, you are always welcome in my house. But keep out of my life. Clear?"

"Now, Daniel. Don't be cross, and don't jump to conclusions." She adjusted herself to show more thigh, which I hadn't thought she could, and went on. "I asked the girl about her plans, knowing how proprietary you can be, and she told me what she just said to you about everything keeping until tomorrow, and she said that she had no objections to driving us to dinner."

"As though she had a choice." I was about to mention that she had a name, and that courtesy required its use, when Charlene interrupted me.

"My brother is quite taken with the girl. He says she's the best he's ever had."

"Your brother is a very lucky man, and he should learn to keep his love life private."

"Now, Daniel. Let's not fight and spoil our dinner. Besides, I have a favor to ask you, and I don't want to feel guilty about asking it."

"Swell." I had more to say, but Mitzi had rolled up to the restaurant and the valet, recognizing both car and driver, nearly killed himself running in front of the car to be ready to open the door for Mitzi. I considered telling her to stay inside and let him handle the doors, but I knew she liked the attention and I figured it might make Charlene - as Charlie's proxy - a little jealous. I was wrong, of course.

The valet not only stared at Mitzi as she bent to hold the door for Charlene, he took his time looking up Charlene's skirt. Not to be outdone by another woman, Charlene took her time getting out of the back seat, showing so much thigh and garter belt - and package, too, knowing Charlene - that I wasn't surprised when he reached past Mitzi and offered Charlene his hand. He escorted her to the curb and, not kidding, bowed.

Mitzi closed the door behind them and walked around to offer me the courtesy of acknowledging my existence, then made sure the valet saw that she wore nothing under her seamed tights. I thought he would stroke out right there, but he managed to walk her back to the driver's door. As Charlene and I started up the walk to the restaurant's front door, I heard him asking her what time her shift ended.

Charlene muttered, "I hope the little slut takes off her shoes. I wouldn't want to come outside after dinner and find holes in your upholstery."

"Can it, Chuck. The girl is just about in love with your brother and trust me, she has no interest in other men."

"And you know this, how?"

"Good evening. Do you have reservations?"

We had reached the hostess stand and the same woman was working as last night. Since Charlene had made the reservations in her own name, the hostess was confused, or perhaps concerned that we would have to wait for a table. As it turned out, neither.

"Charlene Sweda."

"I don't see your name, Mr. Compton."

Charlene's elegant finger traced her own name, clearly visible, then rose with the hostess' eyes following its richly lacquered nail until it turned and pointed to Charlene, herself.

"I am Charlene Sweda. Mr. Compton is my guest tonight." She held the hostess' eyes as a snake holds its prey. "Is our table ready?"

A smarter girl would have been afraid. But the hostess was, as Charlene later remarked, generic. No, I am not sure what she meant. I am sure, however, that standing there, watching her with the hostess, I thought of Charlene as a woman, only, and not at all as a cross-dressing hit man. Watching her walk to the table did nothing to change that illusion and, as we were seated, the Charlene who had knocked on my door those long years ago suddenly reappeared.

Wit, charm and a forceful personality overwhelmed our waiter. He wandered around like a teenager with a crush on his English

Literature teacher, and I swear he sighed whenever Charlene let him fill her water glass. And then, drinks before us and dinner ordered, she asked her favor.

"Danny, old man, I need a favor."

"You mentioned that." I sipped vodka and waited, forcing her to come out with it.

"I have to go out of town to see some people. I'll be gone a few days, and someone has to watch Patricia. I thought perhaps you would be willing to help out."

"Are you nuts?" Apparently my voice carried. People at the next few tables looked around, trying to find the speaker.

"No, dear boy, I am not nuts." She sipped her Scotch and smiled over the glass rim. "I simply think you can help me out with a small problem."

"Right. You want me to babysit a spoiled brat while I'm keeping her mother in servitude."

"At least you've quit calling her a slave."

"No matter what I call her, she has no place else to go." I leaned forward to emphasize the point. "Charlie and his poker buddies took care of that."

Charlene supported her chin on her left hand, played with her drink with the right. "How about, Patricia stays with you and Mitzi, and Mitzi takes care of her?"

"How about you send her home to her father?"

"I beg your pardon?" Charlene sat up, truly puzzled.

"Send the little snot home to Willie, let her see what a prize he is. It's not like he'd gamble her away - even those perverts wouldn't let him do that, and if they got a load of her royal attitude they would for sure stay away." I shrugged. "Maybe they'll even have her jailed."

"You are a caustic, cynical man."

"Selfish, too." I sipped, waiting for the comeback.

None.

Charlene looked out at the river, smiled, looked back at me. "I always wondered how you could be a lawyer and stick up for others, but not be able to stick up for yourself."

"And?"

"You've turned out quite well. I'm not ashamed of you at all." She raised her glass in a spontaneous toast. "To my cousin, who fought for my honor on the playground and now fights for children in the courtroom."

Sure, why not? "You realize, the only reason I'm in Kiddie Court again is that you shanghaied me into handling Benny Randolph's case?"

"Of course, dear boy." Her pinkie found its way into the corner of her mouth, and she gave me a smile somewhere between cynical and wistful. "Even a draftee can be a hero."

I sat back and let the waiter serve dinner. Then, "Let her stay with Willie, and tell her that she has to check in with Mitzi every day, morning and night."

"I'll think about it. But maybe you should ask Mitzi what she thinks."

I sighed, "The waiter didn't bring the steak sauce, and I figure I have about as much chance of getting him back here as I do of getting you to agree with me. So, you get somebody with the A-1, and I'll agree to leave it up to Mitzi. Deal?"

"Sometimes, Daniel, you are so reasonable that it scares me." She raised her hand almost a whole inch before the waiter saw it and came running over, panting. She gave me a wicked smile, then rubbed the back of her hand along his arm as she asked him to, "Please bring Mr. Compton the A-1 before his steak gets cold."

As he was about to run back to the condiment stand she stopped him with just a touch of pressure on his arm which she managed with a subtle turn of her wrist. "And I would like another Scotch, when you have time."

Who here thinks the A-1 came to the table before the Scotch?

The rest of the meal wasn't worth comment, unless you get off on stories of adolescent flirtation aimed at an adult woman in the presence of a grown-up and testy man. Our exit was a replay of last night's exit and tonight's arrival. Without Patricia to provide the offensive juvenile commentary, it would have been almost amusing except that I was tired, I had been looking forward to a pleasant dinner at home and after all, how many times can a man watch a college boy drool over a woman who could be his girlfriend's mother?

After Mitzi had delivered Charlene, she took me home and as I promised Charlene, I asked her what she thought. Naturally, she thought she should have Patricia stay with us for the few days that Charlene would be out of town. Then she asked me if I knew when Charlie would be back and I told her the truth.

"Beats the hell out of me, Mitzi. Beats the hell out of me."

This time, Mitzi asked me to let her stay with me for the night, and of course I said yes. Same terms, same reason: one feeling lonely, one being kind.

* * *

"Good morning, Mr. Compton."

"Good morning, Mitzi."

"Your coffee, sir."

"Thank you, Mitzi."

"I'll lay out your suit, now. We will be having waffles and sausage for breakfast."

"Very good, Mitzi. Thank you."

TEN

Once again, a small crowd gathered as Mitzi strolled around the Town Car and opened my door. This time, though, no Lydia. On impulse, I asked Mitzi what she had planned for dinner.

"A pork roast, sir, prepared with spiced apple rings, and vegetables."

"Ah." I nodded appreciatively. "What time do you plan to serve?"

"How many will there be for dinner, sir?"

Apparently, I had nodded transparently, too. "Plan on one more and we'll see how it goes."

"Yes, sir." She shut the door behind me and said, "I had planned to serve at seven, if that pleases you."

"That will be fine."

As I walked away she said, "Good luck, Mr. Compton."

I turned to thank her. She winked and returned to the driver's door, got in and drove away. I watched her disappear up the street and wondered if there was time to send her for some sensible shoes, just in case.

I made it safely to my office even though Lydia wasn't there to escort me, and there she was at her desk, working hard already. As I entered the office she paused, checked her watch and stood. She picked up a file and moved around her desk, engrossed in her work and unaware that I was there until she nearly ran into me.

Holy crap!

If you remember, yesterday morning I suggested she try shorter skirts and higher heels. Nobody thinks she did that, right? Instead, she was dressed pretty much as she always was, except that she had done something to her face and hair.

Movie stars should look so good.

"Mr. Compton." Icy challenge, redolent of injured jealousy.

"Please have dinner with me tonight."

I could see conflict in her eyes. Should she acquiesce because she wanted to have dinner with me, or should she refuse so as to make a point and stay in control?

"I have plans."

"Oh. Tomorrow night?"

"I don't know." Her mouth twitched; she was fighting a smile. "A girl likes some notice so she can make arrangements."

"Pick a night. And if your plans change tonight, let me know. Dinner is at seven. Your place is reserved."

Her head came up in a genuine double-take, eyes wide. She had no idea what I was planning, she was eaten by curiosity and she wasn't about to let go of her jealousy. But then, "Where is dinner tonight?" Her curiosity was stronger than her pique.

"At my house. Pork roast, vegetables."

"Let me get this straight." She looked away, smiling, then recovered herself and went on. "You are inviting me to dinner at your house tonight?"

"Yes."

"You can cook?"

"Hardly. I have a maid now, and her duties include cooking. She is quite good, if you would care to come." I reached for the file - company business - which she carried. "What's this?"

"Not your case." A quick answer and a deft move to keep the file away from me.

"My law firm, my office, my case." I held out my hand.

"Bruce is doing a favor for his mother."

Did I mention that Lydia has always struck me as a nimble minded, facile tongued liar? Bruce's mother has her own lawyer, and she and Bruce speak to each other twice a year: Christmas and Mother's Day.

"Oh, I see." No need to push it. "Is the coffee ready?"

"On your desk."

"Thanks." I figured, as much as I would get out of this conversation, I already had. I walked to my office and left my briefcase on one of the side chairs, sat down in my own chair and picked up my coffee mug. Screw it. I spun around and stared out the window at the horizon, where Toledo's East Side met the sky.

Ah, the poetry! Horizons and such are so evocative of the deeper meaning of life, which for me centers on why Charlene wants me to save Benny Randolph, and why she thinks Patricia Watson is worth the air it takes to fill her lungs.

Long years ago I sat in my sister's apartment in Manhattan and looked out at the gray winter sky where it stretched off toward New Jersey. Before that, I sat in her apartment near Cabrini Terrace and looked out over a skyline with at least one copper dome that glowed in the sunset like a scene from *Mary Poppins*. I remember riding in the car when we moved north, coming to the city from the Jersey Turnpike. The Empire State Building, red orange in the sunset, stood against the skyline and the EL moved along in the foreground, and when I said it was an electric engine I got the usual, "My son is stupid," response from my mother.

Typical.

There was a real electric railroad engine hauling a real train, and the backdrop was the real NYC. The whole scene was as perfect as a souvenir post card, and I was the one member of the family who was actually glad to be moving to the Empire State. Even as a little kid, I wanted to go north, wanted to live in the mountains and know the City. There's only one "City,"and it was right in front of me.

And trains! Three years old, I had trains. Wind-up, push-along; tracks or none; Marx and Lionel. I had them all, except American Flyer, and the kid up the street had those. Mine were always steam engines, not diesel. But what I wanted was an electric engine, like they used in the cities. I wanted an electric engine like I saw on television, like they used in New York City, and there in front of me was the real thing, pulling a train. It was the perfect moment, and if I had kept my mouth shut it would have been mine without blemish. But I had to say so, had to point out the electric engine. After all, if you can't share your moments with your mother, well, what's the point? So I did and she pointed out that I was too stupid to realize that electric engines belong in Lionel train sets. But I said, no, it was real, look at it, and the fight was on. Just another example of why, years later, my sister said, "If you had just learned to stop arguing, you'd have been hit a lot less."

I brought that up because I wanted to, and because it comforts me to remember that, as bad as things were, I've had moments that others never will. Of course, others had their moments, too, and had real families to share in them. Others had parents whose daily homecoming was a happy time: "Daddy's home!" Others had doors they could close, and be confident they would stay closed, safe from the Motherhood Gestapo: "Just making sure that you are all right. You were so quiet." I had my moments and I shared them with myself, except for those moments I had with Dwight after I failed to save him from the bullies.

I bring that up because I wonder if Benny Randolph would truly want to leave his mother's home, if he had the chance to live there. Or would he want to go to another home with people who might find in him a perfect, lovable little boy, smart and precious and deserving of the best that life has? I wonder because, the way I was raised, by the time I was old enough that others should have noticed that I was wacked out, I was also too far along the coo-coo track to be helped by do-good outsiders. I would have rebelled and acted out, and I would have carried on until they gave up and sent me back to the hell that was my home.

I had a sister; Dwight did not. Maybe that was the difference, that I had an older sister to keep me sane. Never mind the rest. My conscience was clear.

I spent the rest of the day working through my plan, making last minute adjustments and running through what would likely be the response from Stannard, from Willis, from the court. Lefty Martinez owed me another report, and once I had that in hand I would be ready to drop the axe on CSB.

"Stannard, your ass is mine."

Feeling focused and tough, I listened to the intercom while Lydia informed me that if my driver - and she about choked on that - was coming for me at six, I should get a move on. But I was on a roll and I am the boss, and no matter how much I want to be more than that to her, I had things to do before I left.

"Go down there and tell her to wait. I'll be about fifteen minutes late."

"I ... I ... I have plans. I told you that."

"I didn't say you had to hold her hand, and I didn't forget that you have plans. All you have to do is tell her I will be late, tell her to wait, then go wherever you want to."

I clicked off without waiting for an answer. The sooner I finished my work, the sooner I could go home and have dinner. I had finally figured out that if Lydia wanted to have dinner with me she would say so, and since I had already asked her twice there wasn't anything else I could do but wait until she accepted. Or, I could give up and move on, but my instincts told me we were jockeying for position, establishing control. But I hold all the cards in this hand: I told her to pick a day, I have a maid to cook for me and drive me around, and I know she's interested. Lydia, not the maid. Mitzi's interest in me has nothing to do with anything beyond security.

So, I finished up and went downstairs. Lydia wasn't at her desk, and when I reached the first floor I made sure to take a roundabout path to the front door. No Lydia, but Mitzi was there at the passenger door, looking fine in her chauffeur's togs.

She stood there in a loose "parade rest" position, feet slightly apart, hands behind her in the small of her back. She was absolutely stable in those outrageous shoes, completely comfortable in her very short black skirt, sheer white silk blouse and stylish chauffeur's cap. The sheer black of the seamed tights finished the ensemble nicely, and I decided that I should someday call Wang Ho and congratulate him on his fine work. Of course, the fact that she is exceedingly attractive, possessed of excellent legs and a fine figure, a very pretty face and nice hair provided an excellent canvas for the clothier's artistry.

As I approached, she snapped to and reached for the door handle. "Good evening, Mr. Compton."

"Good even, Mitzi. Apparently we will not be having a guest this evening."

"Yes, sir. I was informed."

I got in and she shut the door, went to the driver's door and got in, started the engine and fastened her seatbelt, then pulled into traffic. "May I say something, sir?"

"Sure." I had nothing better to do than watch the scenery go by, so why not converse with my driver?

"I think she's interested in you."

"I agree." The route registered. "Mitzi, this isn't the way home."

"No, sir. Not directly. Dinner will keep."

"Should I ask?"

She held up her own cell phone. "It's a good thing you still have a car phone. My cell was turned off because Willie didn't pay the bill." She paused for the cross traffic, then turned. "Nice move, making Miss Svenson come down personally instead of using the car phone."

I nodded, appreciating the compliment. I thought that was better than saying I hadn't thought of telling Lydia to call the car. "Are we going to the cell phone place to pay the bill?"

"No, sir. We are going to the Ford dealer so that you can pick out a smaller car for your personal use."

"Maybe it would be cheaper if I just paid you a salary."

"It isn't that I haven't thought about that, but at least until the last of it hits the fan, Willie would stick out his hand or the bill collectors would take it away from me. Then what? As long as you keep me around, I can stop worrying about losing my home." She looked up at the rearview and smiled, then went back to her driving. "Besides, that won't get you Miss Svenson."

She had me there, for sure. "This smaller car for my personal use, that's going to help me get Miss Svenson?"

"It won't hurt."

Again, she had me there. In fact, I had been thinking along those lines myself. *What woman*, I had asked myself, *wants to be on a date with a chaperon, especially when the chaperon isn't much older than she is, herself?* "This smaller car: you have it picked out for me?"

She cut her eyes to the rearview again as she answered, "I have something in mind, but we can see what you come up with by yourself, if you want."

"Mitzi, is it just me or is your speech turning normal?"

"Normal, sir?"

"Yeah, you're talking like a person instead of a character in an old movie." The light dawned. "That's it! You watch old movies and mimic the servants! The characters, I mean."

"Yes, sir. Miss Sweda was quite specific that I had to remember my place."

I saw her shiver as she answered. "She scared you, I take it?"

She didn't answer until she had stopped at the next red light. "She terrified me, sir. She said things to me that ..." Her voice trailed off.

"What did she tell you?" I kept my voice level, but I was thinking, *Charlene you bitch.*

"She told me the flat out truth. My idiot husband has gambled away most of our money, and he has upped the mortgages on the house. Except that we haven't filed any papers, we're bankrupt. Going bankrupt won't help me as long as I'm married to him because he will just keep gambling and anything I can earn will go to pay his bills." She stared straight ahead as she spoke, and if her voice shook I didn't hear it. "Charlie took me as collateral, and he was staying with you but he had to leave town. He left me with you because he owes you money, so I'm your slave now, she said. Then she laughed, and said that you're the nice one and then she ... no one ever scared me like that."

"I'm sorry, Mitzi."

"Don't be. You didn't do anything except treat me nice." She turned the wheel and stopped; we were there. She looked around at me. "You and Charlie are the only two people who ever treated me like a real person, ever. I have been a slave to someone since I was born. My brother is a genius, my sister is even smarter. I was the middle child, and I was the pretty one, the dumb one. It was my job to take care of them and the house until they were grown up and married, and then I could go have a life. Willie came along and he looked a lot better than staying home to cook and clean for my," she almost spat, "siblings." She paused, then finished with, "Willie wasn't gambling then, and he was fun. If you want to know the truth, being owned by you is best thing that ever happened to me."

She pulled the door handle and said, "We're here, sir. You are going to talk to Roger. He's my cousin, sort of, and he hates Willie.

Let me do the talking, and don't agree to anything until I say so."

She stepped out of the car and stopped to adjust her cap, slammed the driver's door and sashayed around the front of the car - she gave the shop people a better view that way - and opened my door. "This way, sir, if you please."

She led me inside, asked for Roger and then introduced me to him. I followed her lead and thirty-seven minutes later I was the proud owner of a Mustang convertible, deep metallic blue, with everything on it. Turned out, someone ordered it and never came back for it. Nice car though it was, no one would pay the price and so, with a little dickering and my checkbook in my hand, I came out all right. They promised it would be ready Saturday morning and so, for the first time in my memory I was looking forward to the weekend.

As Mitzi held the car door for me I asked, "What is it about this particular car that is going to help me get Lydia?"

She shrugged, "It's a babe magnet, sir."

I sat back and enjoyed the ride, thinking about what she had said before, thinking that we thought alike, thinking that it was too bad that I wasn't interested in her; thinking maybe my maid was becoming my friend. I've never had a maid, or a woman for a friend. Maybe they'll make a movie, *Driving Mr. Daisy.* But for sure, I was about to have a fine home cooked meal, and with Mitzi there to guide me, if I had any chance at all with Lydia, I'd succeed.

"Mitzi."

"Yes, Mr. Compton?"

"Do you have plans for Saturday?"

Eyes in the rearview, a speculative glance. "Plans, sir?"

"Plans."

"You own me, sir. My time is yours."

"I thought maybe you would be taking a day off."

"And do what, sir?" She checked the traffic, and although the light was green, she waited. A car came late through the intersection, and I appreciated her skill and her concentration. "We lost our friends when we lost our money. I've slept with his poker buddies, and any women in their lives want me dead. I have no money except what you give me for the household expenses, and yes, I know you said I should take care of myself, but I feel funny using your grocery money to get my nails done."

"Mitzi, if you were a prize cat or a show dog, you wouldn't think twice about having yourself all primped up. Of course, you wouldn't be cooking and driving, so maybe that's a bad comparison. But you get the point, right?"

"Honestly? No."

"Maybe it's been so long since I ate that my blood sugar is too low for me to make sense."

"Sure, that's what does it."

"Damn, Mitzi."

"Sorry, sir." She stopped the car and opened the garage door, then got out and opened the car door, then walked me to the house door and opened that, too. "Go inside and sit, sir." She pointed to the living room.

Being a good master, I obeyed. Mitzi brought me a lovely vodka-tonic, and I contemplated the changes in my life in the few days I had known her. I let my mind wander down moss-draped paths of Southern DNA, wondering how I came to own a slave in modern day Ohio. I let my thoughts turn to Lydia, and how she hadn't really argued when I sent her to talk to Mitzi; how she hadn't mentioned the car phone, even though the number is on her speed dial.

Dinner was truly, truly marvelous, and at bedtime Mitzi came to see that I was properly tucked in before she went to her own room. She looked rather middle class in her gown and mules, and I was willing to bet Willie wasn't having nearly the good time he used to, when Mitzi took care of everything around the house.

* * *

"Good morning, Mr. Compton."

"Good morning, Mitzi."

"We will being having french toast and bacon this morning, and grapefruit. Do you like your bacon crisp?"

"You know I do, Mitzi."

"Sir, if I knew, would I ask?" Eyebrows lifted, reproachful

eyes. "Your coffee, sir."

"Thank you, Mitzi." I took the mug, held it so that the steam brought the aroma to my nose. "Crisp bacon, please."

"Very good, sir."

* * *

"Detour, Mitzi."

"Sir?"

"I'll direct you." And I did, right to the cell phone store.

"Wait for me."

She did, of course, standing by the rear passenger door until I returned.

"Here. Just don't call Australia."

"Thank you, sir." She took the cell phone and let it lie on her open palm, then opened the door for me, smiling. "I don't know anyone in Australia, sir."

"Good. Now, let's go to work."

She wheeled along with her usual competence, delivered me safely to my office building and opened my door with her usual crispness. Standing there in her short skirt and stilettoes, she attracted a different crowd - later in the morning, you know - as she held the car door. "Here." I handed her some cash. "I decided that we should do something tomorrow to break in the new wheels. This should cover whatever you need."

She thumbed the bills, raised her eyebrows and then looked up at me. "We already paid for the car, sir."

"Funny, Mitzi. Get yourself some sunglasses, treat yourself to a cappuccino, make some plans for tomorrow."

"Yes, sir. Six, tonight?"

"Sure." I started inside, then stopped to ask, "What's for dinner?"

"Leftovers, sir, if you approve."

"I approve." I waved and turned away. "I have to go make more money so I can keep you in the style to which you are becoming accustomed."

"Very good, sir." She shut the car door and returned to the driver's side, and just for the fun of it I looked back and watched her. Too bad we're just friends, too bad she's the help.

Time to work.

* * *

Mitzi was on station at five fifty-five, waiting for me as always at the rear passenger door. This time she wore dark glasses, and with her chauffeur's cap in place she looked almost like a Vogue model on a shoot. The usual suspects had gathered, junior executives and young secretaries, to watch the evening ritual. Amazing, isn't it, how fast a pretty woman in a short skirt holding a car door for a man had become a ritual? And people say nothing goes on in downtown Toledo.

"Good evening, Mr. Compton."

"Good evening, Mitzi."

I got in, she closed the door and walked around to the driver's door. Horny men lusted for her and jealous women loathed her, and we drove away in stylish mystery.

"Did you get your hair done?"

"Yes, sir. Do you approve?"

"Yes. Yes, I do. It looks really good." I was feeling smug, if you want to know. "Lets them all know, mine's bigger."

Her eyes were hidden by the shades, but I could tell by the shift of her facial muscles that she was looking in the rearview. "Anyone asks, I'll be sure to tell them."

"Except Charlie?" Ok, I'm a smart ass.

In the afternoon sun and with her shades in place I could see her blush. "Yes, sir. Except Charlie."

But she was smiling in spite of herself.

* * *

A well-made drink, a pleasant dinner, a quiet evening. Being boring has its benefits.

"Do you think I'm boring, Mitzi?"

She was wearing her maid suit, sheers and lower heels; longer skirt and looser blouse. She had brought my after dinner drink and set it on the coaster as she answered. "No, sir. I think you are a complex and interesting man."

"Sure."

"I mean it." She stood up straight, looked around the living room and then focused on the fireplace. "You keep me as a slave and yet you are offended by the situation. You kept me as a bed warmer for a night, then let me warm myself in your bed. You think ahead, but you live in the moment. You are like a modern Thomas Jefferson."

I looked up at her, nonplused. "Where'd that come from?"

She smiled at me, sadly, wisely. "My IQ test score was two hundred. In my family, that makes me the dumb one."

"In this house, that makes you the smart one."

ELEVEN

"Good morning, Mr. Compton."

So much for sleeping late. I had figured, wrongly it developed, that since it was Saturday and we were going to play with the new car, I would be sleeping in. But no. Promptly at six-thirty, Mitzi was standing there, coffee in hand and dressed in her maid's togs.

"Your coffee, sir."

"It's six-thirty, Mitzi."

"Yes, sir." She busied herself in my closet and dresser, came back with my robe. "I will have breakfast ready as usual, sir. Please don't dawdle because it's Saturday."

"They'll wait for us, Mitzi. How early can they close?" I know, I know: once a smart ass, always a smart ass.

"Close, sir? They are delivering the new car at eight-thirty."

"Say what?"

She strode to the door, full of purpose and intent, paused in the doorway. "I arranged for Roger to bring the car and papers. We'll be on the road by nine."

"Where the hell are we going at that hour, if I may ask?"

"The lake, sir. We are going on a picnic."

"You're going to change, right?"

Want to feel stupid sometime? Ask that question of your maid, whose IQ you couldn't match with help from NASA, and watch how she looks at you. Mitzi shook her head as she stepped through the doorway, and left me to enjoy my morning coffee.

Hah!

It makes perfect sense to me that she has a genius IQ and no real ability to deal with people, especially a husband who is an addict. I have no trouble accepting that she was the dummy of the family, genius that she might be, and that they taught her nothing about men; that she caught the first stage out of Dodge, so to speak, and then the wheels fell off. What troubles me is that I run a law firm, she's a housewife turned maid, and she's the one who figured out that the constructive application of power brings extra service. In plain language, she's the one who knew to tell her cousin to deliver the car to the house.

On the bright side, for the first time in memory I was looking forward to Saturday. As a kid, every Saturday was likely to be an exercise in agony. No, I don't subscribe to the theory that children should never have chores. But neither do I think that every Saturday has to be devoted to mining rocks.

Once in New York, we learned the joys of planting trees and shrubs in glacial moraine. Translation: every hole required that we drill straight down with a steel rod, then get down on our hands and knees and pull out the rocks and clay, and then sift the mess through a frame which my father made from two by fours and wire mesh. The clay fell through the screen into the wheelbarrow, and the rocks stayed in the screen. We carried the screen to the driveway and emptied it in the potholes, then piled up the dirt on big pieces of cardboard from the mover's shipping cartons. With the tree in place, the dirt went back in the hole. All the while, my mother had her whip-tongue going, scolding everyone and criticizing things which meant nothing, complaining that no one took the whole thing seriously while she was just trying to improve our lives and the place where we lived.

Now, years later and hundreds of miles removed I can see that if she had just shut the hell up and let us laugh about the things we were doing, we would have been a stronger family with a chance for us - my sister and I - to have sane childhoods. But then, if your aunt had wheels she'd be teacart. My mother was already whizzing down the road of angry lunacy when we moved, and rural New York was for her a steep downhill slope.

I lay there with my coffee mug in hand, savoring the day's potential. A picnic with Mitzi! No expectations of either by either, no need for me to resort to legalese to make a point. It wasn't a date. It was hours of fun with a woman who could turn heads and who enjoyed doing so. All I had to do was be there to watch the day unfold, sit where she pointed and eat what she presented. But to enjoy all that I had to leave my bed, shower and dress. Besides, my coffee was just the right temperature for easy drinking, and Mitzi would have breakfast waiting.

At eight twenty-five, dressed and fed, I was signing the receipts and registration application, the power of attorney so that Roger could get the title and plates, and any other piece of paper that he thrust at me. Mitzi cleaned up while we handled the paperwork, and then thanked her cousin and sent him on his way. I had expected to drive him back to the dealership, but another driver had followed him to the house and was waiting outside. While Roger was wandering down the driveway to the other car, Mitzi was in her room changing into her play clothes.

I hadn't seen her in anything but her cocktail dress and Wang Ho's creations, and the difference was striking. Suddenly, my maid became a woman, a person; someone who did normal, everyday things like planning a picnic at the lake and having fun. She had traded the chauffeur's cap for a visor and her heels for sandals. The top was sleeveless, but had a matching jacket; the shorts were just that: short. She was the picture of a smart, hot and pretty woman ready for fun. Standing next to her, I felt like the class dork standing beside the prom queen.

"Ready, sir?"

"I guess." Which was true. I guessed that I was ready, because I was standing there dressed, and the picnic basket was packed and on the table. I had no idea where we were going nor how we were going to get there, and if I was supposed to know to pack something, well, we were screwed.

"Shall we go?" Her look was quizzical, as though I was confusing her.

"Sure." I picked up the basket - it registered that this was a day off for her, once she had made the lunch - and headed for the door. I opened it and held it for her. "After you."

She gave me another look, as though I had forgotten my place. "What?"

"Sir?" She pointed at the basket and the door. "Don't you want me to carry that?"

"I can handle it." I nodded at the doorway. "You going to stand there all day, or go out to the car?"

"I thought you would you go first, sir."

"I thought this is supposed to be a day off for you, now that you're out of your work clothes and I'm holding the lunch."

"Really?" She brightened, and I saw how she had looked as a young woman: smart and pretty, unworn by life, unmarked by an ungrateful child. She moved through the doorway ahead of me and her stride was different, too. I couldn't detail it if I had to, just that it felt lighter as I watched her walk.

She went toward the car but not right to it, looked up at the sky, looked around. I swear, she stood on her toes and spun in a half circle, a dancer's move, and then smiled at me.

I went to the car, dropped the basket on the back seat and stood there in the driveway, watching Mitzi bask in the morning sunshine. She closed her eyes and stretched upward, standing on her toes with her arms at her sides, catching the sun on her palms.

It is better to give than to receive.

The warm feeling that came with watching her wasn't from the sun. Seeing her happy, knowing that she was feeling the freedom of safety and non-responsibility gave me a thrill worth more than the price of the car. I waited for her.

She opened her eyes. "We should go, sir."

"If you're ready." I went to the passenger door and held it open. "Drive first, or ride shotgun?"

"Shotgun." She came to the car, her movements full of easy grace. Every movement was worth watching. She could sneeze, I bet, and be graceful about it. She settled in and adjusted her seat, found the seatbelt and then checked her makeup in the vanity mirror on the back of the visor. "It's your new car and you should put the first real miles on it."

I shut the door, thinking about the role reversal. "The way you handle the Town Car makes me think you like to drive."

"Yes, sir. I enjoy it." She smiled again, and added, "I'm happy in my work."

"Sure." Truthfully, I felt a little nervous. It's like not being accustomed to the money. It's a new car, and even though it's mine I still felt intimidated. I went around to the driver's side and got in, found the keys and started the engine. "Here we go."

I pulled around the driveway to the street and paused. As I was about to move into the street Mitzi put out her hand to catch my arm.

"You remembered your wallet, sir?"

"Yes, I did. But thanks for asking." I didn't see a reason to mention that I had forgotten it as I was leaving and had to go back for it. No, there's no hidden meaning there. I haven't stopped carrying it because I have a driver, and I'm not going senile. I just forgot it and she simply asked as any wife would ask any husband. It was happenstance and habit coming together. Serendipity.

"Did you put the cooler in the trunk?"

"Cooler?"

"Didn't I mention the cooler, in the garage?"

"No." I looked over my shoulder and backed up, hit the opener and watched the garage door go up. There was the cooler, sitting in plain sight.

"I'm sorry, sir. I should have said something." She released her seatbelt and pulled the door handle, ready to go for the cooler.

"Mitzi, sit." I didn't see any reason she should be hefting a cooler on her day off. I set the parking brake and went for the cooler, which I put on the back seat with the picnic basket, and got in behind the wheel. "Let's see: wallet, lunch, cooler, hot babe. Ok, I'm ready. You?"

"Do you have your cell phone, sir?" I could tell she was pleased that I said she was hot.

"Yep. How about you? Purse? Wallet? Cell phone?"

She held up her purse. "Check."

"Here we go again." I put down the garage door and released the brake. "You're the navigator, so get us there."

She did.

We went across town and out to the lake until we saw the sign for Metzger Marsh, and trust me, that was no place for a lady. Not that it's a bad place, just that it's a place to fish and, with the proper shoes, to walk and maybe go down to the lake's edge.

We walked along the breakwater, a long concrete jetty where the fishermen sit and cast, angling for, I guess, perch and walleye.

You've gathered that I'm not a fisherman, right? Mitzi went out to the end and stood there, silent, staring out across Lake Erie. I waited, trying to stay out of the way of sparkling lures and of worm draped hooks and hoping my vertigo wasn't showing.

It was the damned narrowest concrete thing I have ever stood on, let me say, and I was getting a little dizzy just standing there. Mitzi was right at home, I guess. She stood there nearly twenty minutes, then turned around and smiled. "Thanks." She sauntered past me, and everyone on the jetty forgot about fishing until she was well past them, except maybe two self-absorbed preteen males.

Back at the car, we turned around and headed east again. Our next stop was Crane Creek State Park, and I was pleasantly surprised that the place wasn't full of screaming kids playing in the water, their mothers hollering threats and warnings, and otherwise ignoring the finer points of social behavior. In fact, the crowd was small and quiet, we had no trouble finding a pleasantly located table and the bugs left us alone.

Mitzi had packed a lunch which put my mother's best dinners to shame, and that was only the beginning. She had filled the cooler with sliced peaches, water, tonic, lime wedges and - I'm not making this up - ice cream. She had put a half-pint of vanilla in a plastic bag, then put that in a gallon plastic jar of ice and salt. After lunch, she produced plastic bowls, divided the ice cream and peaches and served sundaes for dessert, with coffee which she had brought in a small thermos. The whole thing made me wistful.

"You look troubled, sir."

"I'm not troubled, Mitzi. I'm jealous."

"Jealous, sir?" True puzzlement.

"Jealous." I nodded to reinforce the point. "Someday, someone else will come along and win your heart, and then he'll be the one picnicking with you beside the lake."

She smiled and shook her head. "We used to come here when Patricia was little. Willie says I'm cheap, I say I'm thrifty. Besides," she looked around, "I like it here."

"You recognize the trees, don't you?"

"Sir?"

"The way you look at them, you see individuals, not just a bunch of trees."

"How did you know?" She held her spoon halfway to her bowl, her voice level and curious. But her eyes softened, and I was willing to bet that I was the first person in a while to show her kindness.

"It was the way you looked at them when you looked around." I figured, no need to point out that my Scot-Irish blood makes me fey, sometimes. She already thought that I'm half weird. No need to convince her that she should be locking her bedroom door at night.

"My grandfather brought me here when I was a little girl. He was the only one that treated me like a person instead of a slave. I never had to do anything when I was with him." She nodded at the cooler. "He taught me the trick with the ice cream. It's like making ice cream at home, with salt and ice to make brine."

I had a flash of her explaining the chemical process to a child, not Patricia, who was born smart and kind. A child who would grow up with a real chance because Mitzi was its mother and Willie wasn't its father. Even for a flash it was brief; didn't have a chance to see the child's gender.

She played with the peaches in her bowl and she was a child again, so I stopped talking. I let her have her reverie, and looked around at the trees, huge cottonwoods that held the sand in place and shaded the beach. Most people think of cottonwoods as trashy trees because their seeds are tiny, attached to those cottony fibers that fill the air and lie on the ground in rolls, caught by the grasses and shrubs. People also think that they are allergic to cottonwoods, but my former allergist told me that no one is allergic to cottonwoods. It's the other stuff that blooms at the same time, he said. But then, he also brought his boyfriend, the drug rep, into the exam room when he explained that point. Rumor had it he had left town in company with his lover, so maybe he wasn't the man I should have been listening to.

"Penny for you thoughts, sir?"

"You remind me of a dog."

I expected befuddlement. I forgot she's way smarter than me.

"I know what you mean." She nodded and explained it to me that, "You bought a friend, someone who follows your lead but who knows," she shrugged, "lesser things. Those little things that were so important when humans didn't have modern technology to ease their days."

Yeah, that's it. That's what I meant. "What's on the schedule now?"

"You're the master."

I want points for overcoming the temptation to be a smart ass. "Do you want to stay here for awhile?"

A shy smile and, "I'd like to swim a little, if you don't mind."

"Fine with me. If I had a book and a blanket, I'd read and doze."

"I put them in the trunk earlier, so I wouldn't forget them." She stayed busy cleaning up. "I'll get them when I take the things to the car."

"I'm not a cripple, Mitzi, and this is a day off for you." I stood up and stretched. "Of course, I could always wait till you have the stuff packed and then help carry it to the car."

"Thank you."

"Or, if I had swimming trunks, I could go in with you."

"Yes, you could." This time a full, broad smile. "They're in the trunk, too."

We finished the cleanup together and took the basket and cooler to the car, put them and the trash in the trunk and took out our swim wear. We changed in what passed as the bathhouse, then went to the beach and played in the water like kids. The smell of the primitive bathhouse, the stones in the beach sand, the cold water reminded me of the times I had gone swimming at the annual church picnic, changing clothes barefoot on the cold cement floor of the boys' bathhouse, walking carefully across the stony ground, getting in and wishing I hadn't.

Swimming isn't how I'd choose to spend my leisure time, not at all, ever. It's like a friend of mine once said. She could understand horseback riding and car racing, but as for swimming the whole thing left her cold. "Every minute in the water, you're fighting for you life. What fun is that?" But there I was, getting chilled in the summer sun and treading carefully on the stones and mussel shells, and having the

128

time of my life.

We chased, we tagged, we caught each other. We dove and surfaced and generally annoyed everyone else, and we stayed in the water until we were pruned and goose fleshed, and finally I grabbed her and held her in a bear hug, and she shrieked and kicked and laughed, and when I let her go she turned in my arms and we stared at each other, eye to eye. If she had been Lydia, we would have been in a long, lingering kiss. But she wasn't and we didn't, and she knew what I was thinking.

"We'll get her." She winked and took my hand, and we walked hand in hand to the table to dry off.

"You aren't one of those people who likes being touched, are you?" I figured I might as well ask, just in case there was something going on that I was missing.

"You're pretty perceptive, sir."

Ok, there was a shot in the dark that hit the target. Exactly what the target was, I wasn't sure. "But we did a lot of touching out there."

"You're different. You touch me as a friend." She nodded, agreeing with herself. "It's that Jeffersonian thing, I think." She was serious and there was no mockery in her voice. "You know you have no choice but to keep me as collateral for Willie's debt. If you send me home to him, he will gamble me away again and I will be treated poorly. Not just poorly by comparison, but poorly." She looked out at the lake, then put one hand on my shoulder and pointed with the other. "If I were with someone else, do you think I would be here today, like this?"

"No, probably not." I shook my head in agreement, wondering where we were going with the conversation, and feeling a little uncomfortable.

"If Patricia were here today, if she heard us talking about how you bought me as a friend the same way you would buy a dog, you can bet she'd have been throwing sticks in the water and yelling, "Fetch!" She leaned against me and sighed, "Any other man, my husband included, would have laughed and made me fetch."

"You know some really bizarre people." Although, considering my cousin, Charlene, I don't have much room to talk. "Come on. I'm cold, you're cold and there's a lot of shoreline we haven't seen."

"You're the master."

I was getting a little sensitive about the whole master-slave-dog thing, and maybe that was what she meant. I didn't want to offend her, I didn't want to sound stupid, and I didn't think I could ignore her. "Maybe I could be the boss, instead."

"Whatever you say, sir."

I stood and pulled her upright, started for the bathhouse and realized she was still standing there, looking out at the lake and thinking about fetching sticks thrown by an awful daughter. I waited, then decided, *Enough!*

No, we didn't walk arm in arm to the toilets. We walked side by side, and then we realized that we didn't have our clothes and we had to go to the car for them.

"I don't suppose you want to *fetch* our things?"

"Day off. Get your own."

Finally, some fire. We retrieved our clothes and changed in the bathhouse, then met back at the car. Mitzi produced a plastic bag for our wet things, and again her practicality and foresight impressed me. With someone besides Willie as a partner, she would have been one hell of a spouse and mother.

I held the door for here and she said, "Thanks, boss," and settled in for the ride. We rolled slowly out the park's drive to the state route, and with no one behind us I sat there.

"Problem?"

"Nope. But I'm thinking we'll be going east to a restaurant I know of, and they'll bring us food and we can look at the lake while we eat."

"You're the boss."

"I'm thinking that you like to drive, this is a sweet ride, and before we get there you'll be getting itchy." I looked her in the eye. "You drive, I'll navigate."

No protest. In fact, she was out of the car and halfway around to the driver's side before I could get my seatbelt unfastened. Clearly, she was getting itchy.

* * *

Dinner was great. The food was great, the service was great, the ambience was great, the company was great. Everything was great. Yeah, I know. I should find a more interesting way to say that. My late and unlamented mother, who fancied herself a writer, would have you reading, "After a sumptuous repast of tasty viands, we extended our sojourn within the pleasant bounds of this excellent culinary establishment with delicious postprandial libations."

You choose: dinner was great or, we had tasty viands. For me, it's enough that the steak was fine, the fish was excellent: New York strip and pecan crusted walleye.

Mitzi said she enjoyed it, and I believed her. She tucked into her food with a will, and there was no small talk. Finished, we sat back and stared out at the lake, and then almost in unison, we started to laugh. We were at a table by the windows, and our view of the lake was quite good. Except, the dredge was working, clearing the channel and blocking the more scenic aspects of the view, and we hadn't noticed. We were so intent on the meal that we had forgotten the ambience.

We paid the check and left, still laughing.

"Shall I take you home and tuck you in, sir?"

"I think not."

"Not, sir?"

"Not. I think we should find a place and watch the sun rise over the lake. I think we should stay at a motel and get up early, and go to the beach and watch the sun rise." I yawned. "I think we should do it quickly, so I can sleep."

"Don't be silly, sir. It's barely six."

"Must be the fresh air. Or maybe the exercise."

"Could it have been the vodka-tonics before dinner and the Black Russians after, sir?"

"Cold, Mitzi." I yawned again. "How about it? Want to see the sunrise?"

"Actually," she bit her lip.

"Why so pensive?" A few drinks, especially since I rarely have more than two before dinner and none afterwards, and I was feeling generous, expansive and close to Mitzi. I put my arm over her shoulder and pulled her close. No kissing, no fondling. Just a guy to guy hug. "Come on, tell your friend what you want and he'll get it for you if he can."

"There was this one time, and I know I can't go home - you know what I mean."

Even tipsy I knew enough to stay quiet and let her talk. Plus, I had no idea what she meant.

"My grandfather used to take me up to Port Huron to visit my cousins. We went out to the beach at the state park every morning, and watched the sun rise over Lake Huron." She wouldn't look at me as she said, "I'd like to go up there sometime."

"Ok. Sometime. Tonight, we stay out here and tomorrow we watch the sun rise over Lake Erie. You pick a weekend and plan it, we'll go to Huron and watch the sun rise there."

"You mean it, sir?" She faced me and once again, I saw her as a young woman, untroubled; happy. "Really?"

"Would I lie to a friend?" But I was talking to myself. She was already headed to the car, keys in hand.

I followed, speaking to her back. "You drive, I'll get a room."

She held the passenger door for me. "Very good, sir."

"Two beds, right?"

"Unless you want to sleep on the floor." She slammed the door and went to the driver's side, got in behind the wheel and smiled at me. "Sir."

TWELVE

The perfect place to watch the sun rise, Mitzi said, was the rocks to the east of the Marblehead Lighthouse. Because the sun would rise about five thirty-two AM, she said, we should get to bed early so that we would be well rested for a long day of adventure.

She was right.

The lakeshore to the east of the lighthouse is a rock shelf that has been worn and weathered by centuries of wind and water, sun and ice. We stood there in the slight chill of the predawn dark, listening to the slap and hiss of the waves against the rocks and waiting for the details of the lake and shore to appear in the coming dawn.

The eastern sky went from a deep blue-black to lavender; to lilac fading into orange, and then the sun rose over the lake, a huge red ball that burned to blinding white. I stayed just behind her so that she had the tiniest bit of privacy, and I watched her face the sun and hold out her hands to catch its warmth, just as she had in my driveway, not even twenty-four hours earlier. When she was satisfied, she stood up straight and stretched, then smiled at me and offered to show me the bay.

Sandusky Bay lies between the mainland and the peninsula where we stood beside the lighthouse. The city of Sandusky, visible in the distance, guards the entrance of the bay on the south, as does Marblehead on the north. A causeway from Sandusky leads to Cedar Point, the amusement park, also visible. We could see Kelley's Island, away to our left. Further to our left was South Bass Island, home to Put-In-Bay. In front of us, stretching away to the east was the open expanse of Lake Erie.

Sandusky Bay itself is divided about the halfway mark by the Edison Bridge, which wasn't visible from the lighthouse. From the center of the bridge, one can see both sides of the bay and to the east, the railway bridge. The Sandusky River feeds the bay at its western end, and the land there is swampy. There are roads near the bay, but none that are really around the bay, if you follow. So, what did Mitzi mean?

Did she intend that we hire a boat? Did she and Willie own a boat, and she intended to captain it about the bay? Or did she mean that she would drive us to the ferry and go to Put-In-Bay, the summertime almost-anything-goes party town on South Bass Island? All of the above, sort of, it turned out. But first, breakfast.

We found a restaurant where the food was ok and the service acceptable. Afterwards, she drove us to this unprepossessing dump of a marina, waved at the old guy who owned it and pointed to me.

The old guy shuffled out, took my credit card and filled the tank on a small, nondescript craft, old enough that it could have been a lifeboat on the Ark except that it had a motor. He gave us a helpful shove away from the dock and we headed into the marina's channel, and then out into the bay.

I figured, I knew how Tom Sawyer must have felt, hearing about Huck Finn and Jim going down the river on the raft, and deciding then and there to set Jim free and then go rafting and have adventures down to New Orleans. If I lived through this, it would be one hell of an adventure.

Mitzi was surprisingly competent with the boat. For sure, I couldn't have kept up with her. We toured the bay and I learned all about geology and geography, and glaciation and sedimentation. I learned to duck when she yelled, and learned just how it feels to ride under a bridge in places where the engineers hadn't planned for boat traffic. I learned just what a randy old goat her grandfather had been, and what he had done and who to, and where and when.

By the time we docked at Put-In-Bay, I was ready for a bigger boat captained by a man of only average intelligence. But Mitzi wasn't through with her first wind, let alone needing her second.

"Come along, sir." She set a pace for downtown, and I lunged along behind, grateful we hadn't drowned. She dragged me inside the pizza parlor, pointed to the bar and said, "You get the beer, sir and I'll get the pizza."

"Sure, ok. I'm on it."

"Sir?" She held out her right hand, palm up, and with her left hand she pointed at the cash register under the "Order Here" sign.

"Oh, yeah." I handed her some cash and headed for the bar, bought a pitcher of beer and then found a halfway clean table on the restaurant side, away from the pool tables. Happily, we had beaten the noon rush by fifteen minutes.

Mitzi wiped off the table with a handful of wet napkins and then we filled our glasses, sat and swilled beer while we waited for the pizza. I was right: I was having an excellent adventure.

"Did I scare you, sir?"

"Which time?"

She laughed and looked down at the table. "At least you didn't get sick or complain."

She looked up and we locked eyes, friends, both wistful. She wasn't Lydia and I wasn't Charlie, and neither of us could get back the years we'd lost.

"Twenty-nine."

She slid back her chair and stood. "That's us."

I watched her walk to the counter and pick up the pizza, and I watched her walk back. She was a fine woman, well shaped and pretty, and everyone else thought so too. I was smiling when she sat down and began to serve the pizza.

"What?"

"You're pretty, you're hot and you're with me. I am having the time of my life." I raised my glass. "Friends."

"Friends." She raised her glass and we touched the rims, friends.

We ate, we drank, we left. We walked the streets of Put-In-Bay and the roads of South Bass Island. We wandered past cottages and grape vines, and we watched drunken people fall off bicycles and crash golf carts, and we complimented each other on our decision to walk off our lunch. We walked all the way back to the Perry Victory Monument and then rode the elevator to the top. Mitzi went right to the edge and leaned on the parapet while I stayed back by the elevator doors. Height scares me and I had been brave enough just riding with her. Mitzi said so, and I believed her.

Eventually, she coaxed me far enough from the safety of the elevator doors that I could see, far in the distance, a breakwater and some shelter houses. Actually, all I saw was water and a sandbar, but the sooner I said I saw it the sooner she'd let me get back down on the ground, so I went along.

"That, sir, is East Harbor State Park. We're going there next."

Swell. Anywhere that's not three hundred fifty-two feet up in the air.

Seen closer up - and about an hour later - East Harbor State Park was a rocky shoreline with more cottonwoods and a heavy growth of reeds six and seven feet tall. What I thought was a sandbar was a finger of land with a beach and more people, and kids wading out through the shallows to swim. All along the shore, people sat in folding chairs and on the rocks, reading and picnicking. The shelter houses were in disrepair, and the place had the look of Southeast Asia, right down to the snakes - never mind how I know that. It wasn't my finest hour.

Mitzi said it was time to go back to the car, and far be it from me to argue. Just get me the hell away from the excesses of nature and nautical types, and let me sink into rapturous lassitude in the shotgun seat.

Wrong.

Mitzi took me on another death-defying ride back to the marina, gave the boat into the care of Noah's grandson and led me back to the car. Off we went, and the next thing I knew, we were inside the gates of a wildlife park, putting up the top and getting ready to enter the Kingdom of Hell.

As though Mitzi hadn't laughed hard enough when we rediscovered the reptiles of East Harbor, she insisted that we drive through the animal park. Being that I was in the shotgun seat, I was the one they handed the feed bucket. Let me say right here that the feed bucket was a plastic tub such as foodstuffs come in from the restaurant supply house: cole slaw and the like, sized about a half gallon, I guess. These things are apparently quite popular with the animals, given that the first few hundred feet of fence were lined with them.

You like to feel stupid? Get into a tug of war with a camel over a half-gallon of animal feed while your maid, whose idea this was, sits behind the steering wheel of your spanking new convertible - which she picked out to help you score - and laughs so hard the tears roll down her cheeks. You'll be in heaven. I know I was.

I especially enjoyed her replay of, "Gimme the goddamned thing! Let go! Let go, I said!"

"Shut up and drive."

"I can't even breathe." She wiped her tears with her knuckles, checked the rearview for traffic and then collapsed again. Happily, I got the window up before the camel spit on it.

So much for Sunday. We finished the wildlife tour and headed home, and all things considered, I'd had more fun with Mitzi than I'd had in Atlantic City with Charlie.

We rolled up to the garage door just before sunset, with the sky burning orange and purple. I was tired and happy, and a little surprised that Mitzi hadn't crashed the car during one of her recurring fits of laughter. But we got home safe and sound, and went inside to clean up and change for dinner.

I had decided that Mitzi deserved another night off from cooking, and she hadn't argued. We went inside to shower and change clothes for dinner, checked the answering machine and found the message light flashing: three calls.

The first was from Lydia, suggesting that we meet for dinner. The second was from Lydia, wondering where I was on a sunny Sunday afternoon. The third was a hang-up.

Mitzi raised her eyebrows in silent question.

I reminded myself that women prefer aloof men. "I'll be ready in twenty minutes. Think about where you'd like to eat." I headed to my room to shower and change.

"Yes, sir." Mitzi padded along behind me, went to her room to do likewise, and twenty minutes later she strolled into the living room, ready for dinner.

I hadn't thought about Mitzi not having ordinary clothes when I suggested going out for dinner, not that it mattered. She had somehow turned her chauffeur's outfit into a hot dinner ensemble, happily without the outrageous heels.

"Who's driving?"

"You're the boss," she shrugged. "You decide."

"It's your day off, right?" I figured I had her now: her day off, no orders from the boss. Therefore, she should decide.

"Yep. Day off. No decisions, no stress."

"Didn't you just spend the day deciding where we would go, how we would get there, and when we would leave?" At my argumentative best, I closed in for the kill. "Including, might I mention, a close encounter of the animal kind?"

You'd think I'd learn.

Mitzi started laughing again, staggered across the floor to collapse in the closest chair. Gasping, tears running, she gave herself to paroxysms of gaiety, veritable gales of laughter. She mimicked my response to the larcenous camel. "Gimme the goddamned thing!"

"It wasn't that funny."

Helpless, she sprawled in the chair. Unable to speak, she waved and nodded that it was and then wiped her tears with her fingertips. When she could breathe, she pulled herself up and out of the chair, then went to the bathroom to check her makeup. She came out, held up her hand. "Don't start. Just drive."

So I did, and all the way to the restaurant there were little snorts, occasional chuckles and guffaws, and the odd pounding on the dashboard.

Guess why.

Throughout dinner we stayed away from conversation and concentrated on the food, and my thoughts went to my life before Mitzi, and to Charlene the figment and Charlene the real. But mostly, I thought about Lydia.

For years I dreamed that she would want to be with me, go somewhere with me; anywhere. Finally, when she was willing to have dinner, forced by the conventions of life, I had dinner with my maid. Years and years I had spent longing for friendship and now, because my cousin's alter ego had played poker with a compulsive gambler, I had a maid, a chauffeur and a friend, all rolled into one.

Because I had a maid, apparently, I was suddenly interesting to Lydia, the girl of my dreams. Because I was interesting to Lydia, I had to show my aloofness and not call her back; had to have dinner with Mitzi. But that wasn't it, either. At least, not entirely. I had offered and Mitzi had accepted, and she was my friend, and friends don't make dates and then break them just because another offer comes along.

Besides, it had been a great day, a fun day with a friend. As I was thinking all that through, Mitzi looked up and our eyes met. It might have been a brief moment of tender recognition. It might have been a moment in which lives change and destiny comes into focus. It might have been a lot of things, but Mitzi started to snicker, then laughter followed and near-hysterics followed close on.

It was more than I could stand.

* * *

In the morning, we were back to normal.

"Good morning, Mr. Compton. Your coffee, sir."

"Thank you, Mitzi."

"Waffles when you are ready, sir."

"Looking forward to it, Mitzi."

She went about her usual morning routine, laying out my clothes while I savored the luxury of excellent coffee brought to me in bed.

"Mitzi?"

"Yes, Mr. Compton?" She kept at her routine, checking my suit for fuzz and finding the right shirt and tie.

I rested the mug on my belly, thinking through my words. "We spent the weekend together, we've slept in the same bed, you're are one of the hottest, prettiest and most desirable women I have ever known. I had more fun with you in two days than I've ever had with anyone, and yet I have no need to, ah, try to bed you."

She finished laying out my clothes, walked to the door and stopped, waited for me to finish.

"Does that mean I'm getting old, or is it just that I really am boring?"

"I think," she smiled, "it means you are growing up."

* * *

The usual suspects stared at her as she held my door and handed my briefcase.

"You realize, Mitzi, that if you ever change your shoes and skirt, these people will have nothing to live for."

Behind the dark glasses, she was impassive. "I'll have the car serviced, and pick you up at noon. Will you have lunch at home, or do you prefer a restaurant?"

I started to ask her how she knew my schedule, but it occurred to me that I have a calendar that I carry with me and she can read. Ergo, my maid had planned her duties around my day.

"Whatever you think." I frowned, a double take. "Car serviced?"

"Washed, cleaned and gassed so that you can take Miss Svenson to dinner tonight, sir."

"Tonight?"

Mitzi nodded toward the front door. Lydia was standing there, watching us and pretending that she had just arrived and was waiting for me to walk up to the door.

"How did you manage to get here at the same time she did?"

"I think that if we were fifteen minutes earlier, or fifteen minutes later, she would be there, just arriving. You weren't home yesterday and you didn't call her back last night. You aren't available for lunch. You will tell her how much you hope she will go to dinner with you. She will ponder the offer. You will be direct: she is invited, no one else is invited, you would like to spend the evening with the top down, looking at the moon over the lake."

"Huh?"

She slammed the door, said, "Very good, sir," and walked around the car to the driver's door. She paused for dramatic effect, still inscrutable behind her shades, then got in and drove off with her usual verve.

Great. I've been dismissed by my maid.

But there was no help for it, so I went to the front door and Lydia.

"Good morning, Lydia. I'm sorry I missed your calls."

"Did you have a pleasant weekend?" Wounded, icy, curious.

Also, dressed to the nines.

"Yes, actually." I held the door for her, giving her higher status than my maid. At least, I thought so.

Itching with curiosity. "You bought a new car?"

"Yes. Mitzi needs transportation so that she can run errands, and I need the freedom to come and go and as I please."

"So you bought her a convertible?" She pushed the call button for the elevator.

I was willing to bet that her nails were gouging her palms. "Hardly. I bought it for myself. I decided it was time to enjoy some of this money they're throwing at me."

"Oh."

Clearly, she wondered what I had been doing all weekend. Clearly, Mitzi knew more about this than I did. I decided to press on. "I'll be busy at lunch, getting things serviced and all. I think I'll head out this evening in the new car, have dinner, maybe look at the full moon over the lake."

"Sounds nice." Wistful and bitter. Who but a woman can combine such disparate emotions in so short a sentence?

"Nice enough that you'll come along? I could pick you up at your apartment, say seven or so. If you prefer, we can go from here, but then we'll have to come back for your car. Your call."

She dropped her purse on her desk, stalling. "I ... I have to make a call."

"Fine. Is the coffee ready?" Ah, yes. Conflict. Accept the invitation to dinner with the boss as his date or check on the coffee as his secretary. Which to do first?

"I, ah." She flushed pink, deepening to red, and I'm serious. It was the first time ever I had seen her blush.

"I'll be in my office." I left her to her own devices, to make her phone call and fetch my coffee.

Five minutes, then six. Lydia came in with my coffee and hers. "Seven o'clock?"

"Fine?"

"You'll pick me up?'

"Of course."

"I'll be ready. I know you don't like to wait."

I nodded, pleased that she had accepted. After all, I had what I wanted, a dinner date and the chance to show off my new car. "Good. I'm looking forward to it." I looked at my desk, frowned in a boss-like manner, and asked, "Could you get me the Randolph file, please?"

"Uh, sure." Never ever had I told Lydia to bring me a file, first thing in the morning, especially on a Monday. Never had I been so abrupt with her. Her head swivelled left and right, and confusion hung on her like a cheap suit.

I always wanted to say that.

So, I decided that I had been aloof and made my point, and I could afford to enjoy the morning. "First, though, since everything is under control and I'm not in the mood to jump right in, how about sitting down and telling me about your weekend?"

She brightened, reassured that things were still good between us. She moved closer and then sat, and filled me in on her life: who did what that was amusing, who did what that was silly, and how she had really just sort of knocked around all weekend. I listened politely, not really bored but not at all interested. I felt like a husband getting the low-down after a long day at the office, and that pleased me. Until I realized that I had no idea how a husband felt about anything, never having been one. I frowned in reflex at the realization, and Lydia reacted immediately, twisting in her chair so that I could see the top of her stocking and her suspender clip.

I figured I had better let her win the round, so I pretended to look unobtrusively, sneaking a peak at the enticement which she offered. She must have enjoyed being looked at as much as I enjoyed looking at her, because she made sure that every part of herself was shown to best advantage - go ahead, read into that - as she straightened herself and stood, walked - or maybe undulated - to the door.

My heart raced and my ears rang, and if the fire alarm had rung just then I'd have been in deep trouble. No way I was going to get up and walk, let alone run, so I sat and watched her leave, and wondered what she might wear to dinner that could possibly compete with what she was wearing right then.

When I had my heartbeat under control I went to work. The

Randolph trial was coming up soon, and no matter what anybody tells you, overconfidence and lax preparation have cost more trials than incompetence. I checked and rechecked the file, and then I called Lefty Martinez.

According to Lefty, Stannard had smelled a rat and was going full bore with her trial prep, and she had filed seven subpoenas. Even a blind pig gets the occasional acorn, and whatever else one might say about her, Eileen Stannard wasn't blind.

THIRTEEN

Stunned, or speechless: either works. I couldn't have said my own name for love nor money.

Lydia was dressed in mauve and ivory, something light and summery and elegant. As hot as she was, dressed for the office, she was even hotter in the evening. Bare legs with fingernail polish to match her dress, slightly darker polish on her toes; heeled sandals. Subtle makeup and soft curls in her hair, and pearls.

She was ready when I rang the security buzzer. "Just a second," and there she was coming down the stairs and out the security door. "I know you hate to wait."

I had no idea what to say, so I smiled and held the car door for her. Then it hit me, that the top was down and her hair would be blown all over. "Maybe I should put up the top?"

"No need." She took a spring comb out of her purse, pulled her hair back and fixed it with the comb and smiled at me. "Ready when you are."

Since I was ready, we left.

I figured, I wasn't about to go to Charlene's favorite restaurant - the one by the river with the horny hostess - and neither was I going where I had taken Mitzi. Too many men have tried the easy, habitual path when wooing a woman, and failed, found out by the woman that the chosen place was special only because the man knew it so well that the hostess, the maitre d' or the concierge greeted him by name, asked him if he wanted his usual table, and so forth. Nope, not a chance.

We were going to a place where not only hadn't I taken a date, I hadn't even eaten there: the lodge at Maumee State Park. It's a classy place, with a full view of Lake Erie, an extensive menu and conscientious servers. There are wide sidewalks along the beach and through the grounds, and well-maintained boardwalks along the lake shore and through the trees and reeds growing close by. Yes, the same reeds as East Harbor, but no ground contact and no reptiles to step over, thank you.

I'd like to tell you all about the high-class service, the excellent cuisine and the elegant ambience but, truthfully, I spent the evening looking at Lydia. The view of the lake was impressive and she commented on it.

I nodded.

She complimented me on my choice of restaurant.

I shrugged in self-deprecation.

She thanked me for the invitation.

I sighed, "Um, hmm."

She guided us along the sidewalk which runs between the parking lot and the beach, dodging bicycles and dogs, and badly thrown Frisbees. The soft onshore breeze lifted her skirt and teased her hair, and brought memories of riverside walks with Charlene. But this time, the woman with me was real and so she had no need to stay in character, no need to tease and show off.

I thought about asking the usual date questions: where was she from, how did she come to live in Toledo, where did she go to school. I thought about it but since I was already in love; since I was entirely content to walk quietly with her, I asked her nothing.

"Danny?"

"Hmm?"

She pointed to the east. The moon was rising, blood red through the haze of the summer atmosphere. "Not exactly what I expected when you asked me to dinner."

I'd have said, *Ditto,* but someone was walking on my grave and I had a nasty suspicion it was Charlene.

We stood there and watched the moon rise, and as it climbed, the color burned away and the beach glowed in the pale light of the midsummer moon. I was as happy as I have ever been, even counting the weekend just spent with Mitzi. I took that as a good sign, and as unsettling as was the first sight of the moon, having Lydia beside me erased every pain and fear I'd ever known.

You'd think I'd learn.

But Charlene had taught me to live in the moment, so I let my arm slide down to her waist and I kept it there, holding her close and feeling her warmth through my shirt. She raised her arm and let her hand brush my back, brought it up and let it fall on my shoulder. I waited for her to rest her head against me, but in her heels she was my height, and she'd have had to bend. To do that would have been to admit to a familiarity that was beyond any hope I had, and so I abandoned the expectation and turned to offer to take her home.

Apparently, she expected to be kissed.

I say that because she turned to me at the same time, lips parted and eyes half-closed. I preferred her idea to my own.

It was a soft and promising moment, and if Charlene hadn't beaten aloofness into me I might very well have blown it. But I kept myself in check and watched where I put my hands. Maybe it wasn't a chaste kiss, but neither was it steamy. Then we stood side by side and watched the clouds cross the moon and the waves slide onto the beach.

We drove home with the top down, quietly enjoying the new car smell and the anticipation that comes with a successful first date. I held the car door for her at her apartment, she brushed herself against me, kissed my cheek and smiled, "See you tomorrow," and then drifted up the sidewalk to the security door. She turned and smiled again, and disappeared inside, and I drove home, quietly euphoric.

* * *

From three days in Heaven to a week in Hell: Charlene's BMW was in the driveway, meaning that she had decided to bring Patricia to my house two days early.

Swell.

Since I had no choice, I went inside and greeted them, welcomed them graciously to my home.

"Charlene."

"Now, Daniel. I know that look."

"I thought you were coming day after tomorrow."

"My, Daniel." She smoothed my hair with her hand. "You've had a busy evening."

"I had dinner."

"And drove along the lake in that lovely new car of yours, no doubt."

I considered asking Charlene how she knew what she knew, then decided that I didn't care and that if I said anything, she would figure that I did and taunt me mercilessly. Worse, Patricia would think she had a way to manipulate me. I say that because she was standing there listening, as feral as a ferret poised to enter a rabbit hole.

I had to admit, Patricia looked a lot better after the trip to Wang Ho's emporium. Sexy shoes, trim ankles; short skirt, good legs and a nice butt; thin waist, full bust under a fitted blouse. But there was that sharp look about her, as though she had discovered something within herself; as though she was calculating the advantage and how to use herself to get it.

I was looking at Willie, had he been a teenaged girl.

"Well, darlings, I must be off. Daniel, darling, walk me out." Charlene waved goodbye to Patricia, moved to the door and waited for me to open it for her. She was dressed for travel, but I was willing to bet that wherever Charlene was going, Charlie was doing the traveling. So, as I followed her out, I figured that she wasn't headed to the airport.

"Who's flying? You or Charlie?"

"Do you really want to know?" Without an audience, she dropped into her Dwight voice.

"Not really. Not at all, actually. In fact, as far as I know, Charlie left town last week and I have no idea when he's coming back."

"I hear he's in Chicago, wowing all the girls." She stretched upright, thrusting her breasts against her blouse and pulling back the lapels of her fitted jacket to show her nipples. "Unfortunately, I will be traveling alone, a single woman defenseless in a man's world."

"Yeah, right."

"Now, don't be angry with me, Danny." She was Charlene again, coaxing and cajoling, a woman leaving the man she might very well love. A deft move and she was beside me, soft and feminine, making me wish I could accept her logic: flesh is flesh.

My flesh was quite willing to accept that logic; only my mind objected. I felt her lips on my cheek, where Lydia's had been not so long ago, and if I had been drinking I might not have been so upright. Damn Chanel, anyway.

"I'm afraid," she breathed in my ear, "that I have opened Pandora's box."

"Thanks for the warning." As dryly as I could, considering how I felt, I went on with, "I assume you haven't opened Patricia's?"

"Not even tempted, darling." She stepped back, still womanly. "The child has so much potential, but I doubt that she has the character to nurture it, to develop it into something substantial."

With my peripheral vision, I caught movement at the window. Mitzi wouldn't spy on me, but Patricia sure as hell would. "Anything I should know about Pandora?" I moved around her so that I could open her car door.

She paused with her back to the house, then, "Check your Bulfinch."

"Say what?"

She looked over her shoulder, casually disdainful of modern, formal education. "Thomas Bulfinch, *The Age of Fable.* Pandora was sent by Jupiter in good faith, and when she opened the box of blessings, all escaped save hope. Of course," she sniffed, "you may prefer the pessimistic version in which the box contained all manner of ills which she released while pawing through Epimetheus' possessions, and only hope remained."

"If I recall correctly, the prevailing view is the pessimistic, hence the expression, 'Pandora's box.'"

"Just when I thought you were irretrievably dull!" She placed herself in the driver's seat, brought her feet inside with a demure twist and as I shoved the door closed, she held out her hand to stop it. "Be careful, Daniel. And be pessimistic. Leave nothing lying around for her to get into and keep your distance from Mitzi." She held up her hand to forestall any objection. "I know that you have no physical interest in her. Just remember that Pandora opened the box out of selfish curiosity, just to see what would come out. Patricia - our own little Pandora - will do the same."

"Thank you so very, *very* much for dropping her by."

Charlene noted the caustic tone. "Oh, Daniel, face it. You have to save the broken winged sparrows, and Mitzi is just that. Remember that the brown-headed cowbird lays its eggs in the nests of other, smaller birds. When the eggs hatch, the cowbird nestlings are larger and they evict the legitimate nestlings or just take most of the food. The parent birds raise these brood parasites as their own. Occasionally, the parent birds recognize the ploy, perhaps abandon the nest or eject the cowbird eggs. Usually, though, not." She gave me a wearied look and finished, "Mitzi has to face her life. Patricia is Willie's daughter and you know it. I saw the way you looked at her. You recognized her; Mitzi, as only a mother can, has blinded herself to her daughter's flaws. But she is going to see them in living color and very, very soon, I think. Her only chance to survive is that you will be a friend to her." She closed her door and started her car, then lowered her window. "Whatever you do, protect yourself and that budding romance with Lydia. You cannot save the world, after all, and you cannot save anyone who isn't willing to be saved." A cheerful wave, a last "*Ciao, bello*," and she rolled away into the night.

Swell.

But she had it right, all the way along, so I went inside and said goodnight to Mitzi, and left instructions for the morning.

* * *

"Good morning, Mr. Compton." Mitzi came in with my morning coffee.

"Good morning, Mitzi." I sat up and took the mug, happy that my new routine continued, unhappy that I wasn't sure what would happen in the coming days.

"Sir?" Mitzi stood at the closet door, facing away from me.

"Yes, Mitzi." I had no idea what she wanted, but I could guess it had to do with Patricia.

"I was thinking that I would ask you before Patricia got here, what we should do about her." She reached into the closet and brought out my suit *du jour*. "But she's here now, and I was wondering if you would be willing for her to help me around here."

"Mitzi, you do what you think is right."

"Sir?" She turned, frowning, and waited for the explanation.

"You are in charge around here." I sipped coffee and chose my words. "I know that, for all intents and purposes, you have no choice but to be here, doing what you do." More coffee. "She's your daughter, and you have to try to take care of her."

I sat, she stood, both silent.

Then, "I could get her some different clothes and she could help me clean."

"Is she old enough to drive?"

"Yes." Tentative, concerned. "She has her license."

"Make her drive to Wang Ho's, check out how she handles the Town Car. Have him make a suit or two for her, get her some appropriate shoes. Tell her, Charlene said so. Tell her that around here, everybody works." I stared at my coffee, finished with, "What you tell her about being a slave, what you tell her about you and Willie, that's your business. But I'd be careful, Mitzi. She's your daughter and you love her, but she's Willie's daughter, too."

"Yes, sir." She finished laying out my clothes and I finished my coffee. She stopped to take my empty mug, then, "Mr. Compton, if you don't mind I'll take her to the mall and get her something more suitable for a teenager." She didn't move away, obviously with more on her mind.

"Whatever you decide is fine with me. If you need cash," I pointed, "it's on the dresser."

"Thank you, Mr. Compton." She stayed where she was.

"Whatever it is, Mitzi, just say it."

"You are being very kind about Patricia being here, and taking care of her, and you're right. She's Willie's daughter, too. Sometimes, I think she's more his than mine." She bit her lip and said, "I want to take her to the mall because I don't want her to get the idea that she's my equal with you, and if Wang Ho dresses her to work around here, well, she could get the wrong idea. I know you would never do anything improper with her, but she can be," she paused, then, "headstrong."

I could read it in her eyes: younger, prettier, the master's choice. "You do whatever you think is right. You run the house, you run your daughter."

"And you run me?" A wry smile.

"Yeah, right." I looked over at my closet door, where my suit, shirt, belt and tie were waiting for me, then back at her. "Sure."

"Thank you, Mr. Compton."

"You're welcome, Mitzi."

* * *

I drove myself downtown in the Mustang, half expecting Lydia to be waiting at the door as she was yesterday, half knowing that she wouldn't. Then I remembered that when I drove the Mustang I parked in the garage, so I changed course. She was just pulling in, late for work and yes, I know. Paying for her to have a reserved spot close to mine is pathetic. Sue me.

She saw me and smiled, looked away and recovered herself as she always does. But then she smiled again, and this time she didn't look away. I took that as a good sign, although I wasn't sure if she was posing or if she was deciding to be herself. Then wondered if being herself meant she posed, and then I parked the car and quit worrying about it because she was standing there smiling, waiting for me.

"Hi, Danny."

"Hey." I never know how to greet anyone, but I knew enough to smile and not try anything fake. I was happy she was there and I was happy she was waiting, and I wanted her to know that. "Come here often?"

"Goof." She took my arm, shook her head and added, "I'll never have to worry about you being irresistibly smooth."

I was too busy being happily aloof to respond.

* * *

"Danny, Mr. Martinez is here to see you." Lydia stood the doorway to my office, not at all coy and giving Lefty less than the time of day. She stepped aside to let him in, said, "I'll bring coffee," and closed the door.

Lefty looked mournfully at the door and sighed, "I remember when she thought I was good-looking. Oh, well."

He sat, crossed his legs and smiled like a well-fed cat.

I passed on the chance to make a rude reference to his waning sex appeal, waited for him to offer up what he had that was so valuable.

Lydia knocked, opened the door and came in with the coffee. No one spoke.

Lydia looked to me for instructions. I nodded at the door.

She left us alone and Lefty sipped his coffee, grinned and reached inside his sport coat. His hand came out with an envelope, and I had the feeling I was about to pay a lot of money for the opportunity to humiliate Eileen Stannard.

I was right. Even for Lefty, the bill was impressive.

Of course, it wasn't every day that he produced an affidavit of paternity and the official record of the state's putative father registry showing a dead man to be the father of a child who desperately needed that to be true so that he might have a chance at a decent life. The record of the DNA result showing him to be ninety-nine point seven per cent likely to be the father of that child was, well, overkill.

"You going to tell me why you're grinning like Alice's cat?"

He sipped his coffee and then laughed. I mean, a full throated, thigh slapping laugh, like he was listening to a private joke playing in his head. He held up his free hand, switched his coffee cup from hand to hand, almost spilled it on himself and then reached inside his coat on the other side, pulled out a legal sized envelope with Children Services return address printed on the corner. He tossed the envelope on my desk and sat back roaring, beating on the arm of the chair.

I opened the envelope and found that Eileen Stannard was moving to dismiss the complaint in Benny Randolph's case. I understood why Lefty was amused, but not why he was cracking up.

He stopped laughing long enough to sip coffee and say, "When she was sending the original of that with the paralegal for filing, she asked her if she thought it would wreck your plans for the trial. All I could think of when I heard that was the old joke. You know the one I mean."

Am I destined to go through life with people who are constantly reminded of old jokes? Unfortunately, I knew exactly which one he referred to: "Rectum, hell. Nearly killed 'em."

"You are sure that she has no idea what we're up to?"

"Positive, Counselor. Everyone is on board. Her own people hate her, especially since what you did in court got out, and why, and now she's going to dismiss the complaint so that the grandparents can get custody." He looked down at his cup, then up at me. "Of course, you'd know this better than I would, but don't they have to file a motion or something to get custody?"

"Yes, they do. And they either have to file a separate complaint or a motion in this case, and if Stannard dismisses this complaint, there goes their motion."

"Well, I wouldn't worry either way." He stood up, put his cup on my desk and then stretched, rolled his shoulders and grinned like a shark. "Funny how things can get delayed at the last minute."

"Yeah. A real thigh-slapper."

"See you around, Counselor. Good luck in court."

"Thanks, Lefty." Before he was out the door, I had Stanley Willis on the telephone, agreeing to meet with me. I picked up the papers which Lefty had brought, put them in my coat pocket and headed out the door.

"Eileen, your ass is *so* mine."

* * *

I left Willis' office, walked back to my own and found, in Lydia's writing, of course, a phone slip that "Patricia" called. It was the first time that Lydia had put quotations marks around anything in a message, let alone the name. I knew the answer, but had to make the point.

"Why the quotes?"

"Who's Patricia?"

"Mitzi's daughter."

"Why is she calling to thank you for the new outfits?"

I had a bunch of snappy comebacks including: To make you jealous; and, Because I paid for them. I settled on, "Her mother, my maid, told her to.   Patricia is short on social skills and long on attitude."

"Anything I should know?" It was the quietest, smallest voice I had ever heard from her.

"If you get close to her, wear gloves and carry a snake hook." I checked my watch. "Would it be too soon to ask you out to dinner again? Tonight?"

She smiled, slowly, and said, "No, it's not too soon to ask, but I can't."

"Oh." I nodded, accepting.

"It's a bridal shower." She smiled her apology.

I nodded again, headed toward my office with the rest of my messages. "Have fun, leave early if you want to."

"I ... can't. I have things I have to do to get ready for the Randolph trial."

"Ok." I guess I wasn't jealous enough. She followed me into my office and closed the door.

This time, I *really* kissed her. I grabbed her hair at the back of her head - not rough, just a firm grip. When I let her go, she sighed.

I said, "Have fun tonight. Decide when you'd like to go out with me, pick a restaurant, tell me."

"Suppose you have plans?"

"I'll change them."

You'd think I'd learn.

FOURTEEN

The rest of Tuesday was fine. Nothing to comment on, no funny stories, no complaints. Mitzi's cooking was perfect as always, and Patricia managed to behave herself. Things were so fine, in fact, that I decided to play with my trains.

The last time I considered playing with my trains, I got into the vodka and started thinking about Benny Randolph. This time, with Mitzi there to supervise my drinking and provide dinner, I was in much better shape. Plus, although Benny was in my thoughts again, I wasn't preoccupied like I was that last time. Stannard had last touched the ball before it went out of bounds, and our team would bring it back in. The ball was in play down court, and Willis and I were at the top of the key, waiting for Lefty Martinez to steal it from CSB and bring it up court.

Hell, I don't know. Ask Lydia. She's the sports maven. I just decided that it was time for a sports analogy, so y'all wouldn't think I spend all my free time with my trains, which I don't. Sometimes I drink, which you already know.

Tonight, I have a railroad to run.

I wandered to the train room, filled with purpose and resolve. But when I stepped inside and looked around I just stood there, feeling disoriented. This was my own miniature empire and yet, because I had been absent from it for so long, it was a foreign land. I stood in the middle and looked around, getting my bearings.

Playing trains. That innocuous phrase holds quicksand for the unwary, ready to catch and hold and drown him. Or to leak all over the best conjured plans, staining and wrinkling them into uselessness. Nope. No vodka, just me standing there, cold sober, and trying to remember what I was thinking when I did *that.*

"That" is a helical curve which raises the track from one level to another, with the track sort of wound over itself like a flat spring - a Slinky, if you will. The whole idea is to get the track up to the next level without putting it on an angle that nothing will climb. But it had been so long since I built the thing that I could not remember what it was that I was trying to accomplish. Happily, I had a plan book where I keep notes and drawings of all my schemes. Unhappily, I had no idea where I put it.

Equally unhappily, Patricia was standing in the doorway with that look which seems to come with an adolescent's sense of superiority.

"Mother said you play with trains, but I didn't believe her. I mean, you have a job and everything."

"Not quite everything. I can't find the plan book."

Yes, I know. It is a mistake to forget that they, like wild animals, never lose their nature: once wild, always wild. A snotty, condescending adolescent in better clothes is still snotty and condescending.

"Did you look in your toy chest?"

I turned and looked at her, which was just what she wanted. She posed herself in the doorway, a teenaged seductress who looked almost old enough to ... what? Read?

The advantage that I have from my years of eking out a living in Juvenile Court, among other places, is that young stuff like Patricia - jail bait - holds no mystery for me. Immature, self-involved twits are not interesting and neither are they attractive. Sure, there are times when I have seen young girls with nice legs and pretty faces, and I have known that they would grow up and be real heartbreakers. But not one of them ever gave me even a ripple of anticipation, of carnal curiosity. Not even those with actual personalities. Given that I had already had the pleasure of riding to and from Detroit with Patricia, and since I had already seen what she had to offer, well, what? In an even match, her mother was far more attractive to me, and Mitzi couldn't keep my interest when she was half-naked and curled up against me in my bed. And of course, there was Lydia.

"Don't you have school tomorrow?"

"I'm not a child." She tossed her head. "I can stay up as late as I want."

"Lucky you."

* * *

Wednesday morning started as had every other morning since Mitzi's arrival, with the addition of the Mustang as my personal vehicle. Lydia was pleased to see me, perhaps a little sensitive since Patricia was on the premises, but otherwise herself.

"Hi, Danny."

From the first day that Lydia came into my life, from the instant that I saw her bending over the receptionist's desk to sign in for her interview, I was in love. Every time I see her, I think of that day and I smile. I can't hope to describe how she looked or the what and why of the attraction, and I don't care. The way she stood, her feet together and the heels of her shoes touching; the curve of her calf, the lines of her ankles: don't know, don't care. Then she straightened and turned, looked past me, brought her gaze back to me and smiled, "What's it like to work here?"

Every time I see her, I remember every second of that meeting. Watching her stand there, it all played across my mind like a movie on the big screen, larger than life, and when it ended, the real world was waiting outside in the full light of day.

Light brown hair; minimal makeup. Deep brown eyes, clear and bright, sometimes laughing and sometimes soulful; bedroom eyes. Just enough chin, not too much overbite. Scattered moles, little dark spots unnoticed except in bright light or when she stands right in front of me, looking me right in the eyes.

"Are you all right?"

"Never better." I reached out and smoothed her hair. "Every time I see you, it's like I'm seeing you for the first time."

"Forgetful?" The beginning of a sardonic smile.

"Nope, not at all. Every time I see you, it's like sunrise. All the same, each unique. Another chance for happiness."

She smiled and looked away, fighting for control like always. But then she shook her head and looked back at me, still smiling.

"Goof."

But she let me hold her waist as we walked to the office, and she was still smiling when I left her at her desk and went into my office. All in all, it was a very pleasant beginning to the day.

Yes, I know: you'd think I'd learn.

* * *

Since I had driven myself to work and since Lydia was obviously interested, I drew the logical and wholly incorrect conclusion that if I asked her, she'd accept an invitation to dinner. She was sorry, but she had plans. I was about to ask her if any of her friends *weren't* getting married when the word *aloof* rang in my head like a church bell. I said, "Sure, no problem," and that she should let me know if she would like to go again sometime.

She smiled and said she would, that this "thing" had come up over the weekend and she couldn't get out of it or she would, and what about tomorrow night?

Let me check my schedule. Why, yes. I believe I'm free.

This was followed in quick succession by Lefty Martinez calling to say that Benny's mother was on the lamb, by Mitzi calling to say that Willie was demanding that she come home and bring Patricia and then, the absolute topper. Charlene called to say she'd be gone another week.

"You look unhappy." Lydia stood in the doorway, files in hand and smiling in coy sympathy. "Were you that disappointed that I said no?"

"Yes, but that's not it." What else was there to say?

Apparently, anything but that.

"Oh?" She shrugged and turned away before I could explain, and right away I knew I had screwed up again.

It put me in mind of a trial I had once. The opposing party was an unwed mother who claimed that her former man was the source of the family's sexually transmitted disease. On cross-examination, the question to her was whether she had been stepping out on him as she said he had with her. Her answer was, "I don't recall."

As the magistrate said at the end of the trial, "There are only two answers to that question: no, and anything else." This time, I should have let it go with a sorrowful, sighing, "Yes." But no, I had to tell the truth, the whole truth, and ... screw it. Next time, whatever she wants to hear, that's what I'm saying.

Lydia was gone before I was ready to leave, and the walk to my car was as lonely a walk as I have ever taken. I kept the top up for the drive home, disinterested in everything, and taking no joy in the thought of going home. True, Mitzi would be there, ready to offer succor and vodka, with dinner roasting to perfection in the oven. But Patricia would be there too, and even though she was much better behaved since our first meeting, I still had about as much interest in her company as I had in, say, Am-Way. And now the good news: Willie's car was in the driveway.

Swell. Just absolutely swell.

Willie was at his drunken, belligerent best, demanding the return of his women. Mitzi had Patricia inside and the door locked, so I had to decide what to do about going into the garage. Fortunately, I remembered that my cell phone could call my home phone, and when Mitzi answered I asked her opinion.

"Go away, sir, and let him keep venting. He'll get tired eventually and leave."

An excellent plan, I thought, and it would likely have worked if Patricia hadn't decided that her parents were just *too* embarrassing at the same time that the next-door neighbor decided that since we pay lots of taxes for police protection, we ought to have a return on the investment.

So there they were, the township's finest trying to sort out Willie's drunken ranting, Patricia's condescension and the neighbor's dudgeon, all in my front yard. There was no help for it. I had to explain things.

"Drunken, compulsive gambler." I pointed at Willie. "His daughter." I pointed at Patricia, and then toward the front door. "Inside, my maid: his wife, her mother." I pointed at Willie and Patricia in turn and finished, "She's staying here with her mother until her father sobers up."

"Or goes to jail." The cops weren't amused by Willie or Patricia.

"Works for me, but," I pointed at the house, "it'll put her in a bad position, if you follow me." I gave Patricia a sidelong glance to reinforce the idea.

The cops picked up on it and explained to Willie that, "You're screwing up, pal, and you're making things uncomfortable for your wife while she's working. Be quiet, don't let us see you driving while you're drunk and we'll forget this, as a favor to her."

Willie wasn't so drunk that he couldn't understand the idea of a favor from the cops, so he mumbled, "Thank you, officer," and walked away.

I shook hands with the cops, waited till they had driven away and then put the Mustang in the garage. Inside, I found Mitzi in the kitchen, trying to focus on dinner and failing. Given my childhood, I took a scientific, wild-ass guess that she was afraid I'd throw her out, make her go home to Willie.

"How's dinner coming?"

She bowed her head to collect herself, then looked up to face me. She tried to speak but the words wouldn't come. Her fear showed.

"Rough day, huh?"

Confusion clouded her face.

"I was thinking, tomorrow night I'm planning on dinner with Lydia. Maybe you and Patricia would like to spend some time working through things, maybe go out somewhere and have dinner. You know, a mother-daughter night out."

She sighed, and I could feel a deep, maternal pain. "She called me a whore."

"So I shouldn't offer, you take off your shoes I'll rub your feet?" Southern DNA and a New York childhood give one a mixed speech pattern.

No smile, just a dull, puzzled shake of her head.

"I've lost my daughter." Tears started, rolled, streaked her face. "How did I fail?"

You married Willie so you could bail on a bad childhood, you can't find your own way now and so you can't lead your daughter, who is a stone bitch.

But sometimes, kindness overrides the need to be honest and accurate - as it should have today with Lydia.

"You didn't fail her. You did the best you could and trust me, that was plenty. She's a teenager and she has her mother's intelligence. But she also has her father's self-focused view of everyone and everything, and the good news is that so far, she hasn't shown any sign of addiction."

"What?" Fear and confusion, bordering on panic.

"She has plenty of access to liquor, sex and drugs. You ever see her stoned, drunk, high? Does she party all night, have sexually transmitted diseases?"

"No. She ... no ... never."

"I see this a lot in court. You have a teenaged daughter and she's a bitch. So, what's your point? That like saying the mayor's a crooked politician. Name one that's not." I stretched, pretending confidence in my words. "It's been a long day and I would appreciate a drink. I'll be in my chair." I took a step and then paused, "And in case you're wondering, you have a job here as long as you want it. Dump Willie, you'll get paid like any other employee."

I left her for my favorite chair and wished I believed what I had said. But we all know that Willie wasn't done with her, and we can guess what's coming, right?

Mitzi brought the drink, perfect as always. She stood beside my chair, her face streaked with her makeup and her hair out of place. "Dinner will be ready soon. I ... thank you."

"You're welcome, Mitzi."

* * *

Dinner was swell. The food was, to my untrained palate, excellent as always. Mitzi was subdued, and neither of us had any desire for small talk. Patricia, naturally, behaved as though "Snotty Teenager" was a job description and offered negative comments about the meat, which was too done; the bread: mundane; the potatoes: not done; and the vegetables: well, what could she say? The last came with a sniff and a toss of her head.

I refrained from correcting her behavior, first because I thought it would inflame matters, second because it wasn't my place and third, because my idea of correction was to turn her over my knee and beat her ass. All those points seemed counterproductive at best and not worth the effort anyhow, so I sat and suffered silently, and wished Charlene a most unhappy time in Wherever, USA.

After dinner, when I thought Patricia would be helping her mother clear the table, she retired with me to the living room to discuss current events, to give her opinion of the world and its leaders, and to generally prove the point that only pederasts and parents could love a teenager. Then I remembered that pederasts go for boys. With the pool of people likely to find her attractive so drastically and offensively narrowed, I found a new level of self-pity. If Lydia had just accepted the invitation to dinner, all of this would have been Mitzi's problem, except that she would have had no way to deal with the police and God alone knew what might have happened. The specter of her retirement to her own home, dysfunctional as it was, loomed over me. Who knows what a mother will do to protect her child, even when that child would best benefit the world by disappearing.

I considered the refuge of the train room, but abandoned the idea. Mitzi would be done soon with the dishes, and I had no desire to leave them alone. In hindsight, I should have done just exactly that, left them alone to work it out between themselves. But no, being the ever helpful man-child, I offered a road trip: ice cream.

Everybody loves ice cream, and why shouldn't Mitzi have the benefit of my personal wish for a hot fudge sundae with nuts and extra whipped cream? Why should I deprive myself of such a tasty treat on a hot summer evening? Because it was a stupid idea, that's why. Read on.

Yes, I know, *I know*: you'd think I'd learn.

Mitzi was grateful for the suggestion and went to fix herself and change into her casual summer clothes. Patricia offered a scornful, "Sure, it's fun for children," and then she too went to change her clothes, which prompted me to ask myself, *Why do teenagers dress like that?*

Because. They are asserting independence, showing themselves to be separate from us old people, identifying with each other. Hooray for them. But when I was a kid, worn, torn, frayed, out at the knees ragged jeans were just that, rags. Somehow, worn out, ill fitting clothes became expensive *de rigueur* items, without which no self-respecting adolescent would be seen in public.

While Patricia was changing, I told Mitzi to decide which car we'd take and who would drive. Then, giving credence to her confused state and knowing how much she enjoys driving, I tossed her the keys to the 'stang and said, "You drive. The kid can ride in the back and be important."

Patricia, of course, had to comment on the discomfort of the rear seat, the noise of the traffic with the top down and how no one could possibly hear the radio that way, and then I quit listening.

At the ice cream stand, she discovered that the boys thought she was totally cool to ride in such - what? I have no real idea what word they used to describe the Mustang. I heard something followed by "wheels." I suspect it was "bitchin'," but maybe that was because I had been listening to Patricia for the last few hours. Or maybe it was because what had been a bitch of a day wasn't getting better, no matter what I did.

Lydia was getting out of another car at the edge of the lot, the door held by another man. Neither of us could duck, neither of us could speak. Patricia saw the whole thing, and all of it registered in her reptilian consciousness. I didn't have to ask to know that she would be causing trouble just as soon as she could figure a way to use what she knew.

The good news was that Lydia looked stricken, as though she had been caught holding her sister's dope while the cops were banging on the door. The bad news was that Mitzi wasn't wearing her chauffeur's clothes and Patricia looked ever so much like the recalcitrant child acting out with a step-parent.

Swell. Really, truly swell.

* * *

Since my life was fast approaching the toilet anyway, and since we were close to the expressway, I gave Mitzi her head and told her to exorcize her demons.

Mitzi says that the Michigan cops don't bother people who

drive no more that twenty miles an hour over the speed limit because they are looking for the big tickets, for thirty and over. Personally, I figure ten over is just fine, which means I keep it at eighty or less since the expressway speed limit is seventy in Michigan. But Mitzi lives for speed.

We moved north through Ohio at a relatively sedate seventy plus, and when we crossed the state line I felt the G-force of acceleration as Mitzi headed up toward the sound barrier. I was torn between my natural, inborn fear of life and the thrill of speeding along in a roadworthy convertible with a competent driver in command. I checked my seatbelt to make sure it was fastened.

"Afraid we'll crash?"

"Not so much that we'll crash as that I'll be thrown out on a curve." That, and the danger of being sucked out the car by the force of the slipstream passing over us.

The skyline of Detroit, seen through the gathering dusk of a summer night, isn't a substitute for the Manhattan skyline, not that it needs to be. It is its own, the Motor City, the home of Motown. Maybe the affection I feel for it is based on never having lived there. For sure, we used to make jokes about Detroit, where murder was a misdemeanor. But I still get a warm fuzzy whenever I hear its name, perhaps because of winter trips back to NY at Christmas, listening to the barking dogs performing Jingle Bells and the ads for the drug store. To this day I don't know if I was hearing "Big V" or "Bigbee." But I'm sure that every kid in Detroit knows, and everybody within a decade of my age knows the jingle. Anyway, that's what went through my consciousness as we flew north across the Detroit River, the city stretching away to the left and right in the gathering darkness. That and how much I appreciated that the roar of the wind kept Patricia from nattering on about how the boys thought she was a bitchin' woman to ride in such bitchin' wheels, or something like that.

Mitzi tore along, concentrating on the traffic and finding a path through it, her speed constant. Just about the time I was sure the cops would be looking for us, she found a handy cloverleaf interchange and reversed our course. That we had slowed registered only because of the lessened wind noise. Otherwise, we were still moving with the sound barrier, headed south in one fluid, screaming leaning turn, as though we were a wingless WWII fighter plane pursuing the fleeing Hun.

* * *

I should have guessed that Lydia wouldn't have been waiting for me outside, come the next morning; should have, but didn't. So, predictably, I was disappointed that she wasn't there waiting, pretending nothing unusual had happened. I certainly didn't think it was unusual, not the way my life has always gone. Besides, she is popular and always busy, so who am I to presume that just because we had a long, warm dinner and time staring at the moon that she would be waiting, pining for me to ask her out again?

Yeah, I know. It's called a "game." I wasn't supposed to know Lydia was playing, and I was supposed to go along with her plan: go home, have dinner, stay there, miss her. But none of that happened, to her mind, and now in her mind she was busted. As far as I was concerned, her date was completely normal, if ill-advised. It was like she was keeping a safety in place, in case one of us didn't work out. But which one?

So much for the idea that it's always the guy who can't commit.

When I got to the office, I could tell she was there, and I could guess she was watching for me to show up. I say that because her chair was still turning when I walked past it, like she had gotten out of it in a hurry. I figured, she'd bring my coffee or she wouldn't, so I went to my office and sat, and waited. And waited.

No, I don't have a lot of experience at this sort of thing. Remember me, who watches his cousin put on his pantyhose and calls him "her"? Charlene taught me to think through whatever might go on, then draw a logical conclusion.

"It's pretty much always the simple answer, Dan-rod."

What then, was the simple answer? How about, the longer she took to bring me coffee, the more uncomfortable she was?

"Sorry, Danny. Marcie forgot to start the coffee and I had to wait."

That, too, was a simple answer.

"No problem. I just got here a couple of minutes ago."

She put the mug on my desk, but didn't offer to leave. Maybe I was closer with the first answer than I thought.

"Where's your coffee?"

"What?"

I picked up my mug, waved at her usual chair. "Aren't you going to have your coffee and tell me what's going on, just like always?"

"Oh. Yes." She brightened, spun and called over her shoulder, "I'll be right back."

Thank you, Charlene.

* * *

The morning passed as any other, except that Lydia paid more attention to me than I could have thought possible. Everything was absolutely fine until just before lunch, when Patricia showed up in Mitzi's chauffeur's uniform, including the shoes, and made sure that she spoke directly to Lydia, and only to Lydia about something that "Danny" should know.

I heard nothing except for that one "Danny," which was way more than I needed to hear to know that Pandora's box lid was swinging in the wind.

Crap.

I found out real fast that what she had said was, "Take this note to Danny. It's from my mother."

No "please." No "thank you."

FIFTEEN

"There is a directly proportional ratio between the *status quo* and the perceived *status nova* as it develops in response to stimuli, chronology and societal pressures generally, and that ratio demonstrates a consistency which should be expected as the natural and logarithmic progression of personal and institutional existence toward the *status futura.*"

Or, the more things change, the more they stay the same.

Long years ago, I suffered through the humiliation of law school classes taught by overeducated, inexperienced priss-ass twits; by oversexed, unfulfilled dowagers; by once competent, burned out practitioners; and by one especially offensive, long-haired, sandal-wearing, pseudo-intellectual sissy-boy. Guess which one wouldn't say, "The more things change, the more they stay the same." Intentionally. He thought it made him more attractive to the Air Force captain, on educational leave to complete his law degree and transfer to the JAG Corps, or whatever the Air Force calls it.

The more they change, the more they stay the same.

"This came for you." Lydia's tone would have frozen nitrogen. "She's waiting for your answer."

Just a week ago, I was so boring to Lydia that only death would relieve the tedium. Now, with Patricia in my office, wearing a micro skirt, and Mitzi at home running my household, I was on her bad side again. I had done nothing but react to circumstances which had been thrust upon me, and I had provoked her wrath.

But I have litigated in Juvenile Court. There, more than in any other court, one has to be ready to turn unexpected problems to one's own ends. And if I have said it a hundred times, I have said it a thousand: my mother was born in Dixie, and both my grandmothers and all of their mothers and grandmothers before them. If you are not from the IRS, I am not afraid of *you.* Head over heels I may be, but Lydia is a Girl Scout next to my late, unlamented mother.

I checked my watch. "Lunch time. Get your purse."

"What?" Lydia refused to be distracted from her pique.

The note wasn't from Mitzi. Stunned? Patricia's script was precise, yet girlish: "Mother wishes to know your dinner plans."

I held it up so that Lydia could read it. "Well? Dinner with you or dinner with them?"

No response beyond an eye-narrowing scowl.

I checked my pockets for my wallet and cash, made sure I had my watch. "I'm going to lunch. She's driving and you're invited to sit in the back with me and watch the scenery go by. I drove myself to work, and you are invited to dinner with me, no chauffeur." I headed to the door, paused to look back at her. "Well?"

I could see the little wheels go round. If she said yes, if she said no. What to do? Either answer would cost her control, and neither would hurt her. Plus, if she went along to lunch she could keep her eyes on me, and the little slut in the micro skirt.

"Fine. I'll get my purse." She went to the door with the stride of an angry lumberjack, rethought matters and cleared the door like a runway model in full slink.

The more they change, the more they stay the same.

I picked up the phone and called Mitzi on her cell, learned that she was in fact at the house and had sent Patricia to do the marketing. When I pointed out that she was standing in the office, dressed as a chauffeur, Mitzi was angry, apologetic and hurt.

"No problem. I'll handle it. I'm planning on dinner out of the house."

"Yes, sir. And, Mr, Compton, I'm really sorry about this. She was just supposed to do the marketing, and she left here in her own clothes."

"Relax, Mitzi. She hasn't stolen anything and she hasn't crashed the car."

"Yes, sir."

I followed Lydia through the door, faced Patricia and said, "Miss Svenson and I are going to lunch. You will drive us."

Patricia did a double-take, but she knew she was trapped. "Uh, yeah, sure."

"The correct answer is either, 'Yes, sir,' or 'Very good, sir.'

Your mother expects you to perform correctly, and so do I."

Her face burned scarlet, but she said, "Yes, sir."

"And stand up straight."

Lydia came back with her purse and we headed out. We made a little traffic jam at the front door and so I snapped my fingers and pointed, "Door," and waited for Patricia to open it for us, then I followed Lydia and let Patricia shift for herself.

By the time lunch was over, Lydia was feeling quite secure, Patricia looked worn and I was feeling rather pleased with myself, but pissy. Benny's mother was still missing and I was still holding Patricia's note, and a jealous Lydia could be a tiresome Lydia. I took the note, found my pen and wrote, "Miss Svenson and I will be dinning out of the house this evening. DRC." As Patricia held the car door for us, I handed it to her and said, "Give this to your mother."

Back at the office, I left Lydia at her desk with instructions to, "Get Martinez on the phone and bring me coffee, please," went to my own desk and waited for Lydia to say he was on the line. As long as I was being difficult, I might as well lean on Lefty to earn his money and find the errant mommy.

"Lefty."

"Counselor."

"How many FBI agents does it take to screw in a light bulb, Lefty?"

"Huh?"

"All of 'em, Lefty. One to turn and the rest to *find the son-of-a-bitch!*"

"We're on it, Counselor. Honest."

"Screw 'honest', Lefty. If you let her get away, the whole plan is in the toilet. Little Benny Randolph's ass is on the line here, Lefty, and if you think you'll ever have a chance with my cousin, Charlene, you better by God *find his mother!*"

"Yes, Counselor. Everybody in this agency is on it. Honest."

"Good. Find her, sit on her, and find out why the hell she disappeared."

No doubt, he was saying, "Yes, Counselor," when the receiver banged onto the base.

Ok, I'm better. But not so much that you'd notice. I know Lefty does his best, and I know I didn't have to yell. Above all, I know that without his mother, Benny is thoroughly screwed.

* * *

I spent the rest of the day terrorizing the employees, trying not to show my ass while I was showing that "mine" is definitely bigger. Then I reminded Lydia that we were supposed to have dinner tonight and it was her turn to choose the restaurant. Unless she had changed her mind, I would pick her up at her place, seven sharp.

"Ok, Danny."

She left work about five-thirty, just like usual, and went home to beautify herself. I stayed to work on various things, including my plan for Benny Randolph's trial. Since the overall plan for the case did not include a trial, that might seem silly. But like I said before, overconfidence and lack of preparation can send a good case south in a heartbeat. Plus, if Lefty didn't find Mommy, we were screwed. Knowing that made me antsy, and so I had to do something to salve my conscience. Cursing Charlene for getting me into this made me feel better, but it wasn't helpful.

I got so immersed in the process that I was nearly late going to Lydia's, and when she came down she was as hot and pretty as I have ever seen, and I have no desire to write about it. Funny that for years, I could have sat and recited every detail of everything she wore, of every move she made, of every expression and what she could have been thinking, anything to occupy my mind with thoughts of her. I could have written for hours, fitting the perfect word into the perfect phrase. But now, occupied by thoughts of Benny Randolph; now, knowing that she was interested; knowing that I had a friend in Mitzi, I feel like a writer who has lost his edge. I'm not so angry as I used to be. Although, when I think about Charlene, I can still work up a pretty intense head of steam, which in turn brought me around to Patricia, and thence to Willie.

Charlene has taught me *beaucoup* about women. No, I don't know why, when I was a teenager, we used *beaucoup* to mean "a lot," or "a bunch." Things I wouldn't otherwise think about register with me now, like the idea that Patricia isn't so much a threat to Lydia as a reason for her to demand reassurance. She knows I have no interest in Patricia but she wants me to show that I know that I cannot take her for granted. Lydia, that is. And, she wants me to show that I recognize Patricia as someone who does not have my personal best interest in mind.

There's a concept. Patricia, my own present-day Pandora, does not have my personal best interest in mind when she intentionally interrupts my day, sashays about in her mother's clothing, including heels so thin and tall that she nearly falls off them. Casually, I wondered how Mitzi came to be so comfortable in them. Not just able to walk in them competently, but comfortable. Maybe there is a gene that some women have, a combination lingerie and high heel gene which makes them comfortable in stilettos and G-strings. If there is, I know that Mitzi has it and I'm betting that Lydia does too. She is entirely immune to social pressure, and if she has ever felt a need to please me with her clothing choices, it is purely a reaction to the perceived threat offered by Mitzi and Patricia. Even then, she wore clothes which she already owned and which she wore routinely. That, of course, brought me back to Pandora's box.

Maybe the reason that Lydia saw Patricia as a threat was normal female stuff. Maybe, though, it was because she was older than when we met and maybe she was seeing things differently. I could hope so, anyway. I could hope that Lydia was growing up just like Mitzi thought I was, that we were entering adulthood together.

She directed me to the restaurant, this time a small, quiet place where we could sit and talk. But you already know that I wasn't too talkative, and she carried the conversational ball right up to, "Anything wrong, Danny?"

As a callow youth I might have tried to say something meaningful, or something witty. But Charlene has taught me to stick to the truth. "No."

I might have left it there, were I still that callow fellow, but I was with Lydia, the girl who occupied my daydreams and, truth be told, had kept me from the train room on many rainy weekends when I might have otherwise been making serious progress in miniature.

"This thing about Benny Randolph's mother has me worried."

"You really care."

I shrugged, "He's just a client. I hate to lose."

"Sure, Danny." She smiled and looked down at her plate, played with her food. "Whatever gets you through the night."

"That would be you." I shrugged again, "Or thinking about you, anyway."

"I thought Mitzi was there to keep you warm."

Danger! Danger! Danger! Charlene also taught to lie whenever necessary, and to never ever, not *ever* assume that a woman knew she was close to the truth when she said something like that, even if it were entirely harmless.

"Mitzi is the maid, the cook and the chauffeur, all rolled into one. We are building a friendship. We have even joked about her 'Driving Mr. Daisy.' But she does not, I repeat *not*, keep me warm. I'm saving that place for you."

"Oh." It was soft, a single thoughtful syllable redolent of warmth and passion, of heat and promise.

At least I thought so. But what came next had me wondering.

"Did you ever meet someone and think, 'This could be it,' and then you found yourself wondering if she was thinking the same thing? Did you think, maybe she was wondering what kind of history you had? Maybe she was wondering if you were one of those wild, careless boys who had sown oats all around the country?"

"Me? Are you kidding?" I was truly puzzled. Lydia had once said that any woman who thought I was interesting would likely get excited over boiling water. But here she was, acting like I might actually have a past, a life before Lydia.

She smiled again, but pensively. "Suppose you went out with someone whose past wasn't what you thought? Then what?"

I stalled, trying to remember what part of my past wasn't dull, lackluster and devoid of interest. Then it occurred to me that she was also dating the other guy, and maybe he wasn't what she had anticipated. Maybe he was more interesting to her than she had expected and now, instead of choosing between two dullards, she had a choice between me and the Mystery Man, and mystery equals interest.

Swell. So much for growing up together.

Guys are always in trouble with women because we try to fix the problem instead of listening and offering support and sympathy. Sorry, but that's how we are. Plus, being in love with a woman makes some men protective. Some men get possessive, and some of us just give up.

Thanks, Mother.

"Ask him, I guess, about what bothers you. Figure out if you can trust him. If you believe him, go with that. Don't be stupid, but don't be judgmental." I frowned, "Too much?"

The more they change, the more they stay the same.

"It's not too much." She shook her head, smiling. "But is that what you would do? Ask her?"

"I've never had the opportunity, so I guess I can't say. I'd like to think so, but face it. None of us really knows what we'd do in a situation until we're actually in it. Like right now. Nobody ever asked me this question, so I'm kind of making it up as I go along."

"Oh." It was her turn to shrug. "You were so positive, I thought maybe you'd been there."

"Yeah, right." I almost said how this was a record for me, having a second date with someone that interested me, but what was the point? I'd had second dates before, and sounding pathetic was no way to win a real woman. All I'd do was lose my secretary and have to get a new one. "Dessert?"

"Oh, no. I'll get fat and we ought to get home at a reasonable hour so I can get in early tomorrow." She gave me a rueful smile. "All of the sudden, I'm a social butterfly."

"Ok." I waved for the check and so forth, and took her home.

No kiss goodnight, just a soft smile and, "See you tomorrow," and then she was out of the car before I could work the door handle.

I drove home convinced that Lydia would be going out with Mystery Man tomorrow night, Friday night, if you are keeping track. When it rains, it pours.

And pours.

Willie's car was in the driveway when I got home, happily without the police presence that had accompanied his last visit. But that was still more than I needed, all things considered. He wanted his wife back.

I was about to stick out my hand and demand the thousand dollars for which she was collateral, plus room and board for her and her daughter, when he said, "Set up the game. I've got the cash to play for real now, and I'm going to clean you out."

I thought that was silly, especially since I have no idea how to play poker and besides, I wasn't the one who won her from him to begin with. Before I could make that point, he was back in his car and tearing down the street, a man on a mission.

Swell. No girlfriend, no secretary, no maid.

* * *

When I got to work, Lydia was hard at it. Subpoenas and motions were on my desk for me to sign, just like in a real law office. There were letters, too, and the coffee was poured, ready for me. All I needed was a call from Lefty that he had found Benny's mother, and the day would be perfect.

"Danny, Mr. Martinez is on line two."

"Thanks."

Lefty was crowing. He had her, she was sorry she had worried us and she had no intention of hurting her son, no matter how bad a mother she had already been to him. Whatever we needed her to do, she would be there and she would do it.

"Thanks, Lefty."

"No sweat, Counselor. We never fail."

One down, one to go. "I rang the intercom for Lydia.

"Yes, Danny?"

"Get the children in here, now."

"Yes, Danny." There was a puzzled edge, but she had the horsepower to move mountains, and they came pounding into my office to please the boss man.

"I want chapter and verse on the law as it relates to the

provision of necessaries to a spouse and child."

Blank stares.

"A friend of mine, likely to be a client of this office, has been feeding and clothing the wife and child of another man, due to that man's addiction."

Slowly dawning comprehension.

"Our potential client is about to have a showdown with the addict, and he wants to know his options."

Full, knowing understanding; nodding heads.

"He wants to know *today.*"

Sudden scrambling, shoving to be first to answer the boss's call.

I reached for the intercom, but Lydia was in the doorway. "Trouble?"

"Sort of, not really. Willie wants his woman back. I like her, I don't like him."

"You've grown accustomed to her face?" A wry smile; a woman postponing bad news.

"More her pot roast than her face." I had no real concentration right then, so I asked her, "What's on your mind?"

"Just checking on the boss."

"The boss is fine. Unhappy, a little angry, busy. Plus, I have some things to do before the big game tonight. Willie wants to play for Mitzi."

"You play poker?" Raised eyebrows, a startled look.

"Nope."

"But you know how?"

"Not a clue." I looked up. "There's a book, right?"

"Several, Danny, but a book? And the game is tonight? Are you nuts?"

"How long have you known me, and you have to ask that question?"

She had no answer to that, so I pointed to the door. "Go away. I have a lot to do and no time to do it."

I had the phone in my hand before she was through the door. "Mitzi, you and Patricia are going to visit Wang Ho. This is what you are going to do."

She listened and she didn't argue, and I knew right then that she was done forever with Willie, no matter what.

Next I called Wang Ho, and told him what was up.

"A bill? You crazy? You don't pay here, ever!"

"Who said anything about paying? I want a bill, a justifiable bill I can wave at Willie the Loser."

"Oh! I get it now! You legal types are weird, you know that?"

Swell. Wang Ho puts his clammy hand on my cross-dressing cousin's naked ass to adjust his G-string, thinks nothing of it and calls me weird because I intend to screw a gambling addict out of his wife, within the bounds of the law. Swell.

Back to the intercom. "Lydia, did you find that book yet?"

"Er, no. But I'm on it."

Roughly translated, it hadn't registered with her that she was supposed to find a book on how to play poker and get it to me, pronto.

"Good." Mitzi and Patricia were on their way to Wang Ho's, Wang would tend to them as I asked and send the stuff along with them, and Lydia would find me that book on poker. The ball was in play and now I had to wait, and that was the worst of it.

* * *

A little of this, a little of that. I watched how they played, I watched how they bet. I know nothing about playing poker, but I know about men. I know that they do certain things certain ways, out of habit, sometimes out of superstition. Learn the pattern, predict the play.

It didn't hurt that Mitzi was wearing the most overtly sexual clothing I have ever seen on a woman. I don't mean trashy or obvious. I mean, the way Wang had her dressed, if they didn't look they were blind. Even gay men would have looked at her. Patricia's clothing was ten per cent less so, what with her being a child and all.

I had wondered about her cooperation, but I guess I was right. Patricia, who considered me a lame old man and who had discovered that she could look hot and dress hot - hotly? - and attract the attention of boys her own age, now found that money and power were more attractive than bad skin, bad hair and outrageous clothing. After all, not one of her admirers had bitchin' wheels. Add to that the idea that her father, who she so closely resembled in her attitudes and prejudices, couldn't give her a second nickel if she already had the first. No rubbing there.

Anyway, there they were, the two Watson women, tripping around my house in outrageous clothing and stiletto heels, serving drinks and snacks to six middle-aged men who should have known better - well, five. I'm not middle-aged, yet.

Of the crew, only Willie and I were keeping our eyes on the cards. So far, the plan was working. Willie was winning more than ususal, but not so much as to give him the unchallenged lead, and Arnie, Ed, Vic and Sal were too busy watching the women to bet heavily enough to make it particularly interesting. Result? Willie had what he came with, plus a couple hundred.

I had what I started with, plus about five.

About eleven, the cards looked right. A little of this, a little of that and the hand was going around for a two hundred ante.

"Well, that's it for me." Ed tossed in his cards, checked his watch and fingered his chips. "I guess I'll cash out and head home."

"Me too." Arnie was no fool, either. His cards followed Ed's onto the table.

That left Sal and Vic, and neither of them wanted to push the little luck they'd had. "Come on, Sal." Vic tossed in his hand. "I'll give you a ride."

Apparently, Sal had come with Willie.

"Hey, you cheap bastards. You clean me out, now I got a chance to get even and you leave. Some friends."

"Cards weren't hot tonight, Willie." Sal shrugged his apology. "Some other night, I'll take your money."

"You in or out?" I figured it was time to make the point and get rid of Willie, once and for all.

Willie turned back to the game, licked his lips and said, "Yeah, I'm in. Here's the two hundred and I raise five."

"I'll see the five and here's ten."

The others traded looks, and Mitzi looked sick. She knew what was riding on this hand, and she had no idea what I was doing. I wanted it that way.

Willie, fingered his chips, checked his cards, fingered his chips, checked his cards, licked his lips.

Oh, for crying out loud, bet. You know what you're going to do, so do it.

"You're bluffing."

"Find out." I waved at the pile of chips on the table.

Where Willie got the money, I could only hope to guess. What I knew was that he had a pile in front of him, and there was no limit on the betting. He shoved the pile forward and crowed, "Five thousand dollars, and you ain't got nothing like that." He sat back sneering.

"Mitzi."

Just like I told her, she dropped her skirt, turned and presented her ass. Wang Ho had imitated the poker chip tattoo perfectly: one thousand dollars. I reached into my pocket and pulled out his bill and the work sheet that my associates had created, tossed them on the pile.

"Your wife's ass is worth a grand. The bills for what it cost me to feed and dress her and your daughter come to, oh, about forty-three hundred. I'll call it even if you will. In fact, I *call*."

"You can't do that!"

"Can't do what? Ask your buddies. I'm putting shoes on their feet and food in their bellies. Your wife is working here because you lost her to my cousin, and because you didn't win her back the last time you played. She doesn't get paid because, well, why should I? I own her ass until you can pay the grand, plus what it costs to keep her. And now I've got your kid living here, same terms except there's nothing tattooed on her ass." I turned to the others. "She's just a kid, you know."

They traded looks, and they didn't disagree. Plus, they were all feeling a little uncomfortable about what they had been thinking while they were eyeing the minor.

"Well? I called. What have you got?"

"Full house: aces and kings." He leaned forward to rake in the chips.

I laid down my cards: royal flush. "You lose."

I thought he'd stroke out right there.

The boys led him away, babbling and cursing, none of it particularly inventive or amusing.

Patricia had the decency to realize that her father had just gambled away both her and her mother, and I think she finally realized what he had been up to. Maybe not. Anyway, she covered her mouth with her hand and went to the doorway, wide-eyed, to watch them leave.

Mitzi and I stood next to each other, behind her. Mitzi pulled up her skirt, straightened her clothing and sadly, but her relief evident, said, "I thought you didn't know how to play poker."

I shook my head. "Haven't got a clue. But I know how to cheat."

SIXTEEN

Mitzi cleaned up the house while I counted the winnings. Patricia, who should have been helping her mother or displaying attitude, did neither. She took herself to her room and shut the door, presumably to ponder the nasty turn her life had taken right in front of her. I should have felt sorry for her but, well, I dislike her intensely. Too much like her father, too much like every other snotty, entitled teenager I have dealt with.

Just over seventy-seven hundred. How's that for a non sequitur? Not bad for a poker pot, either, considering that five grand of it came from Willie, and only about two hundred of it was mine to start with. I took the pile of bills to my bedroom and dropped it in my sock drawer, wondering what to do with it, as though I hadn't already decided.

I had known many a month when seventy-five hundred was twice what I had expected, let alone collected. Now, it was just about what the firm paid me every week, before taxes. Those young associates are quite impressive, and no matter that they are well paid, a little appreciation goes a long way. I made ten neat piles, each holding two hundred fifty dollars: three lawyers, six secretaries and a paralegal. The bulk of it, the five thousand that was Willie's belonged to Mitzi as far as I was concerned. That left about two hundred for me, and that was just a few dollars more than what I had thrown in the pot myself. All things considered, a fair resolution to a dirty business.

"Mr. Compton?" Mitzi tapped at my door, then pushed it open. She was still wearing her poker party clothes.

"Yes, Mitzi?"

"I wanted to thank you for what you did tonight." She looked away, blinking, and I saw the tears glistening in her eyes. "I know what you ... what it cost you to..."

"You're welcome, Mitzi. After all, what are friends for?"

"Good night, sir."

"Good night, Mitzi."

So what if the girl I love is out with someone else? I can't lose what I never had, and the feeling that comes with helping a friend is worth more than money or sex. In my life, anyway. I turned in and slept, and it was the best, deepest sleep I had known since I was a kid, Lydia and her mystery man notwithstanding.

You'd think I'd learn.

Three thirty-seven in the morning and the phone rings, if it's not a wrong number, it's trouble. It wasn't a wrong number.

Swell.

First I cheated her husband - and Patricia's father - out of the last of his money and made a fool of him in front of his daughter and his buddies. Then I sent him penniless into the night with those same buddies, who had nothing better to do than to go drinking until the bars closed. One round and another, then several until finally, in a remarkably prescient move, the bartender cut him off. Of course, it was closing time, so what did it matter?

One grinding, tearing crash and a dead, bankrupt gambling addict was what mattered. One worthless husband who was barely a father. A genuine gender embarrassment. A human being.

This time I was the driver, and Mitzi and Patricia were the passengers. It was a long, silent trip to the hospital, followed by hours of unpleasant details. Luckily for Mitzi, she works for a lawyer and has a stone bitch for a daughter. For about seventeen minutes, Patricia came in handy. No, the details aren't important, just that there are ghouls everywhere. Patricia ate them like candy.

The cops were businesslike and considerate. Hefty taxes bring respect, and mine are really hefty, so we got a lot of respect and a lot of deference.

No matter the abuse, Mitzi was shattered. She had kept the stubborn hope that Willie would come to his senses, deal with the addiction and rebuild his life and theirs. Hope springs eternal until it is crushed, and nothing is more devastating than the loss of a cherished dream.

Swell.

We settled the details at the hospital just about dawn, then headed to the Watson house. Patricia took the lead, organizing their needs for the funeral and generally handling things. I stayed in the background, figuring that since I had pretty much caused it all, maybe I should keep out of it. Neither Mitzi nor Patricia noticed what I was up to as I drifted around, checking things like the mail.

Obviously, Mitzi hadn't been there for more than the few days she had spent at my house. The foreclosure notice was on the table and I counted eight "Final Notice" envelopes and five delinquent credit card billings. There was a stack of other things, including "discontinuation of service" notices from Edison and the gas company. While the women were in the bedroom, I tried the television: no cable, but the power was still on. I moved to the kitchen and checked: water.

Patricia came back with a handful of envelopes: wills and insurance policies; more work for the associates. Mitzi trailed behind her, shoulders slumping and her steps dragging. I reached for the phone, which was dead, and then found my cell phone. What was I thinking? All I had to do was take out the cell, scroll down the directory listings and call the associates until one of them answered. Then, instructions given, we waited.

Including dressing and traveling, two hours later Mitzi and Patricia had a lawyer for the estate, if there was one, and someone to handle the insurance details. I had Patricia's grudging respect. Apparently, I wasn't just another lame old man with bitchin' wheels.

The rest of the weekend was a nasty blur which reached its climax on Monday, when Willie was commended into God's hands. After the service, we went back to their house for the usual obsequies, and I left Mitzi and Patricia with their neighbors and headed downtown to the office.

When I rolled in to work, I found out how much trouble I was in with Lydia. I had left it up to the associate to tell her what had happened, which wasn't my best move. Lydia had a good idea what had happened and what was going on during the morning, but the fact that I hadn't called her personally was going to be a sore point for a long, long time. She made sure I understood that, right off, but I had the idea that she was angry with herself more than with me.

The fact that she cared was the high point of the last four days, Thursday night's dinner excluded. Too bad I was too busy to enjoy it.

* * *

My job was to keep Eileen Stannard away from the court room and away from the clerk's office. I had already been in there, agreeing with Mr. Willis and the mother's lawyer that Stannard's motion to dismiss should be granted, and now I was out of the case. I didn't have to be in there to know what they were saying.

"Mr. Gilbert, it's your case in chief."

"Thank you, your honor." Larry Gilbert, attorney for the Ecumenical Council Social Services called his witness, Marianne Jackson, caseworker, who testified that Lisa Randolph was Benny's mother. She testified that his father was Charles E. Davis, deceased.

"You're sure about that?" In Juvenile Court, the judge can ask questions too.

Larry Gilbert said, "Yes, your honor. May we have these marked as exhibits?" Then he produced the certified death certificate for Charles E. Davis; a certified copy of the paternity test results; a certified copy of the affidavit of parentage; and the record of the putative father registry. The judge raised his eyebrows, looked at Willis. Willis smiled.

The judge turned to Lisa Randolph, Benny's mother. "Miss Randolph, do you understand that once to you do this, there's no going back?"

"Yes, your honor."

"This is what you want to do? You want to surrender your son to the permanent custody of the Ecumenical Council Social Services so that they can place him for adoption?"

"Yes. I love my son and I haven't been much of a mother to him. Maybe this way he'll have a chance."

"Your son is - was in the temporary custody of the Children Services, correct?"

"They want to give him to my parents."

"And you don't want that?"

"No. My father raped me and I told CSB what he did. They said it was a long time ago and my son is a boy, so he'll be ok. Then they told me they have to consider the family if they place a child, and he'd go there no matter what I said. But he won't be ok there. My father already ..." She broke down.

"Mr. Willis, you represent the Guardian *ad litem*?"

"Yes, your honor."

"Guardian's recommendation."

The guardian, May Lamberton, sat with her arm around the mother's shoulders, comforting her. She said, "I recommend the surrender be accepted and Benny go into the permanent custody of the Council so that he can be adopted."

"Miss Randolph, I know how hard this is for you, believe it or not. All I can say is, you have done the right thing by your child, and it takes a lot of courage for you to do what you did, and you have to love your child very much to do this." Then the judge recited for the record that the surrender was accepted and Benny was committed to the permanent custody of the Ecumenical Council.

I stood outside the courtroom door while this was going on, and I heard almost all of it. What I didn't hear, I could guess.

You see, Eileen Stannard had filed her motion to dismiss the CSB case with the idea that the grandparents would file a private custody case. They would be the only game in town, and Stannard was betting that the mother, their daughter Lisa, wouldn't be able to stand up to them. The case would go to the court's home study department and the investigator would check with the caseworker, who would give the agency's approval. There would be no need to reappoint the guardian and the grandparents would get custody. Everybody wins except Benny, who gets screwed.

But with a little help, Stanley Willis had what he needed to convince the judge that if Stannard wanted to dismiss the case at trial, then there was no reason to wait. Dismiss it now and be done, Willis argued, and let the Council file its complaint for permanent custody, with the mother's agreement and with her counsel beside her in open court. After all, how could Stannard complain if she got what she asked for, on the record and in writing?

Willis had with him the certified, and therefore admissible as evidence, records which proved that Benny Randolph had a legally established father whose fatherhood had been factually supported and who was definitely dead. He had a mother who loved her child, and a child services agency ready to take permanent custody. The game was over. The Ecumenical Council wasn't required to consider the grandparents for adoption, as CSB is required to, and so with the mother's expressed wish that someone else adopt her child, the Council would look elsewhere.

Did I mention that there was already an identified adoptive home, and Benny would be placed there within the hour?

Willis said that the Guardian had been there and checked out the home of Leroy and Marie Jamieson, and they were just fine. Benny would have a chance because he would have a real life in a real home with real parents.

Now if Eileen Stannard will just come a little closer so it doesn't look like I want to talk to her. And here she is!

"Mr. Compton, did you get my motion to dismiss on the Randolph case?"

"Yes, I did. I think that is the lowest, meanest thing the agency has ever tried to pull, and I think you ought to be ashamed, dumping the poor little guy like that."

"Well, we didn't have the evidence to proceed." Stannard was positively condescending, which is her best thing. "If you feel so strongly about it, why don't you file your own complaint?"

I looked around, trying for nonchalance, waiting for Willis to come out of the court room. Nope, not yet. "You haven't won yet, Eileen."

She sniffed in heightened condescension, tossed her head and said, "The court cannot order the agency to proceed. Would you like me to send you the authority on the point?"

"You can send me a full-blown brief and I still won't let you get away with this."

"There is nothing you can do. The case will be dismissed, the grandparents will file their complaint for custody and the child will go to them just like he should. Family is family, and that's where he belongs."

Bet me. I would have said it out loud, and more, but Stanley Willis was nodding to us, holding up his finger as a signal that we should wait a moment, and then he was at the clerk's desk and the clerks were falling all over themselves to do something for him. Eileen Stannard frowned, puzzled, but I knew what was up. They were certifying the court's order that Benny Randolph was in the custody of the Ecumenical Council, and that CSB was to immediately deliver the child into its possession and custody.

"What's this?" Stannard had the look of a cheerleader on the team bus.

Willis handed her the first order. "This is the order dismissing the CSB case."

"What? There was a hearing? Why wasn't I notified?"

Willis shrugged and said, "You won. You moved to dismiss and we stipulated."

I said, "Toyota."

"What?" Her head swivelled from Willis to me, to Willis and back to me. She was beginning to feel the ground slide out from under her. "What does that mean?"

Willis shrugged again.

I explained, "You asked for it, you got it. Toyota!" I couldn't help myself. I always loved that ad.

Then Willis, ever a gentleman, bowed slightly and presented the second order. "This is the final order in the new Randolph case." He nodded over Stannard's shoulder to acknowledge the Ecumenical Council's caseworker and went on. "May I introduce Marianne Jackson of the Ecumenical Council Social Services Agency? She is the assigned worker and she will be placing the child in his new home."

Eyes blazing, Stannard turned on Willis, her voice shrill and maybe a half-decibel below a shriek. "Do you know what *ex parte* means, Mr. Willis?"

"Of course." He nodded wisely. "At two-thirty in the morning, everybody goes home."

Stannard's eyes bulged and she said - this is a direct quote - "Awk. Wok"

When I grow up, I want to be Stanley Willis.

* * *

I left them at the court house, arguing. Stannard was apoplectic and Willis was playing with her like a cat with a chipmunk. The last thing I heard him say was, "Why don't you go to the Court of Appeals and complain that you won and that it isn't fair for the court to give you what you asked for? While you're at it, tell them you were planning collusive litigation and the court, by its high-handed granting of your motion, interfered with your plan."

The Kiddie Court regulars were gathering, shoving each other and snickering, and I remembered long years ago when I would have been in that crowd. But Charlene has brought me a new life, where clients pay real money and Lydia answers my phone and Mitzi cleans my house and cooks my meals.

What I didn't mention before was that I had read very carefully Mr. Davis' death certificate. I went back and checked the dates and my notes, and the only question left is why Charlene, after sending Mr. Davis to meet his Maker, decided that I had to save his son. But I can answer that without even asking.

Charlene took money from Mr. Davis. A life for a life.

So. I walked back to the office alone, thinking about all that. I have been in love with Lydia since the second I saw her. She exists and I love her, and if I weren't so boring I'd be the kind of man who wouldn't tolerate stupid games. I'm in love with Charlene, the woman who doesn't exist, and if I were more intellectually developed, I'd get past the part where Charlene's body is male and I'd live in the fantasy.

Right.

Lefty Martinez was waiting at the office, standing at Lydia's desk and trying to promote dinner with her, explaining the plan. In his version, he was the key player. I let him have the glory of the moment, because it didn't matter and without his detective work the plan would have been little more than a passing fancy. Plus, Lydia wasn't about to go out with him, no matter what.

"Counselor." Lefty nodded, grinning. "I hear it worked."

"Spies in the court house, Lefty?"

"Everywhere, Counselor. Want to hear how come the grandparents were late filing their complaint for custody?"

"No, but I have the feeling I will anyway."

Lefty laughed and nodded, and turned back to Lydia and self-promotion.

I went to my office and sat, contemplating, and then reached for the phone to call Mitzi and check on her. She was fine, and glad I called. No, she didn't want time off. She liked her job, and she thought that staying busy was better for her than sitting around bemoaning the loss of what she never really had.

Then she added that, if I didn't mind, Patricia was going to help out. Apparently, when properly motivated she was a competent cook, and Mitzi vouched for her skill as a driver. "She's not as confident as I am, not yet, anyway. But sometimes I think you're happier with a conservative driver."

"You're in charge, Mitzi. Do whatever you think is right. But keep in mind that maybe this weekend, you two should go somewhere and talk this through."

"I'll think about it, Mr. Compton." She paused, then, "Do you have dinner plans?"

"No. Figured I'd ask you what you had in mind and go from there."

"I think we should stay busy, and Patricia makes a very good chocolate cake, if that sounds good to you."

"I'll be home at the usual time, Mitzi, and chocolate cake sounds tasty."

"Yes, Mr. Compton. Thank you."

"You're welcome, Mitzi."

We rang off, and Lydia was in the doorway.

"What's up?"

"You did a good thing, Danny."

"Going home to dinner is a good thing?"

"I suppose it could be, but I was talking about court."

"Oh." I shrugged. "All I did was cause trouble. Lefty dug up the dirt and Willis piled it on. I could never have done what they did."

"Maybe not, but what you do, you do well. And you did what had to be done to save that little guy." She backed out of the doorway, paused and said, "And it wasn't because you hate to lose, either."

She moved away before I could ask her to come to dinner at the house, which I decided was a bad idea anyway.

I went back to my files, working listlessly, staring off across the river. I did almost nothing, wasted time, remembered the ten piles of cash and called Lydia for envelopes. No answer, so I walked out to her desk.

She was gone.

Marcie said that she had to go somewhere and meet someone, and I was busy so she just left.

"No problem. I need some envelopes."

She brought them, and I put the bills in each one, handwrote each employees's name and "This is just to say 'Thank you.' I appreciate what you do, even if I never say so. DRC." Then I handed them out, starting with Marcie, whose children always need shoes or braces or something.

Why do women cry when they're happy?

* * *

Dinner was tasty as always. Mitzi makes a hell of a pot roast and Patricia bakes a mean cake. Plus, although she and I really dislike each other, she has developed the ability to feign respect for her mother's employer.

Yes, employer.

After dinner, while they were cleaning up I sat in my favorite chair with a very nice after dinner drink and considered my options. Likely, Charlene would cruise into town and take over Patricia's education. I could hope, anyway. Mitzi, as the sole heir and beneficiary under Willie's will, inherited what little was left and she would get the proceeds of the one insurance policy he hadn't cashed in. There wouldn't be enough to live on, even if she were willing to spend it all. But if she stayed with me and took care of the house - and me, of course - then she wouldn't have any expenses. Whatever I paid her would be hers to save or spend, and Mitzi wasn't a wastrel, from what I had seen. In the meantime, there was the five thousand I had taken from Willie.

"Mitzi, could you come here?"

"Yes, Mr. Compton?"

I made my pitch and she agreed, said it was more money than she was worth. Then I gave her the envelope with the poker money and said I thought she and Patricia should take the weekend, go somewhere and bond.

Why do women cry when they are happy?

SEVENTEEN

So passed Monday. Tuesday, Wednesday and Thursday were uneventful. Lydia was almost her old self, Mitzi and Patricia were acting very much like mother and daughter, and Lefty Martinez discovered that he had other clients. Mitzi drove me to work and Patricia drove me home. People stared and rumors started to fly about my harem. Otherwise, nothing changed until late Thursday afternoon.

"Danny, will you do me a favor?" Lydia was almost subdued as she went on. "I hate to ask, because it's this weekend and I know you probably have plans, and it's kind of an imposition even if you don't."

I had already told her that whatever plans I had, I'd cancel them for her. Granted, that was if she said we could have dinner, not if she asked a favor. "Sure. What do you need?"

"You're sure? It's really kind of personal."

"Favors are always personal."

"Not like this one." She laughed and my toes curled. "This one is a whopper, and I'm asking you because I need someone to help me who is absolutely trustworthy and, well, reliable."

Is "reliable" a polite way of saying "boring"?

"Mr. Reliable, at your service." Calm and aloof, willing to accommodate the lady, not falling over myself to be with her.

"Could you come to my apartment, say about five?" She gave me the softest look I have ever seen on a woman's face. "It'll take at least four hours, maybe longer."

I could feel myself twisting around her little finger. "Should I bring dinner, show up a little earlier?"

"You don't have to do that." She shook her head, smiling. "I'm imposing on you enough as it is."

"It's not an imposition." Her smile was contagious, and I liked the way it felt. "We both have to eat, and I thought maybe you would have more time for whatever it is you want me to help you with."

"You're sweet." She put her hand under my chin and I swear

she sighed, just a little and very softly. "But five o'clock would be fine." She walked away, not at all briskly, and left me smiling like a dope.

I was going to spend Saturday evening with Lydia. Then it occurred to me that she declined dinner because she already had plans, and I would be in the way if I showed up too soon. But I didn't care, because I would be with Lydia.

I have no idea what went on after that, except that Mitzi said she had made plans to take Patricia to Port Huron in Michigan, because her grandfather had taken her there many times and they had watched the sun rise over Lake Huron and ... then I quit listening.

I would have the house to myself from Friday morning until Sunday night.

Mitzi would leave food in the fridge for me to warm.

They would take the Town Car because that was more practical for their road trip, and I should have the new car in case I had a date.

Whatever you say, Mitzi. Be careful. Be safe. Good luck.

* * *

Come Saturday, I was up and ready to go a little earlier than I needed to, since I wasn't due at Lydia's until five in the afternoon - ok, a lot earlier: dawn. I dressed carefully, making sure that I was presentable without being dressy. I wanted to give the impression that it was just another manly weekend day spent helping a friend, being reliable.

I rattled around the house, pretending to be relaxed and appreciative that with the Randolph case settled, my life was my own again. Right. I paced until I figured out I could waste the same amount of time behind the wheel, enjoying the feel of the open road. I checked to make sure everything was secure, took a jacket in case it was cold by the lake and headed off to East Harbor. I figured maybe I could stare at the lake and find solace. It seemed to work for Mitzi.

Along the way, I pulled into a drive-thru for a disposable, forgettable lunch, then headed off to the park. I enjoyed the feel of the Mustang, but the ride? Not so much as you might think. My mind was on Lydia and what kind of favor she was seeking, and watching the lake made me sad.

I felt that I was losing Mitzi without gaining Lydia, and I felt a little pathetic. Then I thought about how Lydia had looked when she asked me to help her, and I thought about Lydia needing a favor on a Saturday night. I thought about how she was the most popular person I had ever known, and then I thought about how she had looked in the moonlight, and how she had looked at me. Then I thought about how, if she wanted me for four hours or longer on a Saturday night, I should stop feeling sorry for myself and go to her place. Saturday night with Lydia had been a dream since the second I saw her, I had been invited by her to spend Saturday night with her, and staring at the lake and feeling pathetic was a violation *ipso facto* of the Guy Code.

Never mind what *ipso facto* means. Besides, maybe it's *per se*. But I didn't care. I was on my way to Lydia's on a Saturday afternoon, and it was her idea.

I parked outside her apartment at twenty before the hour, prayed that she wouldn't walk past her window and think I was pathetic. Finally, it was five of, and I figured I could legitimately go inside.

I got out of my car, reached for the electronic lock button and set off the alarm. I looked around to make sure she wasn't looking out the window, laughing at me. Not to worry: I was so nervous I had parked at the wrong door, and had to walk around to the right one.

As I reached for the button to ring her intercom, the door swung open and one of her girlfriends from the restaurant popped out, said a surprised, "Oh," and then giggled, "You're Danny. She's waiting for you. Go on up."

I went through the door, stopped and turned and look at her as she trotted to her car. She waved as she got in, and I let the door shut, went up the stairs to Lydia's apartment and knocked on the door.

I could hear her walking toward the door, and I realized that I had been worrying that she wouldn't be there. Reliable people often show up when and where asked, and the people who asked them aren't there because a better offer came along. Or maybe it's just me. Maybe I bore people in the anticipation and they realize death would be a relief, and they decide not to subject themselves to pain.

But she was there holding the door open, smiling. "Hi, Danny! Come on in."

I could tell she was wearing heels just by how tall she was. It was the first time I had seen her with her hair in curlers and with no makeup on. And by "no makeup," I mean that her face was slathered with cold cream. She had on a long robe, kind of ratty, nothing like I would have expected. When I looked down, finally, toward her feet, what I saw didn't make sense: brown.

"You are so sweet to do this for me, and if you get uncomfortable and don't want to go through with it, I'll understand."

A lesser man might have quailed at the sight, but I've seen Charlene the same way and with her man parts swinging free. Nothing compares with that sight, let me tell you. "I'd do anything for you, and you know it."

She closed the door behind herself and leaned against it. "I made fresh coffee and a cherry pie. I thought we might want a snack later, but don't be bashful. Any time you want it, take it." She wrinkled her nose and smiled, "I don't think of you as company."

As I looked around her apartment, I felt the vertigo start: Charlene could have decorated the place. It was womanly but without frills; comfortable, solid. Yes, I overpay her. But if she did this on her income, then she is very good with her finances, which shouldn't be a surprise to me, since she oversees the books at the office.

"Danny?"

"Wow. You're good."

"Pardon?"

"I was just looking around at how you decorated the place. I'm impressed."

"Thank you. I used to work for a decorator before I got the job with you. I was pretty good at it, but he made other demands on me and I ... wouldn't." A slight shrug, a little shake of her head and that part of the conversation was closed. "If you don't mind, you could help me straighten the bathroom."

I had no idea what to say or do. I was where I wanted to be, and my thoughts stopped there. "Ready when you are."

In her eyes, I read, *Wanna bet?* I followed her to the bathroom,

194

and saw that she had the floor covered with a plastic painter's drop cloth, that she had three large plastic tubs on the vanity and some sponge paint brushes and a blow dryer. There were brown and white streaks on the plastic sheeting and the outsides of the tubs, and the brushes had obviously been used in something brown and something white. The bathroom reeked of ammonia, and maybe I wasn't so ready as I thought, but I'd die before I'd admit it.

"First we have to get rid of this mess."

She directed and I helped. Between us, we gathered up everything and got it into a plastic garbage bag. No sweat and I wondered, *What was the big deal?*

She turned to face me. "You sure you're ready for this?"

I nodded, because I figured anything I tried to say would sound stupid.

"Ok, here we go." She dropped the robe and she was absolutely bare.

Oh, my God!

When I say "bare," I mean, *bare*. Not naked: bare. She was covered in latex body paint, and no part of her was concealed. Her belly was white and her body, arms and legs were brown; everything but her hands, neck and face. I clung to these details so I could keep my sanity. I thought I'd faint, but I managed to shrug in complete nonchalance.

There was a tiny flash of indecision in her eyes, and then she said, "I'm going to a Christmas-in-July party tonight, as Rudolph. A friend of mine," she giggled a little, "helped me get ready."

I fought the urge to run, to remonstrate. I knew that she wouldn't think of it, let alone do it to her boss, but old terrors live longest and die hardest, and I had the awful feeling that two hundred of her closest friends were assembling outside her apartment door, ready to burst in and make fun of me. I nodded, and prayed I could walk. "What do you want me to do?"

"Go with me. Be Santa."

That's the favor? Go to a party with the girl I love?

"Well? Will you?"

"Sure."

"Then let's get you ready." She looked me over with the appraising eye of a horse trader, nodded and stalked to her closet. She whipped open the door and produced - of course - a Santa suit in my exact size.

I prayed, *Let it fit.*

Which it did, right down to the sandals.

Lydia led me back to the bathroom and put on the beard and mustache - no silly, hang-from-the-ears fake beard for her, no sir. Genuine, theatrical quality fake whiskers, which she applied with sure, unhesitating strokes. Then she frowned, got out her makeup kit and started doing things to my eyes and cheeks.

When she was happy with the way I looked, she went to work on herself. From the cold creamed monster that had met me at the door to a fresh faced and pretty woman, to an absolute knock-out. I couldn't get a deep breath watching her transform herself.

Even with the red clown nose she was gorgeous.

Finally, she nodded at herself, reached into a vanity drawer and pulled out one of those Christmas season novelty hair bows with the reindeer antlers, arranged it in her hair and then smiled at me. "Ready?"

"Sure."

"Too bad there's no one to take a picture."

"You have a camera with a self-timer?"

She did, but she handed it to me with a puzzled look. "How do we do this?"

We found a way to stand in front of her drapes, put the camera on a shelf of the etagere and smiled. *Voila!*

Then she looked down at herself and screamed.

"The hell?"

"I've been running around here half-naked, and forgot to finish dressing for the picture."

Well, *I* was confused.

Lydia disappeared into the bathroom, came out with a bit of fake fur in her hand and said, "Here. Help me with this."

It was a very small G-string with a fake fur panel for the front and a tail flap for the rear. Yes, the tail was brown on top and white underneath. I knelt and she balanced with her hands on my shoulders while she stepped into it, then wiggled herself while I pulled it up along her thighs.

"Thanks." She reached down to bring it the rest of the way, and the hula she did as she adjusted it made the whole day worthwhile.

"No sleigh bells?"

"Damn." She ran to the kitchen and came back with a bell-studded collar, which she handed to me. "Here." She turned and held up her hair so that I could buckle the collar, shook her hair free and checked herself in the mirror. She reached back and grabbed my wrist - I decided she was becoming possessive - and checked the time. "We'll be late. I should drive."

Hell, yes. "Sure."

She looked around, again contrite. "I can get bossy." She turned away, muttering something about "ironic," and then said, "Sometimes you fluster me."

"Now that you're dressed, do you want to take another picture?"

She walked up to me and dropped her head onto my chest, smiling. "My dad will like you. Nothing rattles you, you never raise your voice when things don't go right, you're never flustered." She looked up. "We have time, so if you don't mind, I'd like another picture."

"Ok, but I want a copy of the first one."

"You are such a brat." She shoved me with her finger and then we made Kodak a little richer, clowning for the self-timer. When she was satisfied that we had a good picture, suitable for public release, we went down to the car.

Lydia frowned when she saw the car wasn't where she expected, but she said nothing as we walked around the building to where I had parked. We found the car and I shrugged and said, "Sorry. They all look alike to me."

She shook her head, smiled and said, "Smooth, Danny."

I held the door for her and she slid behind the wheel, took the key and put down the top while I was walking around to the passenger door.

Possessive and impatient.

She drove us to the party with dash and panache, Rudolph chauffeuring Santa in his convertible. What better way to get to a Christmas-in-July party?

The party was in an upscale subdivision, and the uninvited neighbors were gawking at the guests. But when I held the door for her and Lydia stepped out, paused to adjust her antlers and then took my arm, there was a moan from every adult man in eyesight.

She led me to the host, kissed his cheek and introduced me as, "Danny."

For tonight, I'm not her boss.

The music system was high-end, with a decent D-J running it. *Felice Navidad* was playing as we stepped away from the host. Lydia led me to the punch bowl, and waited demurely - ok, ok. Considering she was wearing a latex body suit and a G-string, she was demure. I handed her a cup of punch and she thanked me, and every move made those bells jingle.

Not that she was the only reindeer in the crowd. But no one else had the stones to wear latex and a red nose. She was the star of the show, and she made it clear to all that she was with me.

I should have been composed and in charge, the man. I would have been but, as hot as Lydia looked, next to Charlene she was chopped venison.

Yes, Charlene. Back earlier than anticipated and in her glory as Mrs. Santa Claus. "Daniel, darling!"

I stood there, mouth open and my arm around Lydia's waist, stunned.

Lydia growled.

Charlene bounded over, singing along with the music and, with what she wore, she had my complete attention. White patent leather sandals, all thin straps and spike heels; white thigh-high fishnets and a red micro skirt, slit to show her stocking tops. All this was topped with a white see-through blouse. Between the skirt and blouse, I had no idea how she kept her falsies from showing. Her hair was tinted the exact shade of Lydia's and fixed in the same style. A red felt Santa cap, edged in white, completed her ensemble.

Guess how manly I felt writing this, considering what was happening down south. I was standing next to Lydia, who had gone to so much trouble to get me there, dressed as Santa and having eyes for her, only, and thinking about my cousin, the cross-dressing hit man.

But once again there was no time for discussion and debate. Charlene hooked my arm, dragged me onto the dance floor and away we went, two independent Clauses - grammatical humor, that - dazzling the crowd with our foot work.

Did I mention that Charlene made me take dancing lessons? Something about, if we were going out together I would have to keep up with her.

To the crowd I was just the guy who came with Rudolph, a prop. Rudolph and Mrs. Claus were the stars, and guys were shoving each other to get in line to dance with them. This went on for a while before they managed to free themselves and come toward me, back at the punch bowl. They faced off, ready for a catfight, and two guys I didn't know suddenly joined us.

"Looks like you're one over the limit, Santa."

Swell. Two drunks at a party where I don't know anyone and no one knows me.

"Penalty for that, you lose 'em both. Right?"

I turned to Charlene, just in case. "Friends of yours, *Cousin?*"

In case she might miss it, emphasis added.

But Charlene was with me. "No, Cousin. Strangers."

"Fine."

Charlene had anticipated, long years ago, that we might go out someday and be accosted. She maintained that it would look damned peculiar if she had to whip their asses - meaning those who might accost us - while I stood there and wrung my hands. So, she insisted that I take lessons.

"Daniel! My hero!" She clapped her hands and checked her Lady Bulova: forty-seven seconds. "Just like Nakajima-san taught you!"

"Can it, Chuck."

"Cousins?" Lydia stood akimbo, spitting angry. "You two are *cousins?*"

"Now, darling." Charlene smoothed her hair, reached out to straighten Lydia's antlers. "We're all family here."

"My ass!" She knocked Charlene's hand away, for a second I thought that catfight was still on.

But Charlene smirked, admired Lydia's ass and said so, nodding. "Is quite nice."

Lydia made to lunge at Charlene and I got my arm around her waist just in time.

The D-J switched from Christmas music to AC/DC and *Highway to Hell*, and Charlene went dancing away with her hands over her head, pumping with the beat. "Ciao, darlings!"

I let go of Lydia, who turned on me with, "*Cousins*? You let me make a fool of myself and you two are *cousins*?"

I offered one of those moves where you take your hands and trace your own body to make a point. "I'm wearing makeup and a Santa suit, and these are all your friends, not mine."

That calmed her enough that I could ask, "Would you like to dance?"

"I suppose you took lessons for that, too?"

"You know I did."

* * *

I drove us home, meaning to my place. Without Mitzi there, I figured I might as well show Lydia where I lived.

She stepped through the door and froze, mouth open. She shook herself, stepped inside and gave the place a once-over. I could tell that she was favorably impressed. "Did you decorate this place yourself?" Clearly, she was stunned.

"Nope. Charlene took care of it." I thought about lying, decided not to. I figured, tell the truth now and no need to worry later. "She knows the builder and the decorator, anyway, and she picked out the colors. Me, I'd still be choosing red and green, all primary colors."

"Actually, green is a secondary color." Lydia moved as though she were in a daze, looking around and noting how everything matched and complimented, and the colors were coordinated.

"Would you care for a drink?" I gestured toward the couch, expecting her to say, *Sure, why not?*

Instead, she said "I don't believe this. It is really tastefully done."

Then she reached out to balance herself against my shoulder, caught the G-string and pulled it down her legs and kicked it away. She looked at me and shrugged, said, "Wedgie."

We'll skip ahead over some of the details.

* * *

"I'll never be a conventional lawyer's wife." She rolled over so that she could sit on top of me.

"I'll never be a conventional lawyer." I pulled up my legs, caught her under the arms and pulled her backwards so that I could sit up between her legs.

"Is that a proposal?" She was quite limber and had no trouble adjusting herself so that her legs were around my waist.

"Is that an answer?"

"Do I still work at the office?"

"If you want to. It's not like we need the money."

"And Mitzi?"

"You run the office, she runs the house."

"I don't know that I like the idea of her being around."

"Get this straight: I want an equal partner, not a competitor."

"What does that have to do with Mitzi?"

"She's my maid. She's my friend. You want to keep your friends?"

"Well, of course. But my friends don't sleep in my house."

"She'll move on someday."

She sniffed, "The sooner the better. Maybe I can help her decide."

I've had self-defense lessons, remember? I moved a little, rolled her over and turned her over my knee and spanked her.

She bounced away, rubbing her injured tush, looking thoughtful. "My dad is going to love you."

FINIS

That was two weeks ago. I have been sitting here writing this, enjoying the calm, cursing myself for taking on the project and neglecting the trains. I could have built a whole city in the time it took to write this. But for the first time in five years, everything is peaceful, and it should be for at least a while longer.

Charlene has taken Patricia on a trip across the country, apparently serious about the role of Auntie Mame. Mitzi is mending herself after long years of spousal neglect, and guilt over her own poor parenting skills. The associate who answered the phone and so became Mitzi's lawyer is quite taken with her, and she is trying to explain to him about age differences and dating the boss's maid. But she smiles a lot, even when she is shooting him down.

Lydia is still my secretary and she says it'll take the national guard to get her out of here. She now subscribes to *Bride's Magazine*, and she and Marcie have their heads together a lot, sighing and giggling. What is it with women and weddings, anyway?

Every now and then, she looks in on me and says, "You did a good thing, Danny."

You see, a courier just showed up here with a box. We get boxes here all the time, but not like this one. It came with a note: "Mr. Stanley Willis offers his compliments to Mr. Daniel Compton, on behalf of Benjamin Rodney Jamieson."

The box held a crystal paperweight with a pair a spurs engraved on it.

You did a good thing, Danny.

I'm kind of wondering how good a thing I did, though. Who names a kid *Rodney?*

Coming soon, the second volume chronicling the lives and loves of Daniel and Charlene,

Pandora's Box

ONE

Unless you know more than my cousin Rodney thinks you do, which I guess you could, you don't know anything about me. Right away, let me say that ain't exactly what I wrote. The editor changed it so you would understand what I meant, because sometimes I write like I talk. Being that I grew up in Brooklyn, lots of times when I talk I don't say things the same way they're spelled. Like, *dis* and *dat* instead of *this* and *that*. You maybe wouldn't think it would be such a big deal - I didn't - but it turns out that when people read stuff, it ain't so easy to make sense outta stuff written in dialect, which is what the editor says it is. Me, I thought it was English. Anyway, it turns out that guy, Bernard Shaw, tried writing dialect when he came up with *Pygmalion*, what was *My Fair Lady* in the movies, and he gave up on it. So the editor asked, "You think you're better than a real writer?"

So I said, screw it.

Anyway, my cousin Rodney is a lawyer, one of those upright, conscience-laden types who is always trying to be right. He's hooked up with his secretary, Lydia, who is hot. Maybe not so pretty as he thinks she is and for sure smarter than he knows, but hot. And not at all anal-retentive like Rodney, whose real name is Daniel Rodney Compton. Plus, she has a jealous streak and she can get dramatic. Knowing Rodney, she's got nothing to worry about except her own temper, if you follow, and whenever anyone gets melodramatic, we call it, "Goin' Lydia."

By the way, I didn't write "anal retentive." I wrote, "She don't have a stick up her ass, like Rodney." I'm getting the idea this editing thing is going to get old real fast, so enjoy the classy English while it's around.

Anyway, my cousin wrote about how him and Lydia got together, starting from when our mutual cousin, Charlene, came back to town. There's another subject, our cousin Charlene. Rodney - he hates when I call him that - thinks nobody but him knows Charlene is a guy, thinks nobody knows what Charlene does for a living. Rodney wrote that crap about how he can know what Charlene does and not be in trouble because he's Charlene's lawyer. How come Rodney thinks he can write it out that he's a lawyer for a transvestite hit man and not be in trouble, I got no idea. Me, I just claim I lied on account of it sounded good.

About the Author

Charlie Rowell was born in south central Georgia, grew up in New York's Hudson Valley and graduated from Hope College in Holland, Michigan, graduated from the University of Toledo College of Law and joined the private bar as an independent practitioner.

He was first appointed by the Juvenile Court as a guardian *ad litem* for children alleged to be abused, neglected or dependent in February, 1975. He has served for 28 years on the Citizen Review Board of Juvenile Court, presently chairing Board Number Two.

After nearly twenty-eight years in the uniformed service of the State of Ohio, he retired with the rank of brigadier general (OH), DSM (OH).

He lives with his wife of thirty-five years on ten acres of first and second growth trees; also raccoons, woodchucks, deer and birds.

Cover design & photography by Jimages, Inc.
Cover model - Robyn S.
Stylist - Lindsey Drew Miller